THE KEEPERS ARE COMING

I pulled up in front of my house, killed the engine, and ran inside, slamming closed the door behind me and locking it.

I leaned against the door, shaking.

What now?

It wasn't long before I had the answer.

A pair of bright headlight beams cut a path through the darkness. I pulled back the curtain to see a large grey vehicle shaped like an old bread-delivery truck crawl past my house, its driver sweeping the street with a hand-held searchlight. The truck came to a stop and the driver killed all lights. It took my vision a moment to adjust afterward—the light had shone directly in my face at one point—and by the time I could focus clearly the driver was out of the truck and looking in my yard. It was already dark so I wondered how he could see.

An SUV came around the corner, its headlights shining on high, enabling me to both see the driver and read the name on the side of the truck.

Neither came as a surprise.

He was impeccably dressed, expensive suit, tie, bowler hat on his head.

The side of the truck read: KEEPERS.

Other books by Gary A. Braunbeck:

IN SILENT GRAVES

KEEPERS

GARY A. BRAUNBECK

LEISURE BOOKS NEW YORK CITY

A LEISURE BOOK®

September 2005

Published by

Dorchester Publishing Co., Inc.
200 Madison Avenue
New York, NY 10016

ISBN 0-8439-5577-5

Visit us on the web at www.dorchesterpub.com.

For Ron Horsley
So long, and thanks for the air freshener;
you have no idea...

And in memory of Oscar Horsley (1998–2005)
"Schlermy lay there like a slug.
It was his only defense."

KEEPERS

"Who'll tell the tale?" said the child to the magician. "People should be told."

"Never mind," said the old man, smiling like a beaver. "For centuries and centuries no one will believe it, and then all at once it will be so obvious only a fool would take the trouble to write it all down."

—John Gardner, *Freddy's Book*

I

CARSON AND
THE MAGIC ZOO

ONE

"Hey, Gil—your air freshener's standing by the side of the road." Cheryl adjusted the focus on the new binoculars and then laughed.

"My whosee-whats-it is huh?"

"You'll see when we catch up to him in a minute."

Traffic in our lane wasn't moving nearly as fast as it was in the other two—in fact it was barely moving at all. We were coming back from the grand opening week of my second "novelties and collectibles" store, this one in Columbus, and had gotten into Cedar Hill just in time for rush hour—lucky us.

"Why are you messing with those things?" I asked, nodding toward the binoculars.

She shrugged. "I don't know. Maybe I was hoping for a glimpse of the mysterious lion, or tiger, or *bear*, oh my."

I grinned. Over the past few months there had been several reported sightings of various animals wandering Cedar Hill; a lion on the cliffs at Black Hand Gorge, a tiger in the woods of Dawe's Arboretum, a Kodiak bear lumbering through Mound-builder's Park. I half-expected the next report to be of an elephant near the Twenty-first Street exit. The reports were being dismissed as pranks, but it was still fun to follow them on the news and in the pages of the *Ally*. My nephew, Carson, says the animals come from ". . . the Magic Zoo."

"So, no exotic circus animals out there?"

She smacked my arm. "Don't make fun of me. You never know what might or might not be true."

I checked the rearview mirror to see if I could make it into another lane, but the traffic was coming so fast it was impossible to gauge my chances.

"You sure you're not going to mind this commute?" I asked.

"Not at all. I *like* driving. I'm just sorry that I had to bother you for a ride home today. At least you didn't gripe the way Larry did when I asked him to bring me over this morning. My car is supposed to be out of the shop tomorrow."

"It's no bother. Besides, I wanted to come over and check out how my new Columbus manager was handling things."

She turned toward me. "And how *is* the new manager doing?"

I grinned. "You're doing one hell of a job, Cheryl, and you know it."

I own and operate The Packrat's Attic, a store that specializes in hard-to-find movies, LP records, film posters, CDs, and various other paraphernalia, both from the present and days gone by. Want an 8-track tape *and* a player? An original one-sheet lobby poster from the first release of *Star Wars*? Maybe the soundtrack to *Saturday Night Fever* on pristine vinyl? Then you come to The Attic.

The original Cedar Hill store had been so success-ful, thanks in large part to Cheryl, that I'd gambled on opening another one in Columbus and handing her the reins. So far it was paying off; the new place was a big hit, especially among baby boomers.

Cheryl looked through the binoculars once again, giggled, then pointed toward the object dangling from the rearview mirror. "Okay, I give. What the hell is that thing, anyway? I've been seeing a lot of them around lately."

"It's an air freshener. Apple-cinnamon-scented."

"Well, *duh*. Thanks for pointing that out, Mr. Obvi-ous. I mean, what's it supposed to be? Some guy in a derby with an apple in front of his face. *Sheesh.*"

"Actually, it's a bowler hat, and the air freshener is a reproduction of a painting called *The Son of Man* by René Magritte. He was part of the Surrealist move-ment, like Dalí and Escher. He used that image of a man wearing a bowler in several of his paintings. His work has been reproduced a lot—posters, coffee mugs, air fresheners, you name it. Hell, *we've* got prints of his work for sale at the stores. Most people recognize his work on sight, but have no idea who *he* was."

She stared at me for a moment, and then smiled. "And how is it that *you* know about him?"

I shrugged. "I once minored in art history at OSU during previous life. Also World Languages and American Literature. No, I never got a degree in any of them."

"You're kidding?"

"If I were going to make a joke, don't you think I'd pick a *funny* subject? Something like Art History tends to make people's eyes glaze over and clear the room of humans."

"I've worked for you for five years, Gil, and I never knew that about you."

"It never came up before."

She shook her head. "That's no excuse. You ought to be more forthcoming with people. Especially your friends."

Not wanting to get into another one of our discussions about my social life—or, more specifically, my lack thereof—I nodded toward the binoculars. "You should stop playing with those and put them back in the case. They won't be much of a birthday present for Larry if you break the things before he's had a chance to use them."

"I will not break them . . . but even if I did, my hubby would love them, anyway. He'd *return* them for a pair that worked, but he'd love me for the thought. Besides, he was such a grumpy pants about bringing me over this morning, I figure I should get to play with them first."

"Remind me to never get on your bad side. I'd hate to—"

I spotted him standing by the side of the highway.

Since traffic in our lane was all but crawling, I was afforded a better-than-average look at the old fellow: early seventies, gaunt-faced, reed-thin, dressed in an impeccably tailored suit, he stood with arms held rigidly at his sides, wearing a bowler hat as if he'd been born with it on his head. Cheryl was right; throw in a floating apple the size of a softball, and you'd have *The Son of Man* in the flesh.

I checked my watch. It had now taken almost ten minutes to move less than half a mile. At this rate, it would be getting dark by the time I got to the group home to pick up my nephew.

"What do you suppose he's doing?" asked Cheryl, leaning forward.

Up ahead, the old man was turning to the left, then to the right, lifting his hand to shield his eyes from the sunlight, and for a moment I thought: *He's looking for me.*

(Where did that *come from, pal? Jeez-us, but you've been entertaining some weird notions lately. Well, weirder than usual. Maybe it's time you talked to the doctor about changing meds . . . except the last time, remember, she mentioned the word "neuroleptics"? That's all you'd need at this point—a goddamn antipsychotic drug pumping through your system day and night for the rest of your life! As if you needed any more excuses to not trust your own memories. Hey, speaking of, remember when . . .)*

Blinking the thought away and silencing the voice, I inched the car forward and watched the old man.

Just standing there, all Dapper Dan, looking for something along the road, but also looking behind him every few seconds.

"Is there someone else back there?" asked Cheryl. "Maybe his car conked out on the access road and he climbed up the side of the incline to flag down some help. Maybe his wife's in the car down there and she's sick or something. Oh, God, Gil, do you think he needs help?"

I didn't answer. I *couldn't.*

7

Something about this seemed familiar, but I was damned if I could put my finger on it.

"Gil?"

I blinked, then looked at Cheryl. "Yeah . . . ?"

"Are you okay? You looked . . . I don't know, kind of out of it for a second there."

("Out of it"? Oh, pal, she has no idea . . .)

"The mind wanders."

She studied me for a moment, then began slipping the binoculars into their case. "I think you need to get out more. I think you need to meet someone. I think I'm going to set you up with one of my friends."

"What happened to your concern for strangers by the roadside?"

"This makes me *nervous*, Gil, and I tend to babble when I'm nervous. An old guy like that standing by the highway . . . this can't be good. So I've decided to babble about setting you up with someone. It calms me. Deal with it."

I continued staring out at the old man.

I knew this image. *Goddammit*, I knew it—and not just from the Magritte prints or my air freshener, but from real life.

Okay, not this guy, of course not *this* guy, but another one just like him . . . right?

(Listen, can you hear that? The sound of something back there in the old brainpan waking up and looking for the light switch? Hello? Hello? Is this thing on . . . ?)

I couldn't pin down the expression on the old man's face; one moment he looked almost blissful, then he'd glance behind him and appear nearly frightened. Maybe Cheryl was right, maybe he'd left his sick wife on the access road in their broken-down jalopy.

Blissful and frightened.

What the *hell* was going on, and why was the sight of him ringing so many rusty bells in my head?

I hate it when this happens, and it has been happening a lot lately.

(That's because the meds ain't working like they're supposed to, pal. It's coming back to you and you don't want to remember that night, do you?)

Fuck off already, thanks very much.

I was four car-lengths away when a gust of wind snatched the bowler from the old man's head and bounced it across all three lanes of traffic.

Amazingly, the hat wasn't struck or flattened by any of the cars. The old man slapped a hand on top of his skull to find that, yes, *drat!*, the bowler was indeed gone, and in a series of movements equal parts stumble, slide, and run, he darted into the river of oncoming cars.

"Jesus Christ!" said Cheryl. "He's not even *looking* at the traffic. Oh, God, Gil . . . that poor old guy."

But I wasn't watching him anymore.

I was staring at the dogs.

Just before Magritte-Man had darted after his bowler, two huge black bull mastiffs came bounding up the incline behind him, snarling and snapping. Each dog easily weighed 120 pounds and stood just under three feet in height.

They looked insane; rabidly, violently insane.

And it seemed that Magritte-Man was the focus of their fury.

I had just enough time to say, "What the—?" before hitting the brakes because the car in front of me swerved to miss the car in front of it, which slant-drove across the lane to miss another car as *it* barely missed the old man, who by now was well into the center lane where the traffic was moving much faster but was also better-spaced. He almost had the bowler in his hand when another, stronger gust of wind blew his frame in one direction and the hat in another.

He looked upward, face devoid of expression, watching helplessly as the bowler performed a bouncing, twirling, oddly graceful aerial ballet on its way back to my side of the road.

The dogs were pacing back and forth, looking at him—no, make that *glaring* at him. They were so tensed, so *angry*, that even from this distance I could see the muscles rippling across their backs and the tendons standing out on their short but powerful legs. One of them bared its teeth, then began barking and snarling, jerking its head from side to side, spraying ribbons of foamy spit from its mouth.

They're after him.

Still not checking the traffic, Magritte-Man moved in the direction of the hat as if in a trance, arms reaching upward, imploring.

Everyone, including me, was sounding their horns and rolling down their windows to shout at the old fellow to watch himself, get out of the way, move it fer chrissakes, you crazy son-of-a-bitch.

The dogs were howling, jumping up and down, looking for a break in the traffic.

The bowler landed smack-center on the hood of

my car, skittered up against the windshield, and caught on the edge of a wiper blade.

The dogs snapped their heads in my direction.

"Get it for him, Gil. Hurry before the wind comes up again."

I nodded at Cheryl, and then—checking to make sure the lane was clear—opened my door to get out and retrieve the damn thing, hoping like hell the dogs wouldn't decide that since they couldn't get to Magritte-Man, I'd do as a consolation prize.

There was a break in the farthest two lanes of traffic, and for a moment the dogs had a clear path to their prey and Magritte-Man had a clean shot at making it back to this side of the road.

He took a step forward, saw that the dogs were doing the same, and froze.

Looking at me, Magritte-Man gave a little wave and mouthed what looked like *Hello, Gil.*

Another wave of traffic came screaming down the road.

The minivan in the center lane laid on its horn but never slowed, even when it became obvious that the old man wasn't going to move out of the way in time.

Cheryl screamed a warning to him, but her voice was drowned out by the blaring of horns, the squealing of tires, and the howling of the dogs.

The minivan hit the old man head-on, crumpling him against its grille and dragging him several yards before whatever forces govern such human catastrophes saw fit to release his destroyed frame and spin-roll it several feet, scattering small and not-so-small pieces along the way before it stopped with a sudden, silent, wet finality.

The dogs stared at the old man's mangled form, backed away, looked at each other, ceased their snarling, and sat down.

Staring at him.

Looking contented.

In the car, Cheryl was crying. I couldn't blame her. I felt like crying, as well.

Hello, Gil . . .

I honestly don't remember retrieving the bowler, but the next thing I knew I was standing over the old man—

—who was somehow still alive.

I knelt down and offered the hat to him—I couldn't think of what else to do.

He reached out and touched my shirt with a bloody, demolished hand. My heart tried to squirt through my rib cage, and then something else happened but even as it was happening I felt removed, distant, an observer watching this from miles away.

The old man spit up blood, getting a lot of it on my shirt.

The dogs watched us; God, how they watched us.

Magritte-Man tried to speak, almost made it happen, but in the end settled for thick, wet whisper.

". . . eepers . . . are . . . ming . . ."

I leaned down toward his shredded, pulped lips and said, "What?"

He gripped my shirt as a wave of pain hit.

"Do you know me?" I whispered to him.

Something flashed across his eyes. Recognition? Acknowledgment?

By now other witnesses were pulling over and getting out of their cars.

I looked at the old man. "What did you say?"

Across the road, the dogs' ears pricked up.

"*. . . the Keepers are coming,*" said Magritte-Man.

Then: "*. . . you'll remember . . .*"

He released his grip on my shirt.

And died.

The Keepers are coming.

I lowered my head and looked away. I didn't want anyone to see me crying.

Two

Cheryl and I waited. We answered questions. I was looked over by EMTs, told my story to at least four police officers, gave them my contact information, and was finally allowed to go.

Cheryl and I were climbing back into the car when I noticed the dogs were gone.

. . . and realized that I was still holding Magritte-Man's bowler hat.

Replaying the almost-comic dance the old man had done in time with the bowler's elegant pirouettes as he'd pursued it to the death, I couldn't help but think that if he had gotten away safe and sound it would have made a funny, slightly absurd story to tell at work, or to my nephew Carson; but there are punch lines, and then there's *the* punch line.

I approached one of the officers and handed him the bowler. "He was chasing this," I said, as if it explained everything in excruciating detail.

"Hey, we were wondering what happened to that thing," she said, taking the bowler and dropping it into a large, clear plastic bag that contained what appeared to be the contents of the old man's impeccably tailored pockets.

"Who was he?" I asked.

The officer didn't even make eye contact: "We can't release that information until we've contacted the next of kin."

"But I was with him when he . . ." My voice trailed off as I watched two men load the black-bagged body into the coroner's wagon. "He grabbed my shirt and looked at me. He tried . . . tried to speak to me. I've got his *blood* on my clothes. I was the last thing he saw before he died, and you won't even tell me his *name?*"

The officer shrugged. "Policy. Sorry, sir."

And left me there.

THREE

Cheryl didn't speak until we pulled up in front of her house.

"I've never seen anyone get killed before."

"Are you going to be okay? You want me to wait with you until Larry gets home?"

She tried to smile, couldn't, and so just shook her head. "That's all right. I'll go in and just call the kitties. They always know when something's wrong, and they always come to snuggle and make me feel better." She looked down at the binocular case. "Larry'll be home soon enough. Besides, aren't you supposed to pick up Carson?"

I looked at the time. "I might make it if I hurry."

She shook her head. "Sorry, bud—but not in those clothes, you won't."

I looked down at my blood-smeared shirt. "Jesus, Cheryl . . ."

She reached over and placed a warm hand against my cheek. "I know."

We looked at each other, then both of us started

crying again at the same time, and she put her arms around me and I put mine around her and for a few minutes we stayed like that, crying into each other's necks, and it must have looked pitiful to any passersby, these two people blubbering against each other, but I didn't care, I just needed to get it out of me, Cheryl needed to get it out of her, and if you can't lose it in front of a friend in a parked car on a typical middle-class street then what good is it even having friends?

"That poor old man," Cheryl spluttered.

"I know."

"To die like that . . ."

"I know . . ."

"What did he say to you? It looked like . . . like he tried to say something."

The Keepers are coming.

"Nothing, really. It didn't make a lot of sense. I don't remember. All of the above."

Then our splutterfest continued.

Eventually we pulled apart, Cheryl digging some tissues from her purse, handing some to me, both of us trying to make ourselves presentable again and failing miserably.

"Well," she said, "that was . . . just so special I can't tell you."

"I think the word you're trying to avoid is 'embarrassing.' "

She looked at me, flush-cheeked, eyes glistening. "This may sound corny, Gil, but when you went over to him, when you offered him his hat to him, I was *proud* to know you. I'm still proud to know you. Most people wouldn't've done that."

"Please, don't—"

"Oh, shut the hell up and take a compliment for once in your life, will you? What you did took *nerve*, Gil, it took compassion and courage, whether you want to cop to it or not. *God*, I've worked with you for five years, you've come to the house for dinner, gone to movies with Larry and me, and today, today for the *first* time, I feel like I've gotten my first glimpse of the *real* Gil Stewart. And I *admire* him."

"Gilbert James Stewart," I said, offering my hand. "Named after half of Gilbert and Sullivan, my mother being the opera fan; my middle name after James Stewart, the actor, my dad being the movie fan."

Cheryl took hold of my hand and shook it. "Pleased to know you. *At last.*"

I leaned forward and kissed her cheek. "Thanks for saying that."

"I rarely speak anything but the truth. And I'm fixing you up with my friend Laura on Saturday night, so don't make other plans. Ah-ah—I won't hear *any* arguments, understand?" She opened the door and began getting out. "You'll double with me and Larry." A grin. "You're a good man, Gil. So why is it that I have the impression you don't see it yourself?"

I didn't have the heart at that moment to remind her that Carson was staying with me this weekend. She'd remember soon enough.

I watched her until she was safely inside her house, then pictured her calling for the kitties and their snuggling together on the sofa until Larry got home. It was a nice image. A safe image. An image that did not bring with it any echoes of something *way back there* that was trying to make me remember.

Then I thought of my nephew's missing cat, and the feeling passed.

I drove to the end of her street, waited at the stop sign, and out of habit glanced in the rearview mirror.

A dark, hunched four-legged figure disappeared behind a bush a few yards behind me.

Staring, I thought: *No. It couldn't be.*

I opened my door and got out of the car, looking at the bush.

The branches rustled.

Softly.

The street was oddly silent; no birds singing, no dogs barking, no cats yowling.

The branches of the bush rustled again.

Then silence.

I waited a few seconds more, then decided that I didn't want to know. It was probably just the stress and shock wearing off.

I got back in the car and drove toward home. I needed to change my clothes and take a quick shower. I'd call the group home and tell them why I was going to be late. They'd understand. Gil Stewart was *never* late, not when it came to his nephew, so it must be something drastic.

Everything was okay.

I was fine. I was fine. I was *fine.*

Still, I kept glancing in the rearview mirror all the way home, looking for black shapes.

FOUR

The dismal bitch lay on her side in the dry gray October twilight in my front yard, her black wrinkled teats lumped beside her like a cancer growth far too large and malformed for her body to hold inside. Her sides shivered as she labored to pull in air, and the sound of her breathing—wet, thick, ripped-raw painful—was too close to another sound I'd already heard once today and did not want to hear again.

I climbed out of my car and slowly approached her, all the while looking over my shoulder, half-expecting to see the black mastiffs from the highway.

It appeared this was my day to deal with dogs.

Her coat was patchy with mange, her eyes bloodshot and mad; when I came closer, they narrowed into slits and a low growl came from her throat. I could smell her from ten feet away, a ripe, sick, sweetrotten smell. Underscoring the smell was a moist kneading sound, soft but persistent; as I reached out toward her she jerked to the side and a flap of flesh held in place by the thinnest thread of tissue fell back. Beneath it, maggots teemed in an open wound whose too-bright blood seeped outward into her fur like the ever-expanding strands of a spider's web, some of it dribbling onto the lawn and trickling toward my feet, forming rivulets in the grass.

I couldn't help but think of the old man on the highway, and it almost cut me in half.

"It's okay, girl," I said in what I hoped was a tender voice. "It's okay, shhhh, there, there, just let me take a look so we can make it all better, okay?" I continued on like this for what seemed like an hour but was probably less than a minute. Once I thought she might let me touch her long enough to see if there was a tag on her collar but she made a snap for my hand at the last moment, startling both of us.

I've never done well when it comes to ministering to sick or wounded animals. I guess it stems from an incident that occurred when I was a high-school sophomore, one of those "It Happens" incidents that you think you'll eventually get over but never really do, even though admitting to it some three decades later feels embarrassing . . . but the sight of this pathetic animal on my lawn caused this particular instance of "It Happens" to happen across my memory once again.

(See there, pal? You can remember things if you want to. If you'll just go a little further back . . .)

Go away, please.

After school I had a part-time evening job at Beckman's Market, a local neighborhood grocery store, one of those mom-and-pop operations that had been in the area for as long as anyone could remember. I was cleaning the beer cooler one afternoon—it had been defrosted the night before or something—and there was this big puddle in front of the side entrance door. It was the first thing that the customers saw when they used that entrance, which a lot of them did, so the boss wanted it to look nice.

One customer came in and accidentally pulled the door's spring off its hinge and the thing slammed shut like a vice grip. I started messing around with it but the boss told me to leave it alone, he'd fix it himself in a little while.

A few minutes later another customer came in, followed by this little gray cat. Cutest thing you ever saw, all furry and friendly . . . and evidently hungry; it kept darting over to the produce section, trying to get at the apples and oranges. I thought whoever owned it must keep it on one hell of a diet.

My boss told me to get rid of it. I picked it up, kicked open the door, and threw it out. I threw it quite hard, on purpose, so maybe it'd get the hint and go back home.

No such luck.

The door started to slam shut just as the cat was making the feline version of a mad dash to safety back inside.

It never had a chance.

The door slammed right on its neck. I was only a foot away and heard something crack. Then another customer came in and the cat did not so much *fall* back out as . . . spasm.

I opened the door and saw the cat choking to death. It just kept kicking and coughing and spitting, making horrible, heart-sickening sounds . . .

and it never once closed its eyes, just kept staring at me the whole time like it was my fault. It spewed blood and vomit from its mouth while its other end evacuated all manner of pained foulness.

It had to have been a horrible, agonizing death. And all I could do was stand there and watch it happen.

My boss made me toss it into the trash out back. God, I was sick about the whole thing: I didn't mean for it to die, but now here I was, scooping this dead cat into a shovel and dumping it in the trash. It should have been on its way home to a bowl of milk or a can of tuna. It should have been rubbing up against strangers' legs, purring in that warm, please-love-me way that almost no one can resist. But it wasn't lapping milk or rubbing someone's leg; it was lying on top of a trash pile, flies already swarming over its still-warm body, and I was the one who'd put it there.

I dropped the shovel and picked up the cat's body, my thumb brushing blood from the silver tag on its collar, whispering "I'm sorry, kitty," over and over as if the thing were suddenly going to rally and whisper its forgiveness. For some reason, I wanted to wipe all the blood from its tag, I wanted to know its name; it seemed to me, at that moment, that something should be done to make its body more presentable—but to whom or what I couldn't have said. I just wanted to give this poor thing some kind of dignity, I guess, before I tossed it in among the empty egg crates and tin cans. I knew how silly this would look to anyone passing by but I didn't care, I just kept apologizing again and again, wiping away at the tag (which refused to come clean) until its ass began leaking something dark and thick down the front of my shirt and apron.

I spent the rest of the day crying. My boss sent me home early. I was depressing the customers.

(Let's hear it for Mr. Recall, folks. One memory down, one to go . . .)

Are you still here?

(Three guesses, and the first two don't count . . .)

I shook my head. I would *not* stand here and watch this dog suffer. I didn't need that on my conscience.

I went inside to call the pound, who instructed me to contact Animal Control, who told me to get in touch with the nearest emergency veterinarian service, who in turn told me they had no one available to come and collect the dog, could I possibly get her into my car and bring her over? They would have someone waiting to take her right away.

Your Cedar Hill tax dollars at work.

I said I'd call them before I left, hung up, and went to look for something in which to wrap her. It seemed the right thing to do, the decent gesture, a last act of kindness before we parted ways.

I didn't bother changing my clothes; my pants and shirt were already ruined with blood and the fetor of fresh death was still all over me.

I dialed the number of the group home and got one of the on-site habilitation specialists who works there, told her that I was running late, it was unavoidable, and to please tell Carson not to worry, that "UncGil" (his nickname for me) would be there in time for us to make the next showing of the movie.

Gary A. Braunbeck

Standing now in the supposed safety of my home, I realized the blanket I'd selected from the linen closet was far too big for the dog in my yard . . . but just the right size for wrapping an old man's broken body. I put it back at once and selected one of more appropriate size, all the while knowing that something in the back of my memory was trying to wake up and get my attention, but I was moving now, moving right along, and it was important that I keep moving at all costs and not stop to think about anything for too long, so I shut the closet door and made my way outside.

The dog had disappeared.

I didn't panic. It had obviously been in a great deal of pain so it couldn't have gotten very far. Altogether I'd been inside no more than five minutes.

I was just starting around back to look for her when a delivery van pulled into the driveway. It was from neither UPS nor FedEx. I didn't think I'd ever heard of this company—Hicks Worldwide—before, but I wasn't certain. I went to meet the driver, who handed me a parcel the size of a carry-on shoulder bag and asked me to sign for it as he scanned the shipping label.

If he was wondering why there was blood on my clothes, he gave no indication.

"Did you happen to see a dog wandering nearby as you drove up here?" I described the dog and her condition, hoping that would satisfy any curiosity he might have about the state of my clothes. The driver adjusted his wool cap, wiped some sweat from his face, and shook his head.

"Nope, I'd've noticed a dog in that kind of shape. You call the pound?"

"Of course," I said. When it became clear to him that no further details would be forthcoming, the driver thanked me, returned to his van, and left. I carried the package inside and dropped it on the kitchen table and probably would have let it go at that if it hadn't been for the way it was addressed.

The package had been overnighted to me, had a tracking number, and required a signature on delivery. It had my name and home address in order, nothing odd there, but the return address was also mine.

Someone wanted to make damn sure I got this right away. This same someone also (or so it seemed) did not want me to know who'd sent it until after I'd opened the thing.

We live in anxious times; terrorist attacks, mail-order anthrax, letter bombs, all sorts of unspeakable horrors delivered right to your door—or so say the paranoia-mongers who know a populace kept on edge is a populace easily manipulated. I try not to buy into the fear, because once it's got a hold on you, it grinds your voice under its heel until your spirit is mute.

I put down the blanket and opened the package. I only wanted to find out who'd sent it, if it was some kind of practical joke, then I'd go take care of the dog and hopefully get to the group home in time to take Carson to the movie. Just a few extra moments without the blood of another living thing on my hands or clothes. It didn't seem unreasonable.

Inside was a large, well-taped and well-packed cardboard box that revealed two layers of bubble wrap and packing peanuts before finally unveiling the first of its treasures: five record albums, sleeves undamaged, LPs in perfect condition. *Steppenwolf 7*, Yes's *Fragile*, *The Best of Three Dog Night*, Neil Young's *Harvest*, and the masterpiece of masterpieces, George Harrison's *All Things Must Pass.*

I stared at the albums in wonder. I'd long ago lost my copies of the records, had replaced them on (in order) reel-to-reel, 8-track, cassette, and CD. Who the hell would be sending me mint-condition copies of albums in a format no one listened to anymore?

Beneath the albums, each in a clear plastic protective sleeve, were several 45 rpm records: "Brandy (You're a Fine Girl)," "Join Together," "Don't Want to Live Inside Myself," "Ode to Billy Joe," "They're Coming to Take Me Away (Ha-Ha!)," "Cherry, Cherry," and at least a dozen others I'd heard on the radio while growing up. God, the memories that were brought back just *seeing* the titles on the old record labels—Decca, Dunhill, RCA, Cotillion and Reprise . . . a shorthand history of 1970s popular music, here in my shaking, blood-tinged hands. Growing up, I'd become something of an expert on the various changes made to their labels by record companies over the years—the loss of the multicolored lines on the Decca label, the way the Reprise logo got smaller and smaller, how Capital went from black to the coolest green with its circle-within-a-circle to just a boring shade of pea-puke that shamed my turntable's aesthetic. I was the only person I knew of who noticed or even cared about trivialities such as this—

—except for Beth.

Beth.

I looked through the LPs and 45s once again, my arms shaking more and more as it began to dawn on me that these records were not thrown into this box at random; they were selected with a great deal of attention, a private meaning in their arranged order, chosen as *she'd* choose them.

Or would have.

All of these had been among Beth's very, *very* favorite albums and songs. Beth, my first and truest friend; Beth, whom I'd loved more than anyone else before or since; Beth, whom I'd last heard from one sweltering summer night over twenty years ago; Beth, who'd been missing and presumed (later officially declared) dead for a majority of my adult life.

For a moment her face superimposed itself over the old man's, and why not? I'd been the last person to see either of them alive.

Over the years I had managed to convince myself that Beth wasn't really dead, she'd just run off to some exotic foreign place without telling anyone and was living there under an assumed name, maybe as an artist, or underground writer, or something just as gloriously bohemian. That would suit her; just say, "Fuck you!" to the world at large and vanish into a new country, a new identity, "finding herself" until she was confident enough to come back and say, "Ha! Fooled those complacent smirks right off your faces, didn't I? Boy, have I got a story to tell *you!*"

I gently placed the records aside, making sure to stack them so they wouldn't slide off onto the floor; already I was planning on pulling my Gerard turntable out of its box and hooking it up to the stereo so I could listen to them until I hit the city limits of Sloppy Nostalgia (our motto: "Wax with us or wax the damn car!").

Underneath another layer of bubble wrap were books, hardcover and paperback; Judy Blume, Kurt Vonnegut, a first edition of Stephen King's *Carrie*, *The Collected Stories of Eudora Welty*, *The Heart is a Lonely Hunter*, a bunch of old comic books—*Spider-Man, Prince Namor: The Sub-Mariner, Hawkman, Ghost Rider #1*.

Heaven; I was in heaven.

There was a 9×12 clasp envelope sandwiched between two of the comic books. I opened it and dumped the contents onto the coffee table.

The first thing to spill out was a present I'd gotten Beth for her twenty-first birthday—a thin gold necklace with a small cameo that opened to reveal a photograph of me and her standing in front of a King's Island roller coaster, taken at one of our yearly summer outings when we were still young enough to believe such trips were what made living worthwhile; next were two condoms, still in their sealed packets (the empty third packet was taped to them); a pair of crescent moon–shaped earrings; a half-empty pack of Benson & Hedges Menthol 100s; a program from a community theater production of *Pippin*; and, most telling of all, a pair of tattered Valentine's Day cards: the first one I had given Beth when she was eighteen and I was twelve: "I Love You Best of All!"; the second was one she had given me shortly before I turned eighteen: "Just wait until you're legal!"

I could still smell a trace of the musk oil with which she'd doused the card, the same musk she used to daub behind her ears and on her neck. It was still the sexiest aroma ever created. At least that's what memory had me now believing.

If I'd had any doubts about who'd sent the package, this card erased them.

Beth was alive.

I suddenly remembered a quote from the poet Oscar Wilde: "One can live for years sometimes without living at all, and then all life comes crowding into one single hour." God, how true that was.

Beth was *alive*.

So much had already happened today that I couldn't fully absorb the meaning of that, and so much was *still* happening that, for the time being, I didn't have the *time* to absorb its meaning.

I folded the envelope and was about to toss it among the other goodies when I felt something else inside, wedged into a corner at the bottom. I reached in and scratched away with my fingernail until the object came loose.

I opened my hand and looked at what lay nestled in my palm.

At first, nothing registered; there was only a vague—

—grabbing my shirt and pulling me toward him, blood seeping into the cotton of my shirt as I lifted the bowler and showed him that it was undamaged, looking into my eyes, his lips squirming in a mockery of communication, sounds that were a burlesque of language, but there was

something there, something that drew him to me or me to him, and he turned his head ever so slightly to the right and I saw—

—impression of memory, a needling sense that this thing was supposed to mean something to me. I felt I should recognize it—perhaps the part of me that did recognize it hadn't gotten to the light switch yet—

(No, not yet, but I'm making my way there, pal, you can count on that.)

—but there was nothing.

Wait, scratch that.

There *was* something but it was ether for all the good it did.

I stared at it for a few more moments, and then was suddenly so . . . weary. That's the only word that even comes close to describing what overtook me. I was at once so exhausted and drained that the idea of making it to a chair or my bed was as fantastic to me as the Fountain of Youth must have seemed to the critics of Ponce de León. I didn't think I'd ever be able to move again. It was the first time in years I'd felt so completely emptied and done.

The stillness in my center was cold and without affection. I felt divided, alone, and dissociated from everything—surroundings, thoughts, sensations; even my body was just so much fodder, a too-fragile, too-temporary, carbon-based cosmic joke of dying cells and memories that would vanish into humus once it was placed into the ground and left as an offering upon which the elements could feast.

(Mayday, Mayday, we're losing contact with you, pal, can't let that happen . . .)

What brought me back was the soft, muffled whine of a ghost.

The dog; I'd almost forgotten about the poor thing.

FIVE

Blanket in hand, I stood in the center of the house and waited for her to make another noise; she did, but there was no way to tell from which direction it was coming, so I went out the back door and began searching around the house, then the bushes surrounding my backyard, and finally, once again, the front.

There was a fresh smear of blood on the bottom step of the front porch.

She'd tried to crawl up to the door sometime while I was going through the package from Beth.

I searched the periphery of house twice more; every so often I'd hear a weak and ragged breath and thought I had zeroed in on her hiding place, but each time I was certain I'd found her there was only a mass of absence with speckles of blood left behind. After nearly ten minutes of this—and no sounds from her—I noticed a few of my neighbors were trying not to be too obvious as they peeked out their windows at my odd behavior and bloody clothes. It occurred to me—Mr. Slow-on-the-Uptake—that it might be a good idea to change out of these clothes if I was going to continue skulking through the bushes in daylight . . . which was now waning fast, as was my energy and resolve.

I called out for the dog a few times with no results, then started back inside to shower and get a change of clothes when I remembered the crawl space behind the trash cans at the back of the house. I hadn't thought of that damn thing in ages.

I made my way around and, sure enough, two of the trash cans had been pushed apart. I squatted in front of the opening, tilting my head at a near-impossible angle to see if I could catch a glimpse of her. I couldn't, so I put the blanket on top of the nearest can and crawled through the opening.

A few years ago I had a major plumping mishap that resulted in my having to move into a hotel for a week while a team of overpriced-and-worth-every-damn-cent-of-it "septic professionals" (that's what they asked to be called, don't ask me, I just live here) tore out and then replaced nearly half the pipes in my house. Part of that involved ripping up a small section of floor between the downstairs bathroom and guest bedroom in order to run a separate flow-line to the new emergency sump pump. Fun, fun, fun. To avoid ripping out any more flooring than absolutely necessary, they asked for and received my permission to dig a tunnel underneath my back porch, one that would run its entire length, starting underneath the guest bedroom and emerging in the back beside the steps.

I was entering at the exit point. Crawling in from behind the trash cans, the ground was fairly level, but I knew about eight feet away there was sudden drop of nearly two feet which could take you by surprise and even cause injury if you didn't know it was there. I hoped the dog hadn't made it that far. The idea of having to pull her ass-first out of that little pit in the dark, in the mud, and with little more than three feet of width in which to do it, was not what I'd had in mind when I got out of bed this morning.

I smelled her about six feet in.

Digging into my pants pocket, I pulled out my cigarette lighter and struck up the flame.

She lay three feet ahead of me, on her side. She had somehow managed to get herself three-quarters of the way turned around (so as to face the way out) before she collapsed.

I whispered to her but she didn't respond.

Pulling forward with my elbows, I pushed the lighter up and out until I could see its flame reflected in her eyes.

Her gaze was unfocused and glassy. Her sides no longer heaved. No sound at all came from her, save for the kneading of the maggots in her wound. If she wasn't dead yet, she would be soon; minutes, possibly. Definitely within the next few hours.

I felt immediately sick—not so much nausea as bile-flavored regret. If I hadn't been so lost in the 70s nostalgia craze-in-a-box I might have caught her in the front yard and prevented her from ending up here in the damp, dismal darkness. And if I'd ignored my boss and fixed that door right then and there—

(See how easy it is to take a stroll down Amnesia Lane, pal? Why keep running away? Why not just take a deep breath and dive in, head-first?)

—I keep telling you: Shut. The. Fuck. Up.

"I'm so sorry, girl," I whispered to the dog.

She grunted.

"Hello, you," I said. "I didn't think you were still with us."

This time she actually blinked, then raised her head a little and issued a soft whine. I could see the blood clotting in one of her nostrils and a layer of something once moist but now desiccated and bruise-hued coating her lips.

Water.

I couldn't do anything else for her while she died, but I could get her something to drink. There was no way I'd be able to wrestle her from under the porch without hurting her worse or her tearing and biting the hell out me; even if I could manage it, so much time would be lost that she'd die in the car on the way to the vet's.

No, let her die here, with a cool drink on her tongue and someone near to mark the moment of her sleep.

I began to reach toward her, thought better of it, then said: "I'll be back in a few minutes, girl, okay? You just rest there, that's right, rest. I'll bring you something to drink."

I had to crawl out backward, so it took a minute or so. The farther away from her I got, the softer her whining became. The strange thing is, the softer her whines, the more they became the only sounds I could—or wanted—to hear.

I found a large, clean mixing bowl and filled it to the rim with water and ice cubes, then scavenged some leftover steak from the refrigerator. Maybe she wanted a last meal, maybe not, but goddammit, if she was going to die underneath my porch she was going to have a choice about it.

Back outside and crawling, this time with a flashlight to guide the way as I pushed the bowl of water and plate of food forward inch by muddy inch.

She'd moved again, forward this time, about a foot and a half. The flashlight beam caught her eyes and turned them into a pair of small glowing embers. They moved left, right, then vanished for a few moments as she closed, then reopened them.

"Here you go, girl. You hungry? Got'cha some water, nice and cold."

She pulled forward, using only her front paws. Her back legs were splayed behind her, limp and useless. The fur surrounding her eyes was drenched in thick, mucus-like tears. Even in agony she recognized a treat, knew that this was Something Special. I pushed the bowl and plate closer. She looked at my hand and growled, so I let go and pulled away as she lifted her head over the water bowl and tested it with her tongue. She remained like that for a moment, head dangling over the bowl, some of the water dripping from her mouth, breathing heavily.

I remembered a scene from some movie one of the employees had been playing on the display monitors today: a little girl running away from home encounters a dog whose owner beats it mercilessly, then ties it to a pole in the backyard during a rainstorm. The girl waits for the owner to finish beating the dog and go back inside, and once she's alone with the animal she unties the rope holding it in place and tells it to go, but it won't. It looks at her in utter confusion as she tries to get it to leave, pulling at it, pushing at it, pleading with it to go, to get away, but it only sits there, staring with longing in its eyes at the house where its owner lives. "You can't love him," she weeps. "You can't, you just can't!"

"Did you love them?" I whispered to the dog under my porch. "Did you sit in rainstorms and cry for them to bring you inside? Did you love the belt they used on you? Did you lick their hands when they were done?"

Her ember eyes (brown with gold flecks, I saw for a moment), met mine and she started drinking the water in earnest. I moved the flashlight beam to see if I could make out what was etched on her collar tag but her head was too low.

"I'll do what I can for you, if you'll let me." I reached toward her again; this time, she lunged, snarling, jaws snapping. I jerked back and up and slammed the top of my skull against one of the pipes. The world went supernova before my eyes, and by the time the pain had fully registered I was staggering back to my feet behind the trash cans.

Gripping my head, I dropped the flashlight and teetered against the largest can, knocking it over and falling on top of it. The supernova faded into the light of a single star rolling back and forth, back and forth, slowing as the universe imploded, slowing, then lay there glaring at me.

I got to my knees and grabbed the flashlight, turned off the starlight, and stumbled back into the house. Maybe dogs preferred to die the same way as elephants; alone, in some private place with the darkness as their benign, final, best friend.

My chest hitched and my throat constricted. God knows I wanted to cry for both her and the old man, but I couldn't. Dad: *Crying's for girls, boy*; Mom: *Don't let anyone see you like this, I'll never hear the end of it from your father*.

Water.

Beating down as hard as possible.

Let her drink it; let it cleanse me.

SIX

Fifteen minutes later I stood in the kitchen dressed in clean clothes. The water had been hot to the point of inflicting damage. I'd scrubbed at my hands, arms, and chest until the skin was raw but even now I could still feel the old man's blood on me. My flesh was tender and pink and still held a sheen from the water; I'd never looked as clean. But the blood was still there, somewhere under the skin, becoming a part of me, linking me to his image, the absurdity of his last moments, and to his corpse which now lay in some cold basement draining out into the corner holes of a silver table.

I pulled the folding step stool out from the pantry and set it firmly in place, then climbed up and opened one of the highest cabinet doors, fishing around toward the back until I found the old and (for many years now) unused bottle of Johnny Walker Black. This was a masochistic little ritual I performed on those rare occasions when my nerves got the better of me despite my insisting otherwise:

take out the temptation and stare it in the face and see if you're still made of something.

I am not one who believes that the best way to overcome temptation is to expunge its source from your universe, no; to me, temptation can only be overcome when it becomes boring, trivial, commonplace, and the best way to make it mundane is to always have it near and *remind* yourself that it's near. Makes it easier to hold it in your grip and not caress it as you would the hand of a lover, take a good look at it and give it a good look at you, then smile to yourself because you've won and cache it away again until the next time your nerves don't get the better of you.

Don't let anyone tell you that recovering alcoholics live well and happily never wanting a taste again; you *never* don't want a drink, and eventually that becomes easier to deal with—it's when you begin to think that the drink wants *you* that it's time to dust off that sponsor's number and put your pride in check.

I looked at Johnny W., he looked at me, and pretty soon (despite the old man's blood soaking deeper into my core) we decided we'd had enough of each other's delightful company. He went his way, I went mine, and the folding step stool slipped back into its place wondering why in the hell I'd bothered it in the first place.

I opted for a cup of hot chocolate. Powdered instant. Domestically, I have grown slightly complacent in my middle age. And why not? We're born into a nearly ruined world, so the best we can do is make ourselves as comfortable as possible whenever we have the chance; the easier it is to do so, the better. Sometimes. Not always. Just sometimes.

I wandered into the living room, sipping happily away at my yummy Swiss Miss, and began to reach for the phone to call the group home once more.

Glancing out the front window, I saw the two black mastiffs sitting across the street, staring at my house.

The Keepers are coming . . .

The phone rang just as my hand touched the receiver, startling the living shit out of me.

I dropped the hot chocolate, spilling some of it on my pants, cursed, then answered, listening as the anxious voice of the supervisor on the other end informed me that Carson was missing. I told them I was on my way and hung up.

I looked back outside again.

The dogs were gone.

(Maybe they weren't there in the first place, pal. Maybe they're just flashes of memory. You remember those flashes, don't you? The ones you're always ignoring. The ones that the meds are supposed to help you understand and deal with. The ones you've spent half your goddamn life trying to convince yourself don't exist, that it didn't happen, that you—)

"Get away from me!" I shouted, kicking the mug across the room where it shattered against the wall.

I took several deep breaths, standing there with my eyes closed until I was certain I had control of things.

There.

All good now.

All better.

I was fine. I was fine. I was *fine*.

There were no other dogs.

No other memories.

Nothing that would come sneaking out of the dark and take me by surprise.

I grabbed my coat and headed out the door.

SEVEN

I became Carson's legal guardian after his mother died from a heart condition that no one—including her, as it turned out—knew she had. ("All these years, I thought it was just *gas*.") My sister was a woman of singular grace who never let anything phase her; hangnails were met with the same dogged composure as broken bones. In all the too-few years she'd been in my life, I don't think I ever once saw her panic. Even when she awoke after an emergency C-section to discover that her child had Down's syndrome and that her peach of a husband had left her because he couldn't handle it, she never allowed any setback or misfortune to best her. I loved her dearly and miss her every day.

Carson spent three weeks every month at the group home; the fourth week—and all holidays—he spent with me. He wanted it that way, and so did I. After seven days, we started getting on each other's nerves a bit, so one week a month was just the ticket for us. And I could visit or call him whenever I wanted . . . which I usually did somewhere around the middle of Week Three.

He was never lonely. That was important to me.

One of the things my nephew and I discovered we had in common was a love of comic books. Admittedly, I hadn't really been involved in the comics scene since the heyday of *Ghost Rider, Aquaman,* and *The Silver Surfer* (though I have to admit to a short-lived renaissance during the early appearances of *Sandman*), but Carson didn't care. Spider-Man united us. We were of one mind when it came to the Green Goblin (he was an annoying wuss), Doc Ock (dangerous, scary, and kind of cool), and Kingpin (very fat and rude but never turn your back on him, uh-uh). Carson always helped out at the Cedar Hill store on those weeks he stayed with me; he was my unofficial Comics Manager.

One of our rituals whenever he stayed with me involved his hauling out his latest batch of comic book acquisitions and reading them to me. Another ritual involved our driving out toward Buckeye Lake for dinner at the I-70 truck stop, Carson's favorite place to eat. (The food is surprisingly excellent.)

As I drove toward the group home, I began thinking how, a few months ago, these rituals had converged.

Carson had adopted a cat that he kept at my house. I had no arguments about his keeping it at the house, as long as he paid for the food and litter from the money he earned working at the AARC sheltered workshop. Besides, the cat proved to be agreeable company at night, was always very affectionate, and didn't shed nearly as much as I'd feared at first.

The cat—which Carson named Butterball—ran away one night as I was taking out the trash and failed to close the back door behind me. I dreaded telling Carson about it as I drove to the group home to pick him up for our week together. I had the radio tuned to Cedar Hill's National Public Radio station where two agricultural scientists were discussing the remote possibility that an outbreak of scrapie was starting to infect sheep in Montana.

By the time Carson and I got back to my house (after cheeseburgers at the Sparta and a matinee at the newly renovated Midland Theater, the pride of downtown Cedar Hill) I knew there was no avoiding it.

I pulled up in front, killed then engine, then turned to him and said, "Carson, I need to tell you something. I'm afraid it might be bad news."

"I know," he said, softly bouncing up and down in the seat.

I grinned for only a moment. "Oh, you do, do you?"

"Uh-huh. Butterball ran away and—hey, you know what? I got some new slippers. They're real warm and—"

"Whoa, Carson, hang on. How . . . how did you know about Butterball?"

" 'Cause Long-Lost told me."

"And who's Long-Lost?"

He reached into his knapsack and pulled out a comic book, then rifled through the pages until he came to a dog-eared page. "*This* is him." He handed over the comic.

The whole thing—front and back covers included—

was drawn in black and white. The paper stock was cheap (some of the ink rubbed off on my fingertips) and it was hand-bound with plastic spirals. A home-made comic if ever there was one.

It was open to a full-page drawing of a creature that was so incredible I was momentarily taken back in time to my first encounter with Bruce Banner's alter ego, The Incredible Hulk. "Wow. That's pretty cool."

And it was. This creature named Long-Lost stood in the middle of a futuristic-looking city where it towered over every building around it. It had the head of rat with a unicorn's spiraling horn rising from the center of its forehead; the snout of a pig, the body and wings of a bat; the legs of a spider; a horse's tail; and two semi-human arms jutting from its chest, one hand gripping a pencil, the other a sketch pad. The more I looked at it, the more details registered; its body was composed of fish scales, its wings were a mosaic of hundreds of different varieties of feathers, its underbelly looked slick as a dolphin's skin, and its spider's legs ended in paws that were a combination of dog and cat.

It was both grotesque and remarkable, the work of an underground artist who was obviously gifted in a way only the truly and happily demented can be; despite all of its disparate parts, Long-Lost as a whole seemed at once organic and correct, as if it should look no other way than this.

"So this is who told you about Butterball?"

"Uh-huh. He's the Monarch of Modoc."

"What's Modoc?"

Carson shook his head and made a *tsk*-ing noise. "Boy, you sure are goofy sometimes." He took the comic from my hand and closed it, turning the cover toward me.

And there it was: *Modoc: Land of the Abandoned Beast.*

"Modoc is Long-Lost's kingdom?" I asked.

"It ain't a kingdom like with knights and stuff, y'know? It's like in the future, only it's not, really. It's like a . . . a *hidden* world. There's people and everything and they all love Long-Lost and he protects them."

I nodded my head and asked him if I could see the comic again. He reluctantly handed it over. I flipped through the pages, stopping here and there to read the dialogue in the various balloons . . . except there wasn't any. In each frame where a character was speaking, its speech-bubble was blank. It was only through the badly printed narration in the squares that I was able to discover that Long-Lost was preparing Modoc for something Very Terribly Important, Don't You Know. (That's how the phrase was written every time it appeared: Very Terribly Important, Don't You Know.) I handed it back to Carson.

"How could Long-Lost tell you about Butterball when there are no words?"

"There's words there. I can see 'em but you can't, yet."

"Yet?"

Carson nodded. "It's a secret."

"Okay." But it still didn't explain how he'd known about the cat. Or how he'd come up with the phrase *hidden world*. I wondered if he even knew what that meant.

"Carson?"

"We gonna go to the Sparta again tomorrow? They make good cheeseburgers."

"The best known to mankind, yes—but I was about to ask you something."

"Okay."

"Is this a joke you're playing on me? Did you sneak out last night and get Butterball and take him back to the group home?"

"Nuh-uh. Butterball went to live at the Magic Zoo."

"You wouldn't lie to me, would you?"

"Yeah . . . but not about this. I lie about Christmas presents—like telling you I don't got one for you. I lie like that. But not this. This Very Terribly Important, Don't You Know."

I decided to let it rest for a while. If this was a joke of some kind, Carson would tell me eventually; if it wasn't, at least he wasn't upset. I only hoped that Butterball was all right. I really liked having that cat around.

Later, after dinner, Carson pulled out a whole stack of *Modoc* comics and sat next to me on the couch, showing me each page of every issue, in order, so I could follow what was going on.

Long-Lost ruled Modoc, a place where human beings and animals lived together in perfect accord. Long-Lost kept everyone in Modoc happy and entertained by drawing their wishes and then making those wishes come to life. It was a good-enough place. But there was an evil hexer, Tumeni Notes, who was trying to cast a spell so that the animals would revolt against Long-Lost and force him to show Tumeni where the Great Scrim was located. The Great Scrim separated Modoc's world from our own. . . . On and on it went, becoming dumbfoundingly complicated as it threw in everything from simultaneous-universe theories to Darwinism and a dash or two of modern DNA research. I found it difficult to believe that Carson—though categorized as a "high-functional" Down's and capable of reading at a fifth-grade level—could understand all of this, let alone keep it straight.

He came to the most recent issue and opened it to the first page, then let out a little gasp and immediately closed it.

"What's wrong?"

"Can't read this one yet."

"Why not?"

" 'Cause I'm not supposed to."

"I don't understand."

Tsk-ing again. "You're goofy. I can't read it 'cause Long-Lost won't let me see the words yet."

"But there *aren't* any words in the first place."

"Are too."

I grabbed up three issues at random and opened them to various pages. "Look at this—Carson, come on! Look! Nowhere, see? Nowhere in any of these comics does any of the characters say anything. See? Just empty space." I was shocked at how angry I suddenly felt.

"I told you already, there're words in them, *you* just can't see 'em."

"Yet," I added, all at once too frustrated to care.

"Uh-huh. Long-Lost does it to me, too. When I get a new *Modoc*, the words aren't always there 'cause he don't feel like talking to me yet. I gotta wait."

"Like I have to wait?"

"Uh-huh."

"Why do I have to wait? Why can't Long-Lost just let me read the same words he says to you?"

" 'Cause he won't say the same thing to you. He told me that, just like he told me about Butterball. He says different things to different people . . . but only if he likes them."

Time for aspirin and sleep.

The next morning Carson woke me at seven-thirty and told me that we had to go to the truck stop for breakfast.

"Carson, my head hurts and I've had about four hours' sleep. Can't it wait?"

"No!" He sounded both excited and slightly scared. "We gotta go now."

"Why?"

He showed me the latest issue of *Modoc*—the one he couldn't read to me the night before—and opened it to the first page.

I was looking at a black-and-white drawing of the I-70 truck stop near Buckeye Lake. There was a car driving into its parking lot. My car. With Carson and me inside. And something that looked like the ghost of a bear floating behind us.

I took the comic from my nephew's hands and turned to the next page. It was blank.

Okay; if Carson wanted to continue stringing me along with his little joke, I'd go with it for a while. It was kind of nice to see him putting this much effort into pulling the wool over my eyes..

All the way to the truck stop, I found myself glancing in the rearview mirror, half-expecting to see some diaphanous form pursuing us; Ursa Major, P.I.

We took our usual booth and ordered. While we waited for the food to arrive, Carson opened the *Modoc* issue and turned to the second page and showed me the "new" panels. They displayed, in order, our arriving at the truck stop, eating, paying our bill, and driving away. There were six panels per page, and in each frame we were joined in ever-developing degrees by ghostly creatures of myth; the centaur, the manticora, the chimera, and a griffin.

What started making me nervous was how the illustrations showed both of us eating precisely what we had ordered: pancakes, sausage, and a large chocolate milk for Carson; a western omelet and coffee for myself.

I knew from his monthly status reports that many of the specialists at the group home believed Carson possessed a gift for artwork. I wondered how he'd managed to draw these panels without my seeing him do it.

Carson was twenty-six, having outlived doctors' estimates for his life by more than a decade. He was getting sneaky in his old age. Or I was becoming obtuse in mine.

For the first time in ages, the two of us ate in silence. We then paid our bill and left.

As we were driving out of the parking lot and getting back onto the road, Carson turned to the next page. So far, only one frame was there. In it, our car was making a right onto Arboretum Road—a good twelve miles away.

"Well, at least Long-Lost is giving us a little time," I said.

Carson turned on the radio. It was still tuned to the local NPR station. This time the subject was "Foot-and-Mouth Disease: Is It Coming Back Again?"

I slowed the car as we neared the turnoff to Arboretum Road.

"We could just keep driving," I said. "Nothing's forcing us to do what's drawn there."

"Long-Lost says we gotta. He says it'll cause all kinds of trouble if we don't."

"Tell Long-Lost for me that he and I need to have a talk."

"He knows. He's planning on having a special talk with you. About me. An' stuff."

And with that, I turned onto Arboretum Road.

This time we didn't consult the comic book. About half a mile down the road there was a large fallen tree blocking the way. We would have to turn around and go back the way we came, and the only way to do that was to turn onto another, much narrower, unpaved side road—which was really more of a glorified footpath—then back out slowly as I worked the wheel.

As soon as we turned onto the path I looked up and realized where we were.

"Audubon's Graveyard," I whispered to myself.

"What?" said Carson.

"Nothing." Which, of course, wasn't the truth.

Having lived in Cedar Hill all of my life, I'd heard of Audubon's Graveyard—it was something of a local legend—but had never actually seen it, knew only that it was located somewhere in the vicinity of Arboretum Road.

I killed the engine and stared out at the small rise a few dozen yards ahead. A couple of pigeons lay there, dead, stiff, wings splayed, eyes glassy and staring up toward the sky they would never know again.

Carson reached over and gently touched my shoulder. "Where are we?"

"It's, um . . . well . . ." *How* could I explain this place to him?

There was a five-acre plat on the other side of that rise which some smartass reporter had long ago dubbed "Audubon's Graveyard," actually thinking the name displayed wit and irony. There were still some locals who referred to this area simply as "The Nest," but it was "Audubon's Graveyard" that stuck.

Since the spring of 1957, those five acres of county-owned land had been the focus of several official investigations (conducted by everyone from the State Department of Health to Federal Haz-Mat teams), and for good reason: twice a year, for a period lasting about three weeks, every bird that flew over the area dropped from the sky, dead before it hit the ground. The soil had been tested countless times for contaminants, as had the air, the small creek that ran through the plat, and even the other forms of wildlife that inhabited the woods surrounding it. Nothing was infected, and only birds were dying. In every case, their hearts exploded. No tests, no dissections, no theories were able to explain why this happened. There weren't even good legends from ancient Hopewell Indian mythology to shed any light on the cause. It was simply what it was: a huge and eerie question mark.

Carson nudged me with his elbow and showed me the next page: there we were, on the other side of the rise, on foot, walking toward the body of a dead hawk whose right eye took up a full half of the panel, while Carson and I were little more than minute, hazy ghosts in the background.

"Carson, I need you to be honest with me, all right? It's really important that you understand that."

"Uh-huh."

"*Is* this some kind of a joke? I know from your supervisors that you have drawing talent. Are you drawing those pages in when I'm not looking?"

"Oh, no! No. I ain't very good at drawing. Sure can't draw like this."

"Swear?"

"Swear."

I looked at the comic book in his hand and nodded my head. "Well, then; let's go see what Long-Lost has in mind for us."

We climbed up the rise, Carson taking care not to step on the bodies of the pigeons.

The sight below made my breath catch in my throat.

Scattered across the field were hundreds of dead birds; purple grackles and blackbirds, flickers, brown thrashers, loggerhead shrikes, bohemian waxwings, multi-colored kestrels, kingfishers, starlings, blue-grays, and a magnificent marsh hawk. I had no idea how any of these birds had died; there were no broken necks, no gunshot wounds, no animal bites. Only their eyes held a clue.

Every set was a deep, disturbing red.

There were not only the bodies of birds, but bones, as well. Neither Carson nor myself could walk more than a few paces without hearing the tiny crunch and snap of birds' bones under our shoes. Carson looked once again at his comic, then unzipped a pocket of his knapsack, moved its contents to the pockets of his coat, and began gathering up as many bones as he could stuff in there.

"Carson, you can't be—"

"I gotta," he replied, thrusting the comic into my hand.

In the new set of panels (Jesus H. Christ, *how* was he doing this so quickly?), Carson was moving through the field, gathering up bones. In the final panel on the page an old barn suddenly entered the picture, albeit far in the background.

I looked up, and there it was; deserted, neglected, falling only slightly to decay.

"Carson, stop, we're going home." I was now seriously creeped out. Unless the fantasy before me is up on a movie or television screen I really have no use for it, nor it for me.

"I *can't!*" Carson yelled back at me. "Long-Lost says I gotta."

"Long-Lost is not driving the car, and Long-Lost sure as hell isn't the one taking care of you, so Long-Lost can go fuck himself!" Even I was shocked to hear that word come out of my mouth, which should have given me some indication of how panicked I was becoming, but at that moment I was too caught up in wanting to get the hell away from there so I could start denying any of this had happened to care about my language.

Carson whirled around and pleaded. "Please, UncGil? I just gotta do this."

"I said no."

Now he glared at me. For a few moments we stood there like two half-assed cowboys in some showdown from a Sergio Leone Western epic, then I stormed across to Carson and grabbed his arm, which was stupid, because my nephew, though not very tall, is nonetheless a beefy and very compact man, one whose physical strength is easy to overlook.

He jerked away and I made to grab him again, but this time he was ready and met my movements with a swinging elbow that caught me in the center of the chest, knocking the wind and about three years of life out of me. I dropped to my knees and began to fall forward, stopping myself with my hands. I stayed that way for several moments, my vision blurry and lungs screaming for air. I looked down at the soil under my hands. I remember thinking how very much like clay the soil felt. I wondered if I could possibly dig up several handfuls and fashion them into clay crutches, because there was no way in hell I was going to able to get up under my own power.

Carson helped me up. He was crying. He hugged me tight, saying, "I'm sorry, UncGil, I'm sorry, I love you, I didn't mean it, I didn't, I didn't, I *didn't!*"

"It's . . . it's okay . . . okay, Carson. Come on, let's . . .

whew! . . . let's get back to the car so I can sit down, all right?"

"I'm sorry."

"I know. Me, too."

Ten years and several rest stops later we were finally back in the car. I leaned against the seat and waited for my chest to stop hurting. I'm still waiting, but eventually I was able to rally, turn the car around, and drive out. We had to wait to turn off Arboretum Road because the traffic was starting to get heavy. On my third attempt we were almost broadsided by the #48 express bus that ran between Cedar Hill, Buckeye Lake, and Columbus, but managed to get back on the road in one piece.

Carson looked behind us.

"What is it?" I asked.

"What bus was that?"

"The number forty-eight express. Why?"

He shrugged—a bit too nonchalantly, but that didn't really register at the time. "I dunno."

Back home that night there was no comic book reading. Carson demanded that I sit on the couch and watch TV and relax, he'd take care of me. I kept telling him that I was feeling much better, everything was okay—just make sure he never hit me again—but he wouldn't hear of it. He was going to take care of me, even make dinner.

Dinner turned out to be grilled cheese sandwiches, underdone on one side, overdone on the other, but seeing how proud he was of his accomplishment, I ate two and told him they were the best grilled cheeses I'd ever had. The truth was, they were. His company did a lot to enhance their taste.

Gary A. Braunbeck

The rest of our week together was more subdued than usual. Except for a trip to a comic book store to see if they had the new *Spider-Man* (I knew damn well he was looking for a new *Modoc*, but didn't say anything), nothing happened to remind me of the events at the truck stop and Audubon's Graveyard. I am very good at denial.

I took Carson back to the group home the following Monday. He gave me a long, hard hug on the front steps before going back inside. I stood staring at the door after it closed behind him. The empty space where he'd stood a few moments before seemed to hum with his absence.

The next few weeks kept me very busy preparing for the opening of the Columbus store. Cheryl, the other employees, and I spent many long hours cataloging the inventory, moving displays, changing the locations of various areas ("I really think the prints should be over here . . . ," "Maybe the movies should be closer to the middle of the store than right up front . . . ," "Is there any way to have the CDs closer to the posters . . . ?"), and generally making ourselves crazy.

The store opened. It was a big hit. I drove Cheryl home from the store one afternoon. We saw an old man chase his hat across the highway. Two black dogs watched everything. I came home to find a dying dog on my lawn. A woman whom I thought to be dead for the past twenty years sent me a package full of memories. And Carson disappeared from the group home.

A day in the life.

(Leaving a few things out there, aren't you, pal?)

Shut. Up.

EIGHT

By the time I arrived at the group home, NPR was reporting that seventeen whales had beached themselves along the Maine coastline, and the local newsbreak reported that a group of hikers had seen what was described as a "dragon" near a wooded area at Buckeye Lake.

Okay, it wasn't an elephant at the Twenty-first Street exit, but it was still funny. I'd have to make sure to tell Carson. After I finished being angry. And scared.

Suddenly so scared.

Cindy, one of the certified habilitation specialists who stayed at the group home, was waiting for me.

The neighborhood was amazingly quiet; no birds sang, no dogs barked, no cats yowled.

"I'm so sorry about this," Cindy said as I joined her on the porch. "He complained about having a headache right after lunch and asked to be excused from afternoon workshop duties today. I sent him up to his room so he could lie down. I went up to give him your message after you called and—well, come on in, you can see for yourself."

We went up to Carson's room. Cindy showed me how he'd tied his bedsheets together and used them to shimmy down from his window onto the roof of the back porch. From there it was simple to grab one of the thick branches of the tree beside the house and climb down to the ground. I shook my head at the sight. Carson might have Down's syndrome but it didn't exclude him from possessing the same adventurous—sometimes even devious—imagination of a typical nine-year-old boy.

"I found this on his pillow." Cindy offered me a folded slip of paper. I opened the note and read it, then became dizzy.

Carson's spelling needed work, but the meaning was clear enough:

Longlost sayz The keeperz are comeing N he kneedz To Talk To yoo.

Leaning on the windowsill and blinking the dizziness away, I saw a hand-sized cluster of what looked like small sticks lying near the roof gutter. If Cindy noticed them she gave no indication. But I knew damned well what they meant.

"I might have an idea where to find him."

Cindy rubbed her eyes, her shoulders slumping in relief. "I was hoping you'd say something like that."

"Have you called anyone else?"

She shook her head. "Only the sheriff. It's standard procedure when one of the residents wanders off—not that it happens all *that* much but—"

I raised a hand, stopping her. "You don't need to defend yourself to me, okay? I'm not upset and I won't lodge any complaints with the AARC board." My guess was she needed to hear that. The Association for the Advancement of Retarded Citizens sponsored this group home, which at any given time was staffed by two specialists and three trained volunteers, all of whom were expected to keep precise tabs on twelve residents. I couldn't blame them. No one can be expected to keep track of twelve developmentally disabled human beings—ranging in age from thirteen to sixty—every second of every minute of every day.

I turned back and examined Carson's room, which he shared with two other male residents.

"He took his comic books."

Cindy looked over at the bookshelf that hung over the head of Carson's bed. "I didn't notice that before." This said in the same tone of voice usually reserved for phrases such as "So what?"

"No reason you should have." I glanced out the window once again at the cluster of sticks and saw the head of a black mastiff duck down from behind a hedge across the street.

I gave my own head a little shake.

No. No way.

I forced a smile onto my face and turned toward Cindy, then squeezed her shoulder in what must have seemed like a condescending gesture and said, "I'll call you in about an hour or so and let you know if I found him."

"If you think you know where he is, then we should let the sheriff—"

"No. If he's where I think he is, the sheriff'd never find him. Give me ninety minutes. There's no use bothering the sheriff if it turns out I'm wrong."

Driving away, I hoped that Cindy wouldn't notice the little cluster on the roof. The significance of the comic books was known only to Carson and myself, no problem there, but the bones on the roof might set some Gothic bells ringing.

I knew where he was. What I didn't know was *why*.

I looked in the rearview mirror and saw the black mastiffs following me.

Whenever I slowed, they slowed.

One of them darted across the road into the path of an oncoming car that slammed on its brakes and laid on its horn.

Jesus.

I wasn't imagining them.

I looked in the rearview mirror again and saw one of the mastiffs running toward me, its teeth bared, foamy spit jetting from its mouth. At the last moment it spun around, claws scraping the asphalt with such power they sliced grooves into the surface, and then it took off at an even faster run toward the car that had nearly hit it a moment ago, legs pumping, muscles rippling, foam spraying, howling and snarling as it pushed forward on its hind legs and leaped into the air, landing on the hood of the car and hurtling its mass through the windshield.

I threw open my door and jumped out. In the distance, the driver was thrashing and screaming as the mastiff closed its jaws on his face. A slash of blood cut across the inside of the car, then another, then another, but still the man fought against his attacker.

The second mastiff ran to the car, repeatedly slamming its head against the driver's-side door, fracturing the steel. Then it rose up on its hind legs and began clawing at the window and handle.

Jesus Christ, it's trying to open the door.

It was a crazy thought, I knew it was a crazy thought, but it was enough to force me into action: I pushed my arm into my car and pulled the trunk release, then ran back and grabbed the crowbar beneath the spare tire, spun around, and ran toward the dogs.

The second mastiff was smashing its head against the side window now, having all but demolished the lower portion of the door, its claws tearing at the handle. And as I came closer I saw—I *saw*—the dog manipulate the digits of its paw to press down the release and wrench open the door.

Dogs cannot cannot CANNOT do that. They can't.

The first mastiff released its grip on the driver's face and the man fell to the side, his bloodied arm flopping toward the ground where the second mastiff sank his teeth into the wrist and began heaving backward, pulling the driver from inside.

Gripping the crowbar in both hands, I pulled back my arms and pitched forward with all my weight, swinging down and connecting with the center of the second mastiff's skull. There was a hard *crack!* when the business end of the crowbar hit home, sending an iron wave up my arm and into my shoulder. The dog released its grip on the driver's arm and staggered backward but didn't fall.

It shook its head, blinked its eyes, then gave me a look that might have said, *Don't you know that hurts?* before lunging toward my crotch.

I spun to the side just before the dog connected and was able to ram the other end of the crowbar into its breastplate before it tore into my hip with its claws and gripped my forearm in its teeth—

—but it did not break the skin. Its jaws had a powerhouse grip on my arm, but the thing wasn't biting into me, wasn't sinking those teeth through flesh and tendon all the way to the bone and ripping my arm from its socket; instead, it began to shake its head back and forth, drenching me in spit, jerking my arm this way and that, ripping through my jacket and shirt with its claws, tearing at my skin underneath, all the while whipping its head from side to side until I could no longer keep my grip on the crowbar and it went flying out of my hand to hit the pavement with a loud, ringing *thud!* and skittered over against the curb.

Once the crowbar was out of my hands and reach, the second mastiff stopped shaking its head but did not release its vise-grip on my arm. It pushed forward, forcing me to stumble back, then shifted its weight until I had no choice but to go to my knees or keel over.

The first mastiff was working on the driver. The man was dead. His face was now a pulpy, bloody mass of glistening meat and bone. His legs spasmed as his bowels evacuated. His fingers trembled, then were still.

The second mastiff released its grip on my arm and backed away a few inches, staring at me. Our faces were now on the same level. That's what it had wanted all along.

I looked at it.

Its eyes were the same deep shade of red as those of the dead birds in Audubon's Graveyard.

Its lips kept pulling back in a half-snarl, a deep, rumbling growl crawling around the back of its throat, ready to explode if I so much as moved.

I could feel the blood tricking down the side of my legs where its claws had torn through my clothes. The old wound on my left shoulder throbbed from the kickback force of the first crowbar strike. My heart slammed against my chest. I gulped for air, shuddering.

The mastiff moved to the side, huffing its harsh, hot breath against the side of my neck, still half-snarling, dribbling thick rivulets of slobber-spit onto my arm.

That's when I knew what was happening.

It wanted me to *watch*.

I remained as still as I possibly could, trying to ignore the pain, the fear, and the sickness welling up from my stomach.

The first mastiff waited until it was sure it had a captive audience, and then, slowly, with a deliberation you'd never attribute to an animal, began to disassemble the driver.

Not tear him apart: *disassemble*.

Using its teeth and claws, it worked on the man's right arm until the shoulder was loosened and the scapula could be easily separated from the clavicle. Once the arm was removed, the mastiff carefully picked it up and carried it to the side of the road, licking the blood from the flesh until it was clean, then came back and began to remove the left arm.

Good God, I thought, *where are the police? Someone*

must have heard all the noise, someone must have seen this and called the police. Where are they?

I saw the strobe-flash of the visibar lights approaching from the distance.

Why weren't they using their *sirens?*

The vehicle approached; large, dark, boxlike.

It could only be something like a SWAT team.

Good.

The dogs looked at the vehicle, then calmly went back to their respective tasks of disassembling the driver and guarding me.

Dusk was coming fast. There was maybe an hour of daylight remaining.

Still, the vehicle shone its headlights directly into my eyes. I blinked, pulled back my head, and tried to turn away, only to find the face of the second mastiff batting its nose into mine to turn my head forward.

There was the sound of a metal door sliding open. A figure stepped from inside the van. It was difficult to make out any features because of the headlights' glare, but I could make out some if his shape.

Not a police officer. Not unless the Cedar Hill Police Department was now issuing bowler hats as official head gear.

He cupped his hands around his mouth and shouted something in a language like no other I'd heard before. It sounded like an amalgamation of languages; guttural clicks of Basque, monosyllabic tones of Mandarin, retroflex consonants of Gondi and Kurukh, even the musical complexities of Welsh.

Over two decades, and *now* my World Language minor comes in useful.

Whatever language he spoke, the dogs understood.

They both stopped what they were doing and trot-ted over to the man with steps that were almost light and happy.

"You need to go," said the blurry figure behind the lights.

"B-but . . . but they *killed* that man!" I said, point-ing toward the body as if the other man didn't have a clear view of it already.

"Raw material is a bitch to get hold of these days, Gil. You'll remember soon enough. Now, you'd best be on your way to get Carson."

I opened my mouth to speak, but the two mastiffs came lumbering out of the light, their red eyes glar-ing, their lips pulled back in full snarls.

I staggered back to my feet, stumbling toward my car, not wanting to take my eyes away from the dogs.

When my opened car door hit me in the ass, I twisted around and fell into the seat, slamming the door closed, putting the car in gear, and tearing away from there in a squeal of tires.

I ran two stop signs and least one red light on my way toward Audubon's Graveyard. How I didn't get pulled over by the police, I'll never know. I only know that I was so far beyond scared that it would have taken the *light* from scared a thousand years to reach me.

I need to concentrate, to find something concrete, something real, something of the world I knew and understood to grab hold of and not let go, to ground me, to let me know that I wasn't cracking up again.

(Again? Did I hear the word "again"? Does that mean you're finally going to let it come back to you, pal?)

Gary A. Braunbeck

Ignoring you.

I pressed a hand against my chest as if that would help slow the jackhammering of my heart, then slid it up to press against my screaming shoulder. Even through the jacket and shirt I could feel the old scar tissue beginning to swell, and suddenly I had it, the one thing I could latch onto, the one thing that might keep me in one piece until I'd found Carson and could start making sense out of all of this.

The promise of seeing Beth again.

Because if it hadn't been for this old wound, I never would have met her . . .

NINE

Two months before my tenth birthday my aunt Amy, who was then eighteen, invited me to go along with her to visit one of her friends who was away at college. Aunt Amy usually took me out at least once every two weeks—a movie and pizza, then shopping at the seemingly endless supply of record stores in Columbus (usually near or on the Ohio State University campus). Even then, people twice my age were aware that when it came to contemporary music—be it rock, folk, progressive ("prog," to those of us in the know), even crossover jazz like John McLaughlin and the Mahavishnu Orchestra, this little geek from Cedar Hill was The Kid to Ask. Whenever Amy was going to have a party and wanted the music to be perfect, she'd come to me to help her record tapes. The deejays at Stereo Rock 92 had nothing on me when it came to instant recall of who played in what band and on what label and when.

The excursion that day promised to be a good one; the new Steppenwolf album was just out and I'd been saving my allowance to buy it. No place in Cedar Hill carried it yet, but I knew I'd find it at the first record store I walked into in Columbus. Amy told me that she needed me to settle a bet with some of her friends about the last couple of Grand Funk Railroad albums, and if I'd come along with her and "put those know-it-alls in their place," *she'd* buy the Steppenwolf album for me. (Amy made it a point to never tell me ahead of time what the "bet" was specifically about, because she knew I enjoyed being put on the spot when it came to rock trivia. I'd been the ace up her sleeve on at least five occasions, and not once had I failed her or been stumped by any of her friends. I liked that. I liked being good at something and briefly admired for it: "Hey, this kid's good. *Really* good. Now get rid of him and let's party.")

The drive from Cedar Hill took forever, it seemed (two hours in a car in kid-time is an eternity, remember?), but eventually we arrived at our destination. I knew something was wrong as soon as we started driving down a side road that led to the dorms.

"Shit," said Amy, banging a fist against the steering wheel. "They've got it blocked off."

We turned around and tried three other side roads but all of them were closed. Finally, Amy drove around one of the roadblocks and ended up on a really nice road lined with hills and trees. It would have been pretty if it weren't for the smoke coming over the trees and all the shouting in the distance.

Just as we were coming around a bend in the road Amy hit the brakes. Several yards ahead sat an ominous looking truck that I recognized as having something to do with the Army.

Amy's eyes grew wide. *"Oh, Lord. . . ."*

I rolled down my window to see if I could get a better view of what was going on. I could hear a lot of people shouting somewhere on the other side of the hill. I could also hear something that sounded like the voice of a robot trying to be heard over the shouting. (I later found out it was a bullhorn being used by campus security.)

A soldier walked around the side of the truck and pointed at our car. Amy grabbed my hand and said, "Stay here," then climbed out to meet the soldier. I sat there looking at the smoke coming over the trees. I wasn't so much nervous as I was impatient to know what was going on, so like every curious, annoying nine-year-old you've ever met, I looked to make sure Amy and the soldier weren't watching me (they were arguing, rather loudly), opened the door of the car, and made my way toward the hill. I was almost to the top when I heard the robot voice shout something I couldn't understand, and then something made the loudest *crack!* I'd ever heard and the crowd screamed.

If you haven't figured it out yet, my Aunt Amy had driven us to Kent State University. It was May 4, 1970, and we'd arrived just a few minutes before the National Guard opened fire on students gathered to protest the war in Vietnam. They were supposed to fire over the protestors' heads, but some did not. All of this I discovered in the days and weeks to come; at the moment all Hell broke loose and invited Purgatory to join the party, I was flat on my face at the top of that hill. I looked up and saw a structure a few yards away and, figuring it would be safe, crawled toward it.

There is a very famous photograph from the Kent State shootings. In it, a young female student is half-kneeling, half-squatting by the body of a student lying facedown on the sidewalk. Her arms are parted at her sides like a celebrant blessing the hosts at Mass; her long straight hair is caught in the wind and flowing to the right. She is in the middle of releasing a scream of anguish that to this day I still hear in my dreams.

In the background, past the people running by in panic, past the lush hillside, through the wisps of dissipating tear gas, up in the corner, you will see a small gazebo. If you are a person who has the technology to do so, and if you can get your hands on a copy of that photograph, then use your computer's photo editing software to enlarge that corner section of the picture. Concentrate on the lower left-hand side of the gazebo, enlarge that a little, and you will see what looks like a small fuzzy animal trying to burrow its way through the gazebo's latticework and hide underneath.

That is the top of my head.

A few seconds after that photograph was taken, I scrambled to my feet and ran back down to the car as fast as I've ever run in my life. When I got there, the National Guardsman who'd been arguing with my aunt was surrounded by half a dozen angry and panicked students. Two of them grabbed the guardsman while another attempted to yank his rifle from his grip. The gun was jerked up, down, and to the side. One. Two. Three.

On two Amy whipped her head around and saw me standing by the car. She started to shout something at me and then three arrived and something exploded. I couldn't see what because I was magically on my back staring up at the clouds and wondering why I couldn't feel my left side.

Here's a piece of information you might want to file away under *Things You Never Want to Find Out for Yourself:* If fired in close enough proximity to a target—even an accidental one like an annoyingly curious nine-year-old boy who should have stayed in the stupid car—rubber bullets can cause almost as much damage as the real thing.

The bullet passed cleanly through my left shoulder, missing bone but making a permanent impression on what tissue it met along the way.

I remember everyone crowding around me. I remember the way Amy grabbed me and kissed me and got my blood all over her nice blouse. I remember the strength of the guardsman's arms as he pushed everyone aside and lifted me up like he was some kind of superhero and ran toward the truck. Then I decided I was tired and closed my eyes.

I was treated at the local hospital, then transferred by ambulance to Cedar Hill Memorial the next morning. I remember none of this because I was unconscious for nearly twenty hours after it happened.

What I do remember is waking up in my hospital room to find Amy there with my mom, a nurse, and a couple of reporters. Amy was so glad to see me awake she broke down crying and tried to hug me, but the nurse said that wasn't a good idea, so my aunt simply kissed my cheek and held my hand while my mom glared at her, and then at me. She didn't have to speak; I knew what was going through her mind: *Do you have any idea how angry your father is about all of this? Do you know how embarrassing this has been to us?*

"I'm sorry," I whispered to her.

"Oh, hon," said Amy, "oh god, what have *you* got to be sorry about? I should have left the minute I knew what was happening! This is all my fault. I'm so sorry."

I turned my head and looked at her. Why was she crying about me?

I was something of a minor celebrity on the floor for a few days after that. I was the Kid Who'd Gotten Shot at *Kent State*. That's how nurses and orderlies broke the ice with me: "Hey, aren't you that kid who got shot at Kent State? Wow."

I knew I'd been hit in the shoulder, but what confused me was why I had this monster bandage running from the center of my chest down to my package. (My father was a WWII veteran, and in his house you never said "pee-pee" or "penis" or "dick"; no, when referring to that area, you called it your "package.")

It turned out that when I'd dropped, I'd slammed down on a large rock at the side of the road and ruptured my spleen. My parents had raised holy hell about having surgery performed in Kent and had insisted it be done at Cedar Hill. I was stabilized and moved, even though postponing the surgery could have killed me. To this day I try to convince myself it had nothing to do with the rates at CHM being nearly twenty-five percent cheaper; haven't made it there yet, but stay tuned.

Soon enough I became less of a conversation piece and just another patient and that was fine with me. Most days in the hospital I was kept comfortable, had plenty of help when I needed to get out of bed, regained my appetite, and had a few visitors; mostly Amy (who not only bought *Steppenwolf 7* for me, but evidently every album in every record store between here and Michigan) and a couple of my teachers from school. Mom came to visit only once after that first day, and then didn't say much or stay long. My father never visited or called. I guessed he was still mad at me.

On those days when Aunt Amy didn't come by, I could always count on Beth, who always seemed to appear just when I needed her, always decked out in her torn blue bathrobe with the words *Grand Hotel, London* stitched out in fading letters across the chest. She boasted that her mother had gotten it for her while in England on a theatrical tour, and the hotel management was more than happy to give such a renowned stage actress as Beth's mother a tiny souvenir. (Even then I suspected that Beth might not be telling me the whole truth; I'd heard a couple of nurses talking about how she lived with her aunt, who was the only relative that could be found. If her mother was such a famous stage actress, then how hard could it be to find her? After all, she'd sent her that bathrobe from *London*, hadn't she? Then I figured that maybe Beth was embarrassed because her mom and dad didn't want her, so she made up things. I guessed that was okay. Sometimes the truth was boring, or made other people feel sorry for you and not know what to say, so they didn't say anything and left you alone. I got the feeling Beth had been left alone a lot.)

Beth had been admitted for an emergency appendectomy when her appendix burst and was in the room two doors down from mine. She'd come by my room in the early days of my stay when I was still the Big Curiosity, but unlike the rest of the patients on our floor, she *kept* coming back.

Beth was sixteen years old, I was still nine (*Ten in July* I'd tell people any chance I got, as if knowing that would make me any less ridiculous in their eyes.); she wore love beads around her neck and told me she had a pair of hip-hugger bell-bottom jeans that she only wore in warm weather because she liked to wear her sandals with them—thank God the appendectomy scar was low enough that she could still wear halters and tube-tops.

My wardrobe consisted mostly of mismatched plaid and paisley.

Beth seemed to be popular at her school (she had a lot more visitors than I did, all of them girls who were her age; and she always brought them over to meet me, and they always said I was cute but I don't think they really meant it). I was a big Zero at my school, what with the plaid, the paisley, and my thick, dark-framed glasses, not to mention my interest in books (Vonnegut), monster movies (Godzilla ruled, still does), and music that wasn't on *American Top Forty*.

Why someone Beth's age seemed to like being

around a kid like me, I don't know. Maybe she cast me in the role of Little Brother She Never Had or something; all I know is that anytime I got sick, or fell down (I fell down a lot the first week or so after my surgery), or even felt lonely, Beth was there before any nurse or doctor, always helping me up, or brushing my hair back with her hand, or giving me a big but not too-tight hug. I liked that. My mom and dad weren't big huggers. They loved me, I knew that (or told myself so, anyway), but ours was not a house big on physical displays of affection. So a Beth bear hug (the only kind she knew how to give) was always welcomed, even when it made me feel like a little baby.

Then one day Beth overhead something between a nurse and one of the orderlies, something about the lab where all the animals were kept. Eavesdropping on adult conversations was something that Beth seemed to do automatically, and when she told me what she'd heard, something about the word "animals" piqued my interest.

"They keep animals here? I thought this was a hospital just for people."

"I guess there's like a whole floor of them over in one of the other buildings," Beth said. "They try out new drugs and operations on them, to help humans."

"How do you get there?"

"I heard the nurses saying that you have to go outside, across the street. But guess what?" She smiled at me, one of those delicious "I've-Got-A-Secret" smiles that become less enchanting the older you get, then lowered her voice to a whisper: "There are *tunnels!* Can you *believe* it? Like those secret underground places in all the James Bond movies. Pretty groovy, huh?"

Having been cooped up in this room and bed for most of the last ten days, I was all for it. "How do we get there?"

"I'm not sure, but I'm working on it. Stay cool."

Beth worked on it, all right. One of the orderlies on our ward was the older brother of a girl Beth knew from school, and was easily talked into taking us there. (I remember that he and Beth had gone into one of the little rooms down the hall to talk about it and were in there an awfully long time.)

The Sunday morning we took off on our little excursion was an incredibly warm one, even for mid-May in Ohio. All of the windows were open but they offered no relief. My gown clung to me as I slipped out of bed (with Beth's help, of course) and put on my slippers and the light hospital robe.

"I *know* the robe's uncomfortable," Beth said, "but I don't want you catching a cold or anything worse—God, I'd just *freak out* if that happened. Just to be safe, here—put on your pajama bottoms. And don't look at me like that, you."

The IV bottle was tricky, a big, heavy thing made of thick glass that clinked against the metal pole from which it hung. At least the pole was on wheels so I could pull it along behind me, but the clinking noise drove me nuts; Beth remedied that by stealing some medical tape from a supply cart and wrapping it around the bottle so that it was attached to the pole. Thankfully, the wheels didn't squeak.

Once I'd gotten myself out into the hallway, Beth,

the orderly (whose name I never knew), and I headed for the elevators.

"We gotta go down to one of the subbasements in order to get to the other elevators," said the orderly, putting his hand in the middle of Beth's back. "Hope you aren't afraid of dim places."

"I'm not afraid of much," replied Beth, pulling his hand away from her. "Except maybe having my time wasted."

I knew there was a basement but had no idea there were floors beneath even that. We went all the way down to subbasement #3. Just seeing that light up above the elevator door gave me the creeps; this was deeper than they *buried* you after you died.

Yeech.

The doors opened to reveal a long hallway with concrete walls and bare bulbs cradled in bell-shaped cages of wire dangling from the ceiling. It was damp and cold and I was suddenly grateful that Beth had insisted that I wear the bathrobe and pajama bottoms.

I remember the walls very clearly. It was easy to see the boards that had been used as forms for the concrete because several of them had warped before the concrete had set properly; they looked like ghosts trapped in the walls, stuck forever between this world and the one they'd come from and now wished they had never tried to leave.

Double yeech.

Beth leaned over and whispered in my ear, "This is where they bring the dead bodies."

"Huh-*uh!*"

"Uh-*huh!* I heard the nurses say so."

The yeech factor was then tripled with the notion that at any moment we could see a dead body being rolled down the hallway. I wondered if any of the bodies from Kent State had been brought here, if they'd been covered up and rolled over the very spot where I was standing. The thought frightened me so much that my fingers went numb. I shook them, confused by the effect. Usually when I got scared, my stomach got all tight and hurt; this was the first time I'd had anything happen with my fingers. Maybe fingers had something to do with real fear, and the stomach stuff was just with pretend fear, like with Godzilla or *The Fly* or *The Incredible Shrinking Man*. I'd have to think on that. Later.

The orderly took hold of one of Beth's hands and guided us out of there in a hurry. The feeling began to return to my fingers as I heard Beth breathe a sigh of relief. I looked at her and she smiled, then took hold of my hand with her free one, the three of us now forming an unbreakable chain.

I felt like someone really liked me. I wondered what the kids at school would say if they could see me now, on an adventure with a girl, a *sixteen-year-old* girl who wore love beads and bell-bottomed hip-huggers and had friends who thought I was cute and actually *wanted* to hold my hand. Wow. (My interest in members of the opposite sex began in earnest during my ninth year, which only served to make me even more of a weirdo among my schoolmates; after all, everyone knew girls were *gross*, they had *cooties* and the last thing you wanted was for one to touch you. I'd thought about asking one of the nurses or doctors where the Cootie Ward was located, just to see if they could kill you like all the other kids said.)

There were things about Beth I didn't really understand, like how she could get so serious sometimes. Once I'd awakened in my hospital bed a few days after my surgery to find her standing over me with two of her girlfriends. I tried to speak but my throat was still sore; she put a finger to my lips, then bent down and kissed me, just like that. Then her girlfriends kissed me, as well. I don't know what kind of a reaction they were expecting, but the look on my face made all three of them go "*Awww*," and then touch me; my cheek, my hand, my shoulder. I never asked Beth about why she did that, or why her friends acted the way they did, because I was afraid that she'd tell me the look on my face had been goofy. Beth was the only person I didn't feel goofy around, and if I'd looked that way I didn't want to know. I would pretend. Like she did about her mother the famous stage actress. That would be okay.

"This way," the orderly said, pointing toward a place where this tunnel split off into another.

He led us through the tunnel that connected with the building across the street. It was a long, boring tunnel, not a creepy one like we'd just come through, and I was happy about that. Boring was good.

Once we made it through the tunnel, we got into another elevator and took it all the way up. I was secretly hoping that we'd skip both tunnels on the way back and just walk outside and cross the street; if the tunnels were part of a great adventure, I'd just as soon go back to being a goofy Zero with iffy eyesight in his mismatched plaid and paisley.

The elevator stopped and the doors opened onto a large foyer. Open windows with a breathtaking view of Cedar Hill took up most of the walls. A cool, gentle wind came in through the windows, fluffing the curtains outward. Up here the ghosts weren't trapped in the walls, they fluttered free, saying hello. Even the concrete floors seemed less threatening. On either side of the foyer were sets of swinging metal doors. We went through the set on the right, and as we stepped through it hit us full-force: the stink of ammonia mixed with the chemical cleaners. It burned the inside of my nose and made my eyes tear up. This probably should have been an omen but we continued on down the hall anyway, fun-fun-fun, following the smells until we came to the doors marked: SANCTIONED PERSONNEL ONLY.

"You okay?" Beth whispered to me.

"I guess. Do you think this is okay?"

She leaned her head to one side and sucked once on her lower lip. "Hard to say, kiddo, but we've come this far, might as well finish it, huh?"

I didn't like her calling me "kiddo" but didn't say anything about it. Maybe she was just nervous. I knew I was.

We pushed open the doors and entered a cavernous room. Equipment of all sorts stolen from every science fiction movie I'd ever seen lined the walls, and in the center stood interlocking pens with metal poles for sides. In two of the pens were pigs, in the other two were sheep. They had no straw for bedding and the concrete floor, dribbled with urine and liquid feces, sloped downward toward a system of drains. My first thought was: *How can they sleep on this floor? It's so cold and hard and . . . messy.*

The animals had been sleeping, but stirred awake when we entered. The sheep bleated and the pigs snorted, both sounding almost human, and circled their small pens. I'd never been so close to either sheep or pigs before, and they seemed enormous, like creatures that the scientist experimented on before accidentally creating a giant spider that broke loose and did all sorts of yeechy things.

Pigs have very human eyes, blue, with round pupils. After staring at you they'll look away and you can see the whites of their eyes. Something about the pigs and the sheep seemed *wrong* to me, and I didn't want to get any closer to them.

The three of us just stood there in the doorway. I remember that things were said, but exactly what and to whom I can't remember. We'd come this far, we'd survived the Descent into Darkness and the Hallway of Frozen Ghosts and wouldn't turn back until we had something to show for it.

A tough bunch, us.

As the sheep paced around I saw that sections of fleece had been shaved away in squares for recently sutured incisions. One of them had what looked like a plastic bag sewn to its side. It was filled with something thick and dark and swirling with small chunks. I turned away.

We moved on to the next room, where dogs had started barking. Half a dozen of them in large cages greeted us joyously as we entered. One of them looked sad and sick and ignored us, but the rest pushed all their weight against the bars as we approached.

As I neared the first one's cage, however, he stopped barking and growled at me. Beth heard this and warned me not to get any closer to the dogs, most of whom looked desperate for attention—just a rub, a touch, a sniff of your hand so I can lick it, please, oh, please-please-please.

At that moment I both loved and despised them, with their shrill yelps and wagging tails and bright eyes. Sorrow and discouragement soaked the room in those loud cries, pacing back and forth, back and forth, back and forth. I was overwhelmed. On each cage door was a chart with handwritten details about the dog, filled with alien words and baffling mathematical and chemical symbols. Instead of water dishes they had bottles attached to the cages with tubes they could lick, giant versions of the ones used by the gerbils at school. Despite the warnings and my own confused feelings, I decided to let one of the dogs lick my fingers through the bars. I knew it wouldn't bite me; it seemed far too lonely.

It was friendly and warm and I just wanted to open the door and take it back to my room. I took a chance and pushed my hand a little farther into the cage so I could scratch the back of its neck. There was a light-blue plastic tag attached to the back of its ear. I bent its ear down, gently, and saw the tag had only three words on it: PROPERTY OF KEEPERS. Below that was a series of numbers. I pulled my hand out and looked back at the silent dog. It was staring at me, unblinking, as if it either recognized me or was waiting for me to figure something out. I smiled at it, feeling sorry for the poor thing, and took a step toward it.

It shook its head back and forth, once, quickly: an emphatic *no*.

Beth and the orderly didn't seem to have noticed, so maybe I'd imagined it. Shaking your head *no* like that was something people did—mostly parents and teachers when they didn't want you to accidentally have fun; cold stare, tight lips, head back and forth once and once only: *No, absolutely not.*

I took another step toward the silent dog. This time I watched carefully. This time I did not imagine it. This time it definitely looked at me and shook its head *No!*

I remained still, then mouthed the word *Why?*

The dog looked away from me for a moment, making certain that no one else was watching, then with its front left paw reached up and bent forward its left ear, holding it like that so I could see the plastic tag: PROPERTY OF KEEPERS.

A sense of adventure almost emerged for a few seconds. *I* knew what was really going on here. They were making the animals smarter, smarter maybe than people, and this dog was trying to let me in on the secret. Maybe because the animals were planning a revolt and would need human friends once they were outside and free? Could that be it? I started to mouth the question but then my silent conspirator blinked, suddenly just a dog again, twisted around, lifted its legs, and began licking itself *down there.*

Beth's hand on my shoulder nearly caused me to shriek. "Hey, don't wander off on me, okay? I'd be pretty lonely if I lost you." Even as a child of ten—

okay, okay, *nine*—I could've swum a hundred raging rivers on the memory of those words.

The next room was lined with cages.

The wall directly across from the door was filled with cages containing white mice, and to the right was an entire wall of cats, cage after cage stacked on top of each other. I'd never seen so many cats in one place, yet it was so quiet. The cats crouched in their cages and stared at us. As we got closer, some of them came up to the bars on their cages and rubbed against them, opening their mouths soundlessly.

"Why are they so quiet?" I asked Beth.

"I don't know."

"Well, shit—I do!" said the orderly, proud of himself.

He went over to one of the cages and worked the door open with a paper clip he took from his pocket, then pulled out one of the cats—a brown Tom—and brought it over to us.

"Look here," he said, grabbing its head none-too-gently and pulling it back.

The fur underneath its neck had been shaved all the way across, and running through the middle of the pink skin was a long scar.

"What *happened* to it?" said Beth, sounding as if she were going to cry.

"You think the folks who work here want to listen to bunch of goddamn cats yowling all day long?" said the orderly, throwing the cat back into its cage and closing the door. "You get this many cats, you cut their vocal cords so they don't make any noise."

"That's *terrible*," said Beth, and I could tell she was trying to hold off the tears.

The cats had the same type of water bottles and charts as the dogs, but their cages were much, much smaller. A lot of them had matchbox-sized rectangles with electrical wires implanted in their skulls. The skin of their exposed scalps was crusty and red where it joined the metal. There were plastic blue tags attached to the backs of their ears, as well, only these were much smaller than those worn by the dogs. It didn't matter; I already knew what they all said.

I gripped my IV pole with all my strength. I looked at all the tubes and wires running into the silent cats, then at the thin clear tube running from the IV bottle down into my arm. I think that was the first time in my life when I realized that, eventually, all of us will be put in a situation where we will be treated as something less than human.

Welcome to puberty, you dumb dork.

One of the cats gently swatted at my hand through a space between the bars, working its mouth as if begging to be petted. I remember how wide its open mouth was, how dark, how if you looked into it long enough you might fall in and be swallowed and then both of you would be quiet forever, never able to ask anyone for a hug or food or to refill the water bottle. I squeezed its paw and quickly let go.

There was the sound of monkeys in the next room, but I wanted to leave. I was scared and sad and my stitches were hurting.

"You *bet* we're leaving," said Beth, putting her

hand on my shoulder and looking at the orderly. "Well?"

"Well, *nothing*," he said. "You two pussies can leave if you want, but I'm gonna go look at the monkeys. I hear they're doing some *really* weird shit with them."

Beth glared at him. "How are we supposed to find our way back?"

The orderly shrugged. "Getting you *back* wasn't part of the deal. You put out, I bring you and the squirt over here. You want me to take you back the same way? You know what it costs."

"You are such a fuck-stick," said Beth.

"Yeah, well . . . you didn't seem to mind it the other day in the linen room."

Beth shook her head, her eyes suddenly so bright. She looked angry, and sad, and . . . something else that I couldn't pin down. *Ashamed?*

"Come on, Gil, we'll find our own way back."

So we left the orderly to his monkeys and whatever else was back there.

She did not hold my hand this time.

At the breathtaking windows, neither of us spoke.

The same in the elevator.

In the tunnels, not even the ghosts said a word.

Once or twice I sneaked a look at Beth, who seemed to be trying not to cry in front of me. I wished she would so I could hold her hand again. It would make me feel better and maybe her, too.

I looked at the tube from my IV.

I thought of the girl I'd seen and the way she'd screamed as she knelt by the body.

I thought of the cats and how they wanted to talk to us but couldn't.

The wires.

The charts.

The dog shaking its head *No*.

Back on the ward, the lunch trays were just arriving and the aroma of sloppy joes, my favorite bestest yummiest lunchtime food ever, filled the halls. I had no appetite. When a nurse asked where we'd been, Beth replied that we'd gone outside for some fresh air because this place smelled like a hospital, and did the nurse have a problem with that because if she did Beth would be more than happy to step outside with *her*.

I just stood there, staring down at the floor, feeling sick and thinking about the way that dog had shaken its head at me.

Now, as I pulled onto the side road that led to Audubon's Graveyard, I tried to remember whether or not that dog's eyes had been red.

I parked the car, popped the trunk, and killed the engine and headlights.

Everything was swallowed in darkness. Even the lights and sounds from the road a quarter-mile behind me couldn't reach in and break the night.

I gripped the steering wheel and lay my forehead against my hands, still trying to steady my breathing.

(I'm telling you, pal, if you'd just stop fighting it and let yourself remember, this would all go a lot easier . . .)

I didn't feel like arguing.

It's not that I "hear voices" or anything dramatic like that; no formless demon from New Jersey tells me that God wishes I'd grind up my neighbors into dog food because they haven't accepted Abe Vigoda as their Lord and Savior or anything like that. I live with—or *try* to live with, anyway—a condition that some doctors and psychologists call "minimization," a fancy term that means (as far as I understand it) you're constantly talking yourself out of something you remember. Think of it as denial's more vicious and immovable first cousin.

In my own case—if the doctors are to be believed—I have spent decades convincing myself that this one particular memory is of something that never happened, and in the process have forced myself to forget it.

Even now, I'm damned if I can tell you what it is.

The only problem with minimization is, if you're successful at it for long enough, you unconsciously begin questioning the validity and even the reality of other memories.

I thought it was all so much bullshit until about five years ago, when I began getting these physical jolts for no reason. I'd be sitting in a chair reading a book, and the next thing I know my whole body has just sort of snapped forward like a rubber band and the book's on the floor and I've knocked over the glass on the side table and I'm shaking like I've got the DTs.

Nerves, I told myself. *Just nerves.*

Then I started talking to myself internally, in two different voices; one of them my own (or what I imagine it sounds like to other people's ears), the other belonging to the smartass me of age eighteen.

And I began having these monstrous dreams, filled with violence and death.

Each of them separately was worrisome enough, but then they began clustering on me; the jolts, the voices, the dreams.

I honestly thought I had a brain tumor for a while, but a series of tests quickly ruled out anything physiological.

So I began seeing doctors, most of whom went right for the SSRIs—selective serotonin reuptake inhibitors—like Lexapro, Paxil, even good old Prozac. Each of them helped for a while, but the jolts and dreams always came back. My current doctor, whose offices are in Columbus, is the leading psychopharmacologist in the state. She determined that the reason none of the SSRIs were having their desired effect was because they needed to be "accentuated" (the word she used, hand to God) with a mood stabilizer such as Lemictol. It took us about six months but we finally hit on the right combination: Seroquil at night, Lemictol and Lexapro in the morning. For the past three years that combo had been doing the trick.

Until the last couple of weeks, when she started talking about trying anti-psychotics.

Christ.

I gripped the steering wheel tighter and rolled my forehead back and forth across my knuckles; the poor man's face massage.

Just a few moments to rally my sorry ass, that's all.

I'd get Carson, take him home, and we'd get through this.

We'd get through this because everything was going to be fine.

I was fine. I was fine. I was *fine*.

Just a few moments to rally and catch my breath, here in the safety of my car, my forehead against my hands, my breathing getting slower, steadier, steady . . . steady . . . there you go . . .

TEN

. . . I wake to the sounds of moaning and bleating. I blink my eyes and stretch my arms, pulling in the first breath of the day. I nearly choke from the fetid stench of wet straw and urine-soaked dirt. I press my hands into the floor to raise myself. I feel something warm and deep. I look down and see the trail of liquid filth that has squittered from the bowels of one of the sick animals chained in this place. Rising, I find a cloth hanging from one of the stable doors and drape it over my shoulder.

Walking outside, I climb the small rise to the side of the building and stop when I reach the well. I work the water pump beside it and soon the spigot spits out a heavy stream of something lukewarm but wet. I lean down my head—careful not to catch either of my horns on the iron—and drench my face and chest. I rub until I feel the filth of the night wash away, then use the cloth to dry myself.

In the distance, from a place just over the rise, I can already hear the groaning of the machinery, smell the metallic smoke rising into the air from the chimneys.

Overhead I hear a crow calling and there is the faint odor of rotting flesh in the air.

Suddenly one of the men is behind me, prodding me into movement with a long device that cracks and sizzles when it touches my flesh. The electricity jolts through my tail, my legs, and up into my chest.

"Get your ass moving, pal!" he shouts, then holds the device above his head, smiling, filled with glory; Jason showing his Golden Fleece to the masses.

It is the orderly from so many years ago, the one who guided Beth and me through the tunnels and to the animals. He looks even meaner than I remember as he snarls, "I got plans to meet some buddies for drinks and I'm not gonna be late on accounta you!"

He makes the device hiss and crackle once again. I twirl the cloth like a rope and snap it forward, knocking the device from his grip. It flies out of his hand and lands in a puddle of liquid excrement. Before he can pull his other weapon from its holster I grab him by the throat and lift him off the ground. I am very strong. He kicks and chokes. It amuses me, the way his dangling feet twist and move in the air. Is he trying to dance on air?

Another voice says, "Please put him down. He's an idiot. It's not worth it."

I turn my head. Carson stands nearby. His hand rests on the butt of his holstered weapon.

I release my grip on the orderly's throat and he drops to the ground with a heavy, wet noise. He coughs, rubs his neck, then looks up at me. "I swear to God, I'm gonna kill you one of these days."

"That's enough," says Carson.

"My ass," shouts the orderly, stumbling to his feet. "I don't see why the rest of us should have to put up with this shit—*you're* the freak-lover!"

Carson glares at the orderly. Here, in this place, he is the man he might have been, strong, brave, articulate. "One more word out of you and I'll turn him loose. There won't be enough left of you to feed to the pigs."

The orderly glowers for a moment, then spits on my front left hoof and begins to walk away.

Carson looks at the puddle of excrement and says: "Forgetting something, aren't you?"

The orderly stops. For a moment it looks as if he might respond in anger, then a shadow crosses his face. In that shadow I see his wife and children, their too-thin bodies, their dirty clothes, the hunger in their eyes.

He nods his head and walks to the puddle. I offer him the cloth. Wordlessly, he takes it, covers his hands, and retrieves his device from the puddle. He leaves without saying another word or looking at me.

"Are you all right?" asks Carson.

I nod.

Carson begins walking over the rise and I follow him. Behind me the other animals, the sick ones with whom I share the building, begin their moaning anew.

We see the dance of life, rippling, flying, running by. There was a time when we were part of the dance, before the fields were plowed over and we were taken to these rooms.

I wish that I could find some pity in my heart for

Gary A. Braunbeck

them, but I cannot. They are ill, their flesh tainted. They can only wait for the walk to the bloody chamber.

As I top the rise I look down and see them in the fields. They graze and sleep. Two are by the fence, one mounting the other. They rut and grumble as one plunges into the other. I look away and see Carson staring at me.

"One day," he says to me, "Zeus looked down from Olympus and saw a mother weeping over her dead child. Not quite grasping the concept of human suffering, Zeus chose to come down to Earth as a child himself in order to find out more about it. The other gods were irritated with Zeus at this time and so played a trick on him—they turned the Earth while Zeus wasn't looking. He landed in the middle of a desert. He wandered as a child for days, then weeks, and began to weaken from starvation. The gods had temporarily stripped him of his godly powers; he was totally human.

"So he wandered, then collapsed, unable to walk from the sores upon his feet. He crawled until he could move no more. He lay there dying. In what might have been the last moments of his life, Zeus heard a strange weeping sound. He turned his head to see an odd beast lumbering toward him. This beast was a cow who had no one to milk her. Her teats were swollen and painful. She saw this child lying there in the middle of the desert and went to him, positioning her body so that her teats were directly above his mouth. Zeus sucked hungrily, drinking his fill of her life-restoring milk.

"The gods saw this and were strangely moved,

and so restored Zeus's powers to him. He brought the cow back to Olympus with him and decreed that she and her like were to be considered sacred, and would be plentiful upon the Earth so that no child would ever again know the suffering he had to endure, and no parent the grief of having to see their children die. The cow lives on Olympus still, grazing in a field beside Zeus's throne."

A loud whistle breaks the still of the morning. Men wander into the fields, each carrying their own device, and begin to prod the beasts into groups, and those groups into lines. They march toward the large building with the smokestacks. The men continue shouting and prodding them until they are stuffed into the corrals. The animals cry out in confusion. Another man walks the length of the rows, tossing handfuls of hay to them. They lower their heads and eat, silently.

At the front of each corral is a large metal door. There are four in all.

A buzzing sound fills the air for a moment, followed by a deafening shriek that momentarily frightens the herds, then is replaced by the chords of soothing music.

The animals, calm again, return to their meal. I can hear the voices of the herd.

Our hearts are pounding together. There is not enough room. Is this a face I am standing on? Is my friend dead? Are we all dead already, or is death still to come? Are we real? Do we exist at all?

I envy them. Their whole purpose is fulfilled just by standing in the field all day, eating, then looking upward at the sky where no gods look down.

The door at the end of the first corral opens. From deep inside the dark place beyond comes a rumbling.

The rumbling room! they think.

One by one, they raise their heads and cry out. More hay is tossed to them but they do not look at it. All thoughts of hunger have fled. Now there is only fear and bodies pressing together, the crushing weight of one becoming that of many. The wooden rails of the corral make clattering noises as their bodies slam against them, but do not break. The rails never break. Such is the care given to the construction.

One of the beasts cries out as blood bubbles from its nostrils.

Another releases the contents of its bowels.

Yet another stomps in crimson-colored urine.

Their fear reaches out and grips my horns, pulling my head forward.

"It's time," says Carson, placing a hand gently on my shoulder.

I march forward, my hooves sinking into the mud. I can feel my muscles rippling under my flesh. I have to remember that I am not the same as them. I must remember this. It is important.

I enter the corral gate, and follow the path that leads me to the right. I walk a separate path that parallels that of the herd. I reach the end and step up onto the platform that has been built for me.

I turn to face them.

I take a breath.

I raise my arms before them.

They stare at me in awe and wonder. This is how

they worship me. How they love me. To them I am a god. Their cud-stuffed prayers are only for me.

I suffer as you do, I say to them. *I have known the loneliness of dark spaces. I have tasted the fruit of betrayal. I know what it is like to stand upright as a man does.*

TWO LEGS! they pray to me. *IF ONLY WE HAD TWO LEGS, WE COULD LEAVE THIS PLACE OF FEAR AND FOLLOW YOU!*

You will never stand on two legs, I say to them. *To stand as a man stands is very hard. Two legs are very hard. Perhaps four is better, after all.*

WHERE ARE WE TO GO? TELL US, SHOW US THE WAY. WE WILL FOLLOW.

I answer them with a cry of my own, one composed of equal parts field-beast and man. They throw back their heads in reply.

I turn on the platform and begin walking inside.

They follow.

The platform extends all the way across the rumbling room. I can travel its length and never touch the soil below. This platform empties onto a wooden terrace at the other end, and there I will walk down the ramp, go around the building, and enter the Corral of the Separate Path once again, then twice more after that. Until all the herd have been led into the dark, rumbling room.

Then I shall be rewarded.

I step through the doorway into the rumbling room. Behind me, the herd moves as one.

My arms still raised, I gesture for them to come. *Come, my children, follow me.*

They enter the rumbling room four at a time. As they step through the door, a man walks up to each of them. These men hold hammers. Hammers smash into heads. Their knees buckle, and with a cry they drop. Chains are dropped from above and secured around their legs. The room roars. The chains are pulled taut and the first four are lifted from the ground. They hang there, in great pain but not yet dead. Another roar, the walls shake, and they begin to move. It is as if they are slowly flying. As they pass by, they look at me. Their eyes are stupid with fear, and I cannot return their gaze. I am not the same as them. I am not the same as them. I am not the same as them.

Other men approach them now, holding something long, curved, and shiny. They lift their arms, these men, and pass the shiny curves through the flesh.

I whisper to them, *Fear not; soon you too shall graze in the fields by Zeus's throne.*

I have to make them believe this, as I must make myself believe it.

There is no other way to survive in this world of no gods.

The line is moving smoothly now, the beasts entering, the men falling upon them with hammers and chains. The room roars and snarls. I walk on. I reach the end of the platform and turn to see the fruition of my leadership.

The beasts hang there with their stomachs split open and their heads cut off. I smell their open flesh and see their dead hooves. On a metal hook I see all of their tongues, cut out and pierced by the sharp metal, pierced through the root and hanging there, mute and bloody.

I lower my arms.

I see their heads lined up on the floor. Someone is cutting off their cheeks with a knife, slicing through their tender flesh. Once this has been done, he kicks what remains of their heads down through a hole in the floor.

Blade passing through them.

Lives there a man who has not dreamt of being as strong as a bull in the fields?

Red running past.

Is there a bull who has never longed to stand as a man and be nearer the sky?

Bubbling up.

Only. You. Remain. Eternal.

Red passing through. The world, this room.

Give to me reign of the fields, the sky, and all creatures who dwell in between.

Split in half, this way and that.

Their cries still screeching through my brain, I climb down the stairs and walk around the building, an abandoning god, and prepare myself for the moment when the sun kisses the ground and the sky bleeds twilight and I am fed on my follower's broiled remains and Beth is allowed to sit by my side.

To stand as a man stands is very hard. Two legs are very hard. Perhaps four is better, after all.

I touch my sides, wishing to stand on two legs. Two legs gives me a tailor. A tailor gives me clothing. Clothing gives me pockets. A place to hide my hands. To keep my paycheck. To store a key to a room with no straw on the ground or—

Eleven

—the top of my skull connected with the roof of the car when I jolted awake, shaking.

Goddammit.

I rubbed my face and eyes as if rubbing would brush away the remnants of the dream, then took a deep breath and looked at my watch.

I had been asleep for almost twenty minutes.

Not great, but at least it hadn't been *hours*.

I stretched my back, rubbed the back of my head, took several deep breaths, and—as rallied now as I would ever be—climbed out of the car. After removing the high-intensity flashlight from the trunk and closing the lid, I began walking over the rise and down toward the graveyard. The flashlight's beam revealed that there weren't as many birds here now, and nowhere could I see any bones.

I headed toward the old barn in the distance. As I neared, the silence surrounding me became almost unbearable. I'd have given anything to hear a bird sing or a dog bark.

The ground around the barn was spotted with deep holes. Someone had been digging. Quite a lot.

The barn door was partly open, so I was able to enter without making any noise. Inside it glowed with warm, bright light, courtesy of at least a dozen oil lanterns.

Carson was at the opposite end. His clothes were covered in the moist, clay-like soil from outside. A large shovel rested inside the wheelbarrow he'd used to haul the dirt in.

He did not hear me as I walked toward him.

He was busy cutting sections of twine from a roll. There were various sizes of branches and sticks in a pile at his feet. There were buckets of water. Rope. Tubes of caulk and a caulk gun. An immense sheet of tarpaulin from which several large pieces had been cut.

I was in the middle of the barn. I could see Carson, but since the stalls on that side ran into the beams and wall that supported the hayloft above, I couldn't see what he was working on.

"Carson?"

He looked at me, smiled, and waved. "Hi, UncGil. I've been taking the bus. The #48 express. Remember how it almost hit us?"

"Yes."

He looked down at something on a hay bale. A comic book. He turned the page.

"Is that the new issue of *Modoc*?" I asked.

"Yeah. I bought it yesterday."

I took a few more steps toward him. "What're you working on?"

"Present for Long-Lost."

"What kind of present?"

"Come look. I'm almost all done."

I walked over to him.

Somehow, he had used the bird bones and clay, the twine and rope, the caulk and several sections of discarded wood, as well as all the twigs and sticks, to build a near-perfect replica of Long-Lost.

It wasn't nearly as big as it was portrayed in the comics—it looked to be just under six feet in height—but it was still impressive. He had cut away sections of the tarpaulin to fashion the skin for the wings. The horn was a stick that he'd whittled to a point. He'd gathered feathers as well, using them to give the body as much texture as possible. The spider's legs were one of the most amazing parts: for those he'd used bone, stick, twine and twig, clay, and remnants of bed sheets, twisting them tightly together so they could support the weight of the rest of it. It was a marvel of design, something I knew to be beyond his capabilities.

"How long have you been working on this?" I asked.

"Long time. Ever since we came out here the first time."

"You've been sneaking out and taking the bus?"

He nodded, and then began wrapping the twine around the bottom of one of the legs. "Uh-huh. That bus runs all night."

So he'd been sneaking out at night after bed check and getting back before breakfast.

A flash of fire burned up my side and I had to lean against one of the stall doors.

Carson looked over and saw me, the state of my clothes, and the blood. He dropped the twine and ran over, putting his arms around me. "You hurt, UncGil? What happened?"

"I had an accident."

"Wanna go to the hospital?"

I shook my head. "No, Carson, I want to take you home where you belong."

He released his hold on me and went back to work. "I don't wanna go back there. I wanna stay here."

"Well, you can't."

He checked the comic book, looked at me, then turned a few pages and shook his head.

"What's wrong, Carson? What's Long-Lost say? What are you supposed to do now?"

"Well," he said, adding the last bit of twine and clay to Long-Lost's arm, "I dunno." He held up the comic. "The next part is about you."

(LonglosT sayz The Keeperz are comeiNg N He kNeedz To Talk To you.)

"I see." I reached out and took the comic book, rolling it up and slipping it into my jacket pocket. "Then we should go home and read it together."

He shook his head. "The animals need me."

"What animals?"

He stopped his work and stared at me. "Don't you know what this place *is*, UncGil?"

The pain was starting to make me dizzy. "No, Carson, I don't. So why don't you tell me all about it on the way home?"

"I'm *not leaving!*" he shouted, throwing a wad of mud at the far wall. "I'm not leaving and *you can't make me!*"

"Don't shout at me, Carson."

"You try an' make me go an' I'll . . . I'll . . . I'll call for 'em."

My stomach tightened. "Call for who? Long-Lost? He doesn't live in this world, Carson. He lives on the other side of the Great Scrim—remember from the first couple of issues?"

He shook his head again, starting to cry. "Nuh-uh, not Long-Lost."

"Then who?"

"The Keepers. They know you're here."

Listen to the cold silence in the center of my soul as he said this.

"I don't know what you're talking about, Carson."

"Yes, you do." He pointed at my pocket. "Long-Lost said that you don't remember like you're supposed to. That's why he wants to talk to you."

I took several deep breaths, forcing the pain away—or at least forcing myself to ignore it as much as possible—and pushed off of the stall door. "I'm not talking to anyone except you tonight, Carson." I started toward the barn door. "Now *come on!* I'm hurt and sore and tired and hungry and I've been worried sick about you and there's stuff going on I don't understand and I want you to be somewhere *safe*, do you understand?"

"But I am safe."

I turned around and kicked open the door with my uninjured leg.

"This is the Magic Zoo, UncGil. They'd never hurt me."

I couldn't move.

I couldn't speak.

111

I dropped the flashlight and staggered backward.

Standing in the doorway, on its hind legs, was a massive brown Kodiak bear. It stood well over eight feet high. Its body was trembling and it was salivating, making a noise somewhere between a bawl and a growl. It threw back its head, then tilted it from left to right. Bones cracked, then it began to hum, all the while reaching out toward me with black claws that were easily five inches long.

It stopped moving, huffed, then trained its deep-red eyes on my face.

A rough growling noise came from behind it, and a moment later the two black mastiffs emerged, one on each side of the bear. Their red eyes burned, if anything, even brighter than before.

"They won't hurt you, UncGil, I promise. You just gotta come back inside and close the door."

I wasn't about to move any closer to that door.

"You had the rumbling room dream again, didn't you, UncGil?"

I turned toward my nephew. "How could you *know* that?"

" 'Cause it's still following you." He stared at me for a second. "Long-Lost showed me in the comic. But I can still see it around you."

I started moving backward.

Slowly.

The bear and the dogs continued staring at me.

When I was a few more feet away, the bear looked down at one of the dogs. The mastiff gave a quick nod of its head, and the bear reached out, gripped the door, and pushed it closed.

At the last moment, before the barn door was fully

shut, the bear raised its other paw and waved at me.

"Here you go, UncGil," sad Carson from behind me. He stood there holding a beat-up wooden stool. "You gotta sit down and talk to Long-Lost."

He set down the stool, then waited for me to move.

"You're talking a lot better than you have been," I said to him.

"Uh-huh, I know. Long-Lost, he says it's because I'm one of the 'special ones.' Because I don't have to be helped by the Keepers, I'm getting there faster."

"Getting where?"

He shrugged. "Don't know yet." Then he smiled the smile of the Carson I'd always known and loved more than anything in the world, came over, and wrapped his arms around me. "I love you so much, UncGil."

I put my arm around him. "I love you, too, buddy."

"That's good. Hey—do you like swans?"

It was one of those non sequitur subject shifts that had always been a staple of conversations with him.

"I, uh . . . I don't know, Carson. I never thought about it."

"Swans are pretty."

"Yes . . . yes, they are."

"Yeah." He let go of me and started walking back toward his art project. "You should sit down and rest, UncGil. See what Long-Lost has to say."

I sat down, wincing from the pain in my hip, arm, and shoulder. Reaching into my pocket, I removed and unrolled the new issue of *Modoc: Land of the Abandoned Beast*.

Before I even pulled the cover back, I felt something brush against my leg and looked down to see

Carson's missing cat, Butterball, rubbing against me and purring.

(Butterball went to live at the Magic Zoo . . .)

I reached down to pet him and he, as always, rolled over onto his back and offered his tremendous belly. I rubbed it, and Butterball's purring grew louder, deeper, more contented.

Then, as usual, he fell asleep like that; on his back, legs splayed in every direction, mouth open. He looked like the cat equivalent of the town drunk passed out in the gutter.

I looked toward the barn door, heard the bear huff again, then unrolled the comic and turned to the first page.

There was an illustration of Long-Lost, this one much more detailed than the other. He was staring directly outward, and the dialogue bubble above his head read:

HELLO, GIL. NICE TO FINALLY TALK TO YOU.

"This isn't possible," I whispered to myself.

I turned the page.

YES, GILBERT JAMES STEWART, IT *IS* POSSIBLE.

I gritted my teeth. "What do you want?"

THE SAME THING THAT PEST IN THE BACK OF YOUR HEAD WANTS, GIL. I WANT YOU TO *REMEMBER.*

114

"Remember what?"

THAT WOULD BE TELLING.

"Then at least explain what the fuck you're supposed to be."

TSK-TSK—SUCH *LANGUAGE*. YOU SHOULD BE SETTING AN EXAMPLE FOR YOUR NEPHEW. BY THE WAY, HE HAS NO IDEA HOW SPECIAL HE REALLY IS. NEITHER DO YOU.

I closed my eyes, squeezing the lids so tight I began to see stars. The stars exploded into faces; Beth, her aunt Mabel, an old man whose face I recognized but whose name wouldn't come to me . . . something with a "W," wasn't it . . . ?

I felt a small jolt surge through my body. I started, shuddering, nearly dropping the comic.

WOULDN'T HAVE BEEN GOOD, GIL, DROPPING THIS. THE FLOOR'S GOT OLD SHIT AND PISS BURIED UNDER THE HAY. YOU SHOULD REMEMBER TO WIPE OFF YOUR SHOES BEFORE YOU GO INTO YOUR HOUSE.

"Am I going to see my house again?"

OF COURSE YOU ARE. AND I DON'T WANT YOU TO WORRY. THE KEEPERS HAVEN'T GONE THERE. YET.

Something hitched in my throat, and for some reason I began crying. "What's happening? And *why . . . ?*"

SHHH . . . THERE-THERE, MY FRIEND. NO NEED TO GET UPSET. I HAVE NO INTEN-TION OF HURTING YOU. BUT YOU'VE GOT TO REMEMBER *ON YOUR OWN* OR . . . OR IT *IS* GOING TO HURT, AND I WON'T BE ABLE TO HELP YOU. I HAVEN'T GOTTEN THROUGH THE GREAT SCRIM YET.

I wiped my eyes and pulled in a hard, snot-filled breath. "I don't understand . . ."

The next panel showed Long-Lost rolling his eyes in exasperation.

OKAY . . . YOU GET *SOME* OF IT, BUT NOT ALL. NOT EVEN *CLOSE* TO ALL—SO DON'T GO THINKING THAT YOU'RE GOING TO BE A STEP AHEAD OF THINGS, BECAUSE THERE'S *NO WAY*, UNDERSTAND?

I said nothing, only nodded my head and moved to the next panel.

WHEN THIS PLANET AWOKE TO SING ITS FIRST SONG, THERE WAS ONLY ONE SPECIES OF ANIMAL LIVING ON ITS SUR-FACE. THIS CREATURE BREATHED AND DREAMED JUST AS YOU DO TODAY. BUT IT WAS LONELY. HERE WAS THIS MAGNIFI-CENT EARTH, FILLED WITH BEAUTY, AND IT

HAD NO ONE AND NOTHING WITH WHICH TO SHARE IT.

THIS FIRST ANIMAL TOOK A DEEP BREATH AND BEGAN TO SWELL IN SIZE, RE-ARRANGING ITSELF FROM WITHIN, THEN SPLITTING INTO TWO IDENTICAL HALVES. THE HALVES MATED, CREATING A THIRD, A HYBRID OF THEMSELVES WHICH IN TURN MATED WITH THEM, PRODUCING OTHER HY-BRIDS. THEY CONTINUED TO MATE AND PRODUCE, AS DID THE PROGENIES, GIVING BIRTH TO EVERYTHING FROM THE MANTI-CORA AND SPHINX DOWN TO THE ANTS AND MAGGOTS—THAT IS HOW THE EARTH BECAME POPULATED.

EVEN AFTER THAT, THE BIRTHING CON-TINUED. SINGLE CELLS FUSED TOGETHER, CREATING METAZOANS THAT EVENTUALLY CULMINATED IN THE INVENTION OF ROSES AND ELEPHANTS AND DEW-GLISTENED LEAVES AND EVEN HUMAN BEINGS. ALL LIFE ON THIS PLANET—PAST, PRESENT, AND WHAT THERE IS OF THE FUTURE—SPRANG FROM THE *SAME SINGLE ORGANISM.* IF ONLY THEY COULD JUST SEE THE JOINING OF ORGANISMS INTO COMMUNITIES, THOSE COMMUNITIES INTO ECOSYSTEMS, THOSE ECOSYSTEMS INTO THE BIOSPHERE . . .

I'M GETTING AHEAD OF MYSELF. THAT AL-WAYS HAPPENS WHEN I WAX NOSTALGIC ABOUT THE GOOD OLD DAYS.

I AM THAT FIRST ANIMAL, GIL: ALL THE REST SPRANG FROM ME. AND THAT'S ALL

YOU'RE GETTING UNTIL YOU REMEMBER THE
REST ON YOUR OWN . . .

    I waited, flipping to the pages further back, which
were blank. I turned back to the last illustrated page,
only Long-Lost was gone; in his place were now six
panels, the first one showing a boy of about nine or
ten lying in a hospital bed while a lovely girl several
years his senior held his hand.
    I recognized Beth and myself immediately.
The next panel had no illustration, just a thought
bubble with a caption that read:

    ALL RIGHT, GIL—A LITTLE NUDGE. CON-
SIDER IT A GESTURE OF GOOD FAITH.
THESE PAGES ARE MADE FROM A SECTION
OF FLESH TAKEN FROM ONE OF MY WINGS.
THEY REFLECT MEMORIES, GIL, BUT ONLY
THOSE YOU'RE WILLING TO FACE. YOU'LL BE
WRITING AND ILLUSTRATING THE REST OF
THIS ISSUE.
    WE'LL TALK AGAIN SOON.

    I went back to the first panel again, only now there
was the caption:

    BETH WAS RELEASED FROM THE HOSPI-
TAL FIVE DAYS BEFORE ME, BUT SHE MADE
IT A POINT TO VISIT ME EVERY DAY AFTER
SCHOOL.

    The second panel was now filled by the young
boy's face—my own—and the caption was situated

close to the top of his head, so you'd know it was he who was narrating.

EVEN THEN I NOTICED HOW SOME OF HER SPARKLE SEEMED TO FADE ONCE SHE WAS BACK IN THE WORLD.

And I stayed like that, on the stool in the barn, while outside a gigantic bear and two black dogs stood guard; I stayed like that, reading the comic through to the last page, then returning to the first and finding that it had altered and was now taking up the story where the last page had left off, and I read the words, and I saw the pictures, and with every new panel the memories were as thick as summer heat around me, and I was . . . powerless.

But there was Beth's face, and soon her voice in my ears, her scent enveloping me, the ghost of her touch rising to the surface from deep beneath the layers of my skin, and I stopped fighting it and let myself—

(. . . *about goddamn time, pal* . . .)

—become lost once again in her eyes, her companionship, and everything that followed. . . .

II

BETH, AND
EVERYTHING
THAT FOLLOWED

1970–1983

Beth was released from the hospital five days before I was, but she made it a point to visit me every day after school. Even then I noticed how some of her sparkle seemed to fade once she was back in the world. It was nothing dramatic, her spirit hadn't been broken in one brutal blow, but even a kid can recognize a soul that's starting to bleed to death from thousands of tiny scratches.

Still, she was always upbeat and affectionate, bringing me comic books or telling me about this groovy new song she'd heard on the radio, or regaling me with gossip gathered during lunch or study hall. She always sat on the edge of my bed and held my hand and made me feel like I was the most important thing in the world. I had never received such unselfish attention from a person before, nor have I since.

"I've been driving for a month now," she said, "and my aunt is *finally* trusting me to use the car when she's not with me. I haven't had any passengers yet"—she winked at me and smiled one of those delicious I've-got-a-surprise smiles—"but that's gonna change on Friday."

"What's Friday?"

She lightly smacked my hand. "Friday, *dummy*, is when you get released. Doctor said you'll be well enough to go home, and *I* am going to pick you up."

"But Mom and Dad—"

"I already asked your mom and she said it was fine."

I blinked. It had never occurred to me that Mom wouldn't want to pick me up, but just as unsettling was the idea that she had given Beth—who was little more than a stranger to her—permission to take me. "Did you ask her when she was here?"

"Nuh-uh. I called your house."

We were unlisted. "How'd you get our phone number?"

Another patented Beth wink. "Vee haf vays of gazzering zee information."

"Huh?"

"Someday you'll understand. Care enough about someone, and you'll find a way to help them, no matter what."

I didn't really understand what she meant by that, but it seemed like this was something she really wanted to do because she liked me. I had to keep reminding myself that this great girl with the long hair and love beads and hip-huggers and gold flecks in her light brown eyes *liked* me. A lot, it seemed.

"Hey, here's an idea—how about after I pick you up, we go out for some ice cream cones?"

"Sure!"

"Then maybe you can come over and eat dinner with the family."

"Oh—did your mom come home?"

A brief, wistful shadow crossed over her face and then was gone, replaced by her bright smile that seemed a little false. "No, it's just me and my aunt and the Its."

" 'Its'?"

"You'll see."

Mom called the morning of my release and said it was fine if I wanted to go over to Beth's for dinner; Dad wasn't feeling well (which meant he was either drunk or hung-over) and it might be best if I didn't come home right away. Too much activity might upset him and we couldn't have that. It made me glad she wasn't picking me up; all she'd do was complain about Dad, then tell me not to say anything.

A little before ten a doctor I hadn't seen before came in and gave me the once-over, told me that I'd need to exercise my shoulder, and gave me a pamphlet explaining how to do it. Half an hour later a nurse I'd never seen before came in with a wheelchair, handed me some slips of paper, and told me that my ride was here. Beth came in right behind her, all Day-Glo smiles and flourescent sunshine.

"Ready to hit the road, little brother?" She winked at me but the nurse didn't see it. "Got all your stuff? Okay, good—what about his prescriptions?"

"He's got them," replied the nurse, who must have been new to this floor because she didn't seem to recognize Beth at all.

"Cool. Mom gave me money to get them filled on the way home." She was play-acting, just like her mother on the London Stage. It was kind of fun to watch.

I was rolled downstairs and to Beth's car—a monstrous green U-boat of a station wagon with wood paneling on the doors. Inside it smelled of cigarettes, sweat, and something pungent that made my nose itch.

Once on our way, Beth reached over and squeezed my hand. "How you feeling, hon? Any pain?"

"Yeah, a little. My shoulder and stuff."

"Let's stop and get your medicine. My treat."

"But Mom said my medicine was going to be expensive."

"Codeine, some stuff for swelling and stiffness, and antibiotics. Twenty-two dollars—I already checked."

I know it's hard to remember, but in 1970, twenty-two dollars was a lot of money, even if you *weren't* a kid.

"That's an awful lot," I said.

"Hey, nothing's too good for my guy. Besides, I've been saving my allowance for years. *And* I worked waiting tables part-time during the summer. It won't leave me broke."

She was my friend, she'd visited me, she was giving me a ride for ice cream, and now she was going to spend *twenty-two dollars* of her own money on medicine for me? What had I done to deserve this? People never did anything for me without wanting something back for it, and for a moment I thought maybe Beth was going to say something like, "Hey, since I did this for you, would you do a favor for me?" But she never did, not once in all the years I knew her.

Prescriptions in hand, we drove over to the Tasty Freeze on West Church Street and pigged out on the Holy Grail of large cones: the two-scoop double-dipped chocolate with sprinkles. Impossible not to eat and wear at the same time. About midway through it my shoulder and arm began to hurt terribly, so Beth bought a small Coke and gave me a pain pill. By the time I finished the cone, I was feeling full and shiny. For all I knew my shoulder and arm were still in agony but, thanks to the pill, I didn't care anymore.

"Oh, great," said Beth, lifting my head by the chin and looking in my eyes. "The first time I'm in charge of someone younger than me and I get him stoned. Let's get out of here before someone calls the fuzz on us."

Back in the car, I noticed how the shine from the sun in her rearview mirror painted a glowing slash across her face. It looked as if she was wearing a golden mask. Whenever she turned to speak to me, the mask would slip around her face and over her ears, turning her hair the color of dreams. "Still with me?"

"Uh-huh," I said, though I felt really sleepy.

"Hey, wake up, Boy Wonder, c'mon." She sounded genuinely concerned. "C'mon, okay? Stay awake. I checked the instructions and it turns out I'm a spaz, I was only supposed to give you *half* a pill, not a whole one. Don't make me have to take you back to the hospital to get your stomach pumped or something, okay?"

". . . 'kay."

"Promise?"

I shook myself awake. Everything was still shiny, but I was more alert now. "Can we get another pop?"

"Ah, caffeine, yes. Smart idea."

We pulled into a gas station where Beth ran into some boy she knew. He came up behind her while she was pulling the bottles out of the freezer-like cooler and put his hand on her back. She whirled around like she might slap whoever it was, but then she recognized him and smiled, pushed her hair back behind her ears, glanced quickly in the direction of the car, and leaned in to kiss him. Even from thirty feet away, I could see their tongues going into each other's mouths. The boy slid his hand down and grabbed her hip, then her ass. She broke the kiss and saw me staring at them, then quickly yanked his hand away and whispered something. They looked over at me and the boy laughed. For a moment it looked like Beth might laugh, too. I didn't know who this boy was, but I hated him.

They talked for a few more moments and then Beth gave him a quick kiss and came back to the car. She smiled at me when she climbed in but didn't look in my eyes like she usually did. She seemed embarrassed—or maybe annoyed that I'd been watching. I took the bottle of pop and swallowed two big gulps. It made my chest and stomach feel all frosty as it went down, and then an ice-bird spread its wings through my center and I wasn't as hot, thirsty, or tired anymore.

We were almost to Beth's house when she said, "I

go out with him sometimes, that guy back at the gas station."

"Is that why we stopped there? So you could see him?"

She blushed. "Yeah. My aunt doesn't like him. She doesn't much like any of my friends." She finally looked at me. "You're the first friend I've had over in a long time."

"I won't say anything to your aunt about him, I promise."

Squeezing my hand as she pulled into the driveway, Beth cleared her throat and whispered, "I'll never ask you to lie for me, I promise."

Beth's aunt Mabel was the most unhappy-looking person I'd ever seen; even though she smiled an awful lot and spoke in a bright, happy voice, the tightness of her features, the worry etched into her skin, and the way she sat as if expecting the other bomb to go off at any moment betrayed her true feelings. This was a sad woman, a cheerless woman, stoop-shouldered and shopworn and heartbroken and chain-smoking. Looking at her made me want to cry; she reminded me too much of Mom.

"How's the lasagna?" she asked early into dinner.

"It's real good, thank you. A lot better than the hospital."

Mabel laughed a thick, chortling laugh composed equal parts of phlegm and sandpaper. "I should certainly *hope* so. Lord! If I can't beat hospital food, I might as well hang up my apron!"

I giggled and took another bite of the lasagna; it *was* quite good, but its rich flavor and aroma were overpowered by the smell of the house, which made me feel sick.

Beth and her aunt lived in a one-story house that was only slightly bigger than a double-wide trailer; two small bedrooms, an even smaller bathroom, a big living room, and a kitchen that took up a full third of their living space. Deep shag carpeting the color of old rust covered every inch of floor—at least I think it was the color of old rust; it could've been light blue for as much as I could tell by looking at it, which I tried not to do because it only made me feel sicker.

A fly buzzed around the lasagna pan and Mabel swatted it away. "Damn things," she mumbled. "I got to replace those screens on the doors."

I was surprised that only one fly had found the nerve to come over; there were so many of them.

Something brushed by my leg and I looked down to meet yet another of the Its—one of the seven dogs that Beth and Mabel shared their home with. That's right, *seven* dogs of various shapes and sizes—from a Chihuahua to a mid-sized sheep dog and everything in between—none of whom seemed to be very housebroken, if the pee stains and scattered piles of dried and not-so-dried poop were any indication.

Imagine what the inside of a kennel left unattended over a sweltering three-day weekend would smell like, add an underlying scent of sour milk and rotten eggs, then spray an entire aerosol can of rose-scented air freshener and you might have some idea how this place smelled. I didn't have to ask Beth why it had been so long since she'd had any friends over; one hour in this house and already I wanted to shower until my skin came off. It wasn't only the smell, it was the *feel* of the place; it felt ruined, the air thick with humidity and animal fur. By the time dinner was finished, all three of us were wheezing to one degree or another. Mabel's constant smoking didn't help matters, but I never said anything; I never said anything to Mom or Dad when their smoking started bothering me, it seemed rude to complain to this bright-eyed sad woman who was so happy that I liked her cooking.

I helped Beth clear away the dishes and wipe down the table. Mabel disappeared into her bedroom with two of the dogs and emerged twenty minutes later in a light-blue outfit, smelling of deodorant and Avon perfume.

"Okay, kids, I gotta head to work."

Beth's face immediately registered alarm. "But, I need the car to take—"

"I know," Mabel replied. "Suzy's giving me a ride both ways tonight, so the car's all yours. But you be careful. Get him home and then come right back."

"Of course."

"I mean it, Elizabeth. I'm going to call you when I get my break and you'd better be here to answer."

Beth shook her head and rolled her eyes. "I *will* be! Jeez-us."

"Don't 'jeez-us' me, young lady. I'm only looking out for your well-being. God knows my sister couldn't be bothered to."

"Please don't say things like that about Mom." Now it was Beth who was stoop-shouldered and shopworn. This hurt, and I wondered if her aunt knew it hurt and that's why she'd said it.

Mabel came over, put a hand on Beth's shoulder, and gave her a quick kiss on the cheek. "I didn't mean anything by it, okay? I'm just a little tired, that's all."

A shrug: "Okay."

"Okay, then." Mabel turned toward me and held out a hand. "It was real pleasure having you over for dinner, young man. I hope you'll visit us again. Often as you'd like."

"Thank you, ma'am," I said, shaking her hand— the first time I'd ever done so with an adult. "You're a real good cook."

"Aren't you sweet." Then she bent down and kissed the top of my head. A car horn sounded out front and Mabel waved to us on her way out the door.

"God!" said Beth with a sudden rush of air. "I swear she must think I'm retarded or something, the way she treats me."

"Where does she work?"

"Huh? Oh—at the nursing home. She's one of the night nurses. She also cooks breakfast sometimes."

I remembered the home from visiting my grandfather there when I was seven, how lonely, exhausted, and used up everyone seemed to be. No wonder Mabel was so sad.

I wasn't sure how to ask this next question, so I just let fly: "Where's your uncle?"

"I've got a couple of them, why?"

"I mean . . . your aunt's husband?"

A quick shake of her head. "Mabel isn't married, she never was. I don't think men interest her much."

"Whatta you mean?"

She mussed my hair. "It's a little hard to explain, sweetie pie. She has friends who stay over sometimes. I don't think she gets lonely. She's got me to talk to and all of the Its for company. Speaking of the Its, want to help me clean up a little? I do this every night after she leaves for work."

"Is it safe? Mabel seemed awful worried about—"

"Mabel worries about everything. We've had some trouble in this neighborhood—some break-ins, a couple of shootings a few blocks over, you know— so she thinks every time she leaves me alone that all these monsters are going to knock down the door and attack me. She even has a gun in one of her dresser drawers—like she's Clint Eastwood, Dirty Harriet or something. There's not going to be any trouble. C'mon, give me a hand."

We spent the next hour picking up—and scraping out—all the poop from the carpeting, then Beth let the dogs out in the backyard by twos and threes so they could relieve themselves as nature intended. (During all the years I knew Beth and spent time over there, that house was always filled with dogs; if one died or got sick and had to be put to sleep, it was quickly replaced by another. Beth and I eventually began to refer to her house as "Doggyship Down.")

I sprayed the pee stains with this foamy stuff Beth took out of the bathroom; she told me to let it set until it dried, then we sprinkled baking soda all around and Beth ran the vacuum cleaner.

Once finished, the carpeting looked a little better and the stench wasn't as strong as it had been.

"That's only because you're getting used to the smell," Beth said. "Live with it long enough, and it doesn't seem that bad."

I wondered how she kept the smell off her clothes; not once during her visits to me did I ever smell the dogs on her, so I asked her how she managed to do that.

"Every week I take five outfits from my closet, wash them at the coin laundry or have them dry-cleaned, then hang 'em up in my locker at school. I get there about a half-hour before school starts and change in the girls' restroom. In the mornings, after my shower, I can usually get out of here before the smell sinks into me." Another shrug. "No biggie, really. I like to look and smell clean when I'm at school or going to the movies or something. If I go out, I do it after school on Friday so I don't have to come back here first. Don't worry yourself, the system's worked fine for a while now."

I nodded as if I were mature enough to understand. She was a wonderful mystery to me.

"Why do you have so many dogs, anyway?"

"Because nobody else wants them. A couple we adopted from the Humane Society, but most of them are strays Mabel or I have found. Just can't turn away a animal in need, I guess. It doesn't seem right that nobody wants to keep them, care for them, have 'em there in the middle of the night to snuggle with when you wake up and feel lonely. . . ."

I thought she was going to say something else but she didn't. We had a couple of brownies, talked a little more about nothing terribly important, and then it was time for me to go.

We were a few blocks from my house when Beth pulled the U-boat over to the curb and put it in park. "Listen, I want to tell you something, okay? Something that's just between us, right?" She was a long way past serious; she seemed almost scared. *"Right?"*

I nodded my head.

"This is gonna sound weird, okay, but . . . I never had any friends when I was your age, I never got to do any of those things that kids your age get to do, right? I always felt mad about that, about missing out on things. Hell, I'm not even sure if I *know* what kids your age like doing 'cause I never did it."

"Could you please not . . . not say that?"

"Say what?"

" 'Kids your age.' "

She shook her head and smiled. "But you *are* still a kid; you're not even ten yet."

"I know, but . . ." I looked down at my hands, which I couldn't feel.

"Okay, I guess you deserve that. If I live to be twice the age I am now I doubt that I'm ever gonna know what it feels like to get shot, so you ought to be entitled to age points for that. Deal—I don't call or refer to you as 'kid' anymore."

"Thank you."

"You're welcome." She leaned over and kissed my cheek. "I wanna know what it is you like to do, I guess. Will you show me that? Will you teach me how to have fun like a person of your age has fun?"

"You might think it's stupid."

Gary A. Braunbeck

She put the car in drive and pulled away from the curb. "Bet'cha I don't."

And she didn't.

Over the next year and a half I taught her (in no particular order): how to build a fort from boxes, blankets, chairs, and umbrellas; how to climb a tree; the fine art of thumb wrestling; how to make a kite from scratch; how to tell if Godzilla was going to be a good monster or bad monster before he even made his first appearance in the movie (not as easy as it sounds); the proper way to build and paint the Aurora monster models; why Steppenwolf kicked Three Dog Night's ass; how *Mr. Terrific* was just as cool as *Captain Nice* but *The Green Hornet* was by far the coolest of them all; why the *Bazooka Joe* comics sucked monkeys but the bubble gum could be re-chewed at least three times before it lost its flavor; and, probably the most valuable tidbit of wisdom I tossed her way, how, if you sat or stood in the proper position and had the right muscle control, you could make a fart last up to thirty seconds and not dump in your pants (eating popcorn at least twenty minutes before attempting this difficult stratagem is immensely beneficial to a successful outcome).

Whenever we were together, which was often, Beth had a childhood, and I had the woman against whom all others would be measured and come up lacking.

But for that night, it was her kiss lingering on my cheek as I walked toward my front door and my father's putting his hand on my shoulder for the first time in an eternity ("How you holding up there, son? Ever tell you about when I got shot during the war?") that made me feel that maybe, just maybe, I wasn't such a worthless little kid, after all.

I spent the next seven years becoming an honorary member of Beth's and Mabel's family. By the time Beth turned twenty-four she had grown into her shopworn beauty and grace with all the poise I'd come to expect from her. In the years since the hospital we had shared every secret, every dream, every sadness, pettiness, fear, hope, want, triumph, and failure of both childhood and adolescence; I knew her better than anyone, and she, in turn knew more about me than any person ever had or ever would. There had been so much between us, so many shared moments and experiences: our first trip (the first of many) to King's Island where she took me on my very first roller coaster ride, then didn't laugh her head off or make fun of me when I threw up as soon as we climbed out of the car; a terrible afternoon a few weeks after I'd gotten my driver's license when I drove her over to Columbus to get an abortion because her boyfriend at the time (all her boyfriends were so physically interchangeable to me they became faceless over the years) had dumped her and quickly skipped town after she told him she was pregnant; the day she picked me up at four in the afternoon on my fifteenth birthday and drove all the way to Cincinnati so I could see my first circus; an Emerson, Lake & Palmer concert where we were nearly trampled to death after the crowd—who'd been standing in near-blizzard conditions for over three hours—rushed the doors when they were finally opened; all the times I helped her to take one of the dogs to the vet, times when I stood beside her after the animal had been given the Last Injection and she needed to say good-bye—then, later, her infectious near-giddiness when the dead pet was replaced by a new one; and, most of all, a certain picnic in Moundbuilders Park on my seventeenth birthday when Beth asked me if I had a girlfriend. When I said no, she leaned in and gave me the sweetest, longest, most tender kiss against which all others would forever be compared and come up lacking, then shyly handed me a birthday card inscribed: *Just wait until you're legal!*

I read the inscription twice before clearing my throat and saying, "Um, I, uh . . . is this a joke?"

She put her thumb and index finger under my chin, lifting my head so she could look straight into my eyes. Whenever she did this, it meant Something Serious was about to happen or be said. "Can I ask you something?"

"You mean besides that?"

"Don't try to be funny, you're not all that good at it."

"Okay."

She kept her thumb and finger under my chin, making small, maddening circles against my skin with the tips of each. "Do you love me?"

I blanked out for a second—what was happening here?—then shook myself back to the Right-Now and said, "Yes, of course I do. We've known each other for—what is it now?—*eight* years?"

"Almost nine now."

I reached up and held her wrist. "You are the best friend I have ever had, Beth. Hell—you're the *only* real friend I've ever had."

She cupped my face in both her hands and kissed me again. "And you're *my* best friend. You've never judged me, or lied to me, you've never been cruel or thoughtless to me, you've appreciated everything I've ever done for you and you've done so many *sweet* things for me, even when I was acting like a real bitch on wheels—"

"Your words, not mine. Go on, I'll speak up when I disagree."

She smiled, moving closer to me. "You know that in high school I was kind of . . . oh, what's the word I'm looking for?"

"Popular?"

She laughed and shook her head. "Well, I suppose that's *one* word for it."

"Friendly?"

She bit her lower lip and shook her head.

"Available? 'Open twenty-four Hours'?" I began to laugh. " 'One Mattress, No Waiting'?"

"You're dangerously close to losing one of your nuts."

"I know, I'm sorry."

"You *do* know what I'm trying to tell you, right?"

"That you were kind of easy in high school?"

"Don't sugar-coat it, kiddo— Oh, shit! I didn't mean—"

"Too late." I held out my hand. "You owe me a buck."

"But we were having a moment—"

"—that will continue once you pony up the dough." Ever since the day she'd taken me home from the hospital, Beth and I'd had an agreement: any time she slipped up and called me "kid" or "kiddo" or any other variation thereof, it would cost her a dollar. She had promised never to call me anything like that again, and my charging her for her digressions seemed a solid way to remind her of the importance of keeping her word.

She dug into her pocket and produced a crumpled dollar bill, which she slapped into my hand with a lot more force than was called for, in my opinion.

Shoving the buck into *my* pocket so the lint would have some company, I smiled at her and said: "You were telling me something about your being easy in high school?"

"Easy? I was a slut. If I'd stayed in college, I'd probably be a real piece—"

"—like you already weren't?"

"—*of work*, smartass. I'd be a real *piece of work*. I spent way too much time in way too many beds trying to convince myself I was worth something. If a guy even hinted that he liked me, I'd pretty much let him do whatever he wanted."

"I kind of suspected that after you banged the orderly that time in the hospital so he'd take us to the animal lab. Well, that, and when I saw you with that bozo at the gas station the first time you took me home for dinner."

"I'm not like that anymore. Since the abortion last year, I've been very careful about who I . . . you know . . . I mean, I haven't been with a guy in that way *since. . . .*"

She wasn't on the verge of tears—Beth almost never cried—but there was a thinness to her voice, a vulnerability that both surprised and scared me.

I touched her face. "You don't have to explain any

140

of this to me. I understand how things were. It never mattered to me. It still doesn't."

She turned her face into my hand, kissing the palm. "That's just so goddamn typical of you."

"What? Did I do something untoward? Did I say the wrong thing? Did I let fly with a whopper of a fart and just not notice—what?"

"You *accept* me for who and what I am. You always have. Whenever one of those dick-for-brains boyfriends of mine would treat me like shit, or embarrass me, or stand me up for a date, you always said or did the right thing to make it better. I could never really *hurt* when I was with you. Sometimes, just knowing that all I'd have to do—it didn't matter who I was with or where we were or whatever kind of trouble I getting into—all I had to do was pick up the phone and call you and you'd make everything better."

"Okay. *And . . .* ?"

She stared at me for a moment, then slightly shook her head. "And you have no idea how great a thing that is, do you? You have no idea how wonderful you really are. All you can see are your weaknesses and failures. You don't see how strong you are already, how strong you've always been. Christ, when I first met you in the hospital I thought you were, like, *my* age. Sure, you were *built* about the size of a nine-year-old, but when you looked at a person—when you looked at *me*—you were so much older than you should have been. Even now, looking into your eyes, you seem so much older than I am. Haven't you ever noticed how people can't keep eye contact with you during a conversation?"

"Always figured it was because I had something stuck in my teeth—"

"*Shut. Up.* You listen now. People can't keep eye contact with you because you see through all the scrims and bullshit. Whether you mean to or not, you just don't look *at* a person, you look right into the middle of who they really are and people can't handle that."

"That explains my jam-packed social calendar."

"See? Just then, that remark—'My jam-packed social calendar.' How many seventeen-year-old guys do you know who say things like that? And wasn't there an 'untoward' in there earlier? Don't answer, it wasn't really a question."

"What's going on here, Beth? I'm confused."

"No, you're not. You're one of the most *un*-confused people I've ever known. I think everything is very clear to you."

I held up the birthday card. "This isn't."

"Yes, it is. You just don't want to admit it."

"Admit what?"

"That you love me."

I sighed in exasperation. "*I already said I did!* That's what started this . . . this . . . this goddamn dialogue exchange from a Harold Pinter play. You're my best friend and I love you."

"But you don't *only* love me as a friend, do you?"

(Mayday, Mayday, sonar has malfunctioned, there's an unexpected obstacle outside the cabin window and—)

—and there it was.

She'd blindsided me and she knew it. Had it been that obvious all these years and I was just too stupid to know I'd been wearing *all* my feelings on my sleeve?

Staring into her soft-brown, gold-flecked eyes I was as utterly and deliciously helpless as any teenager in love has ever been. "You're twenty-four, Beth."

"You make it sound ancient."

"How would it look to your friends? Christ, I'm just a *baby* as far as they're concerned."

"Leave them out of it for now, okay? Fuck 'em. Right now, right here, I want to know your feelings for me."

What surprised me the most was how quickly I answered, and the ease with which the words came out of my mouth: "I've been in love with you since that day you brought two of your friends into my room at the hospital and kissed me in front of them. I was in love with you long before you held my hand for the first time, or told me a secret, or took me to your house, or slipped your arm through mine while we wandered around King's Island. The first time I saw you in your hip-huggers and a halter-top I thought I'd implode from how beautiful you were. Do you have any idea how much I wanted to kill that guy at the gas station because *he* got to hold you and kiss you and all I could do was sit there and watch him do it? You haven't dated one guy that I didn't immediately want to run over with a power mower just to hear him scream. Whenever you hug me, I won't wash the shirt for a *week* because the smell of your musk oil lingers in the material. All my life girls have either made fun of me or treated me like I was their brother. My first kiss I got only because I was at a party playing 'Spin the Bottle'—it pointed at Linda McDonald, who was the new girl at school and didn't know I was the class joke. The only girl who's ever kissed me like she *meant* it is you. I'm never really happy unless you're around, or I know that I'll be seeing you soon. When I'm an old man sitting in a nursing home with oatmeal dribbling down my chin, I'm gonna bore the piss out of the nurses because I'll keep telling them over and over about this girl named Beth who was the great love of my life, but because she was also my best friend I did the noble thing and let her slip away.

"Whoever you wind up with, whichever guy out there has the brains to know he's just met the greatest woman in the world the first time he meets you . . . the two of you can be together for sixty, seventy years, you can have dozens of children and grandchildren and great-grandchildren and build the most unbelievably fantastic life together. But when you're holding his hand at the end and looking into his eyes and seeing him remember the richness and fulfillment and joy he's known because his life has been spent by your side, at that moment, *that very moment*, he won't come *close* to loving you half as much as I do, right here, right now. So, yeah, Beth, I love you, and I'm *in* love with you, and nothing you've said or done in the past has changed that, and nothing you can say or do now is *going* to change it. There? Happy now?"

"Actually," she said, slipping her arms around my neck, "I am. *Very* happy. Because I love you, too. And I figure that if you're going to lose your virginity, Gil, it should be to me."

Earlier, when I said the first kiss Beth gave me that day was the one against which all others would be compared and come up lacking . . . I was wrong. The kiss she gave me at that moment, a kiss just as soft and warm and deep and long and moist as the first, but this time with the hint of hunger on the tip of its tongue and a *heat* around it that you experience once and once only in your life if you're lucky, because it's a heat that burns into the core of your heart and tells you that this is *it*, kiddo, run for cover, this is the Real Thing, Take No Prisoners, give it up, you're doomed, because Love has just kicked your teeth down your throat, ain't it grand?—*this* kiss was the one whose summer taste and autumn passion would linger on my lips for all the rest of my days.

When she pulled away—not taking her arms from around my neck—we both let out a long, hot, staggered breath. She pressed her forehead against mine and stroked the back of my neck, swallowing once before saying, "Oh, *my*," ending that second word on a smoothly descending note of embarrassed laughter that snuggled down in the back of her throat and wrapped itself up in something like a purr; I could almost feel her voice with my fingertips.

"Just wait until I'm legal, huh?"

"Oh, I think we passed the 'waiting' part about thirty seconds ago." She lifted her head and looked into my eyes again. "Before I picked you up today, I rented a hotel room downtown. Can I take you there? Can we leave right now?"

She'd bought two boxes of condoms (three to a pack, and we still called them "rubbers") and bet me a year's worth of back rubs that I couldn't last through one box. I made it all the way through the

Gary A. Braunbeck

first one from the *second* box before she and I didn't so much fall asleep as pass out. I say this not to boast (c'mon, I was seventeen and a virgin; most days I was so horny the crack of dawn wasn't safe) but to give you some idea of how gloriously *unhinged* the whole experience was. It was romantic and primal, awkward and embarrassing, spectacular and funny, life-affirming and depressing as hell, always surprising (she did things with me I didn't think two bodies were capable of doing, even with lubricants), and even a little . . . mystifying. We fell out of bed laughing, we got a little mushy, a lot dirty, very sweaty, and ultimately so sore neither of us walked very fast or very straight for a day or two afterward.

It was wonderful.

And I think I knew the truth about the whole thing before we'd even finished dressing afterward.

"You're giving me a look," she said.

"Why did you do this, Beth?"

"Because I wanted to."

I tied my shoelaces and looked at the floor. I didn't want to see her face when she answered the next question. "This doesn't mean what I think it means, does it?"

"What do you think it . . . no. No, kiddo. And I'm sorry."

"Then *why?*"

"Because I needed to . . . to be with a guy who loved me." She placed her hand against the small of my back. "You don't hate me, do you?"

"No." Which was a lie. At that moment I don't think I'd hated anyone or anything more, but I also knew I'd get over it. This was Beth, after all.

146

A few nights later at dinner Dad remarked that Beth seemed like a decent girl and I should count myself lucky to have found her. Then he looked across the table at Mom and smiled, and my mother actually blushed.

I was stunned. For as long as I could remember, they'd never displayed any tenderness or affection for one another in front of me—as far as I cared to imagine, they'd never displayed any in private, either. They were Just Mom and Dad, the people who raised me and paid for my clothes and put a roof over my head and sent me to school and never missed a chance to remind me that everything I had was because of them. I knew that parents were just like any other couple, that there was love and affection and all of that, but these were *my* folks, for the love of God. *My* folks never talked about anything like this—hell, the only time anything more than the day's trivialities were ever brought up was when Dad was on a drunk and shouting at the top of his lungs about the bills or the condition of the house or how the goddamn company was going to fuck over the union with the next contract.

But this little flirtatious display over the meatloaf . . . this was just *weird*. It made me nervous. And a little queasy.

I went to bed that night without setting them straight about Beth and me. I think my dad was just glad to know that I liked girls.

Later—I guess it must have been two or two-thirty in the morning—I woke up with one of those middle-of-the-night cases of dry mouth that make you think you're going to die within seconds if you don't get something to drink *right now*, and went downstairs to get a glass of juice from the fridge. The living room was dark as I passed by but it *felt* like someone was in there. Probably Dad. Again. They'd been screwing with his hours at the plant and as a result he hadn't gotten back on anything close to a normal sleeping schedule yet. Most nights he'd toss and turn for hours until he woke Mom, who'd make him come downstairs and do his tossing and turning on the sofa. He was usually cranky as hell whenever this happened, so I walked very softly and decided not to turn on the kitchen lights. I drank my juice, quietly rinsed out the glass and set it in the sink, and was starting back toward the stairs when I heard Dad say, in a voice so tired and sad it froze me where I stood: "Did I ever tell you that when I was a kid, I wanted to raise chickens for a living?"

I couldn't have been more anxious if I'd run into an armed burglar. Talks between Dad and me never ended well—one of us always wound up accusing the other of being too pushy or disrespectful or whatever—and the idea of getting into it with him at this hour, especially considering how upset he sounded, made me cringe.

Then I heard Mom reply: "Only about a hundred times, hon. But if you want to talk about it again, go ahead."

When had she come down? I would have heard her—the steps squeaked and groaned like something out of a haunted-house movie. I was surprised that Dad hadn't lit into me about making so much noise coming down here.

Then it occurred to me that maybe the two of

them had been sitting in there the whole time since I'd gone to bed, that maybe Dad was genuinely upset about something other than the usual list of complaints and Mom, to keep the peace, had decided to sit in there and let him talk it out, however long it took.

Something in their respective tones baffled me; they were talking to one another not as my parents, but as a husband and wife.

I realized then that, until the incident at dinner tonight, I'd never actually thought of them as being that way—husband and wife—only as Mom and Dad. It was kind of fascinating, and in my best What-the-Hell-Are-You-Doing? skulk, I crept out of the kitchen and hid myself in the shadows on the stairway. They couldn't see me there, I was pretty sure, but I had a clear view of their silhouettes against the window, where the curtain glowed a dull blue against the diffuse street light trying to sneak in from outside.

Mom was sitting in her chair next to the fireplace and Dad was on the old leather ottoman that should have been put out of its misery years ago. He was leaning forward, elbows on knees, holding his pipe in one hand. If the curtains had been open, he would have been staring out the window, but I knew he'd just been sitting there staring at the curtains as if imagining something really interesting on the other side. I'd seen him do this too many times to count. I always wondered what he thought about as he sat in the dark staring at a set of closed curtains. Why not just open the damn things? At least the view of the street *might* change if a car or dog or neighbor wandered by.

Gary A. Braunbeck

"You gonna tell me what's bothering you?" asked Mom.

"It's stupid."

"Not if it's got you upset like this, it isn't."

Dad fired up his pipe, then pointed toward where I was hiding with its glowing red bowl. "He must think I'm some kind of asshole."

"I don't think he feels that way. He maybe doesn't understand you, but he doesn't think ill of you."

"What about you?"

"You're my husband and I love you."

"C'mon. I'm not drunk so I'm not gonna throw a fit—*answer the question*."

"I think you act like a real bastard when you've been drinking—but it doesn't *make* you a bastard. That's something you really have to work at."

Dad chuckled, puffing on his pipe. Even from where I was hiding, I could smell the sweet cherry-flavored tobacco.

"Think he'll remember much about us after we're gone?"

Mom pulled in a little gasp of air, then said: "Don't you go talking like that. We may not be as young as we used to be, but I'm not shopping for burial plots just yet."

"That's because you don't have to, remember? We paid for them damn things—what was it?—ten, fifteen years ago?"

"Oh."

"*Oh*, she says." He shook his head. "Think a person'd remember something like that."

Mom readjusted her position in the chair, then

asked: "Are you going to tell me what's wrong or not?"

Dad puffed on his pipe again, then wiped the back of his arm over his face. "I told you, it's stupid."

"How about you let me decide that for myself?"

He looked straight at her. "It's just, I been thinkin' about when I was a kid, how I'd always get a whole dime once a month to go spend however I wanted. Shit, I had seven different paper routes I worked, and I handed every penny over to Mom so she could buy groceries and pay the bills—"

"—I remember the Depression, hon. We're the same age, as I recall."

"A dime was a small fortune back then. But Mom, she insisted that once a month I take a dime and go to the movies on Sunday. I could see a triple-feature with cartoons and get popcorn and a soda and still have three cents left for ice cream or something. I used to love those times, y'know. 'Downtown Sunday' was a big thing for me. I'd go to the Midland or the Auditorium for the movies, then walk around the square. Those're some of the best memories I have.

"Anyway, there was this one corner downtown with this old building, and every Sunday I'd see the same three old guys sitting on the steps, sharing a newspaper or splitting up sandwiches, passing around some beer, and they always had this raggedy-ass fat old hound dog with 'em. I didn't know which one of 'em owned the thing, but it never gave me any trouble so I never asked. But any time that dog'd see me coming, he'd waddle over and then just sit there and look at me with those sad eyes—thing looked like it was coming down off a drunk most of the time. I'd usually give it some leftover popcorn or a piece of my sandwich or whatever I picked up after the movie, and it'd eat it, then lick my hand and waddle back over to those three old guys. They always waved at me and I'd wave back. It was like part of my Downtown Sunday routine, you know?

"I thought it was great that here you had these old guys who'd meet each other on them steps and pass the better part of the day with their paper, and their stories, maybe playing checkers or something . . . and they always had that damn dog to keep things interesting. I mean, there was people who'd walk by and make fun of them, or try not to laugh at 'em 'cause they thought they was, you know, funny in the head or something. But I never laughed at 'em or made fun or anything. They had a place to go and spend good time with their friends. I thought that was just . . . just great." His voice was growing thin, unsteady. He took a few more puffs from his pipe and as he did, Mom leaned forward.

Something more was going on here than what I was seeing and hearing. I'd never heard Dad talk about his childhood much, and whenever he did, I always tuned him out after a minute or two. Same thing with Mom. After all, I was young—what the hell did their childhood memories have to do with *me*?

"One day," Dad continued, "I'd had a real good month and so Mom gave me an extra nickel, I thought I was King Midas or something, even bought myself a couple of comic books—I bought a little penny bag of dog scraps from one of the restaurants after I got out of the movie, decided that I was gonna make that old hound dog's day. So I walk over to that corner and the three old guys are there and the dog waddles over as usual and boy, did it get *lively* when it saw what I had for it. So I fed it the scraps and petted it for a little bit, and that's when I noticed that somebody'd stapled this plastic blue tag to the back of the poor thing's ear. I figured maybe the dog catcher had caught it or something and maybe they did this down at the pound before the old guys came to claim it—but I couldn't imagine anyone doing something like that to an animal. So I was extra nice to the dog that day and decided to walk it back across the street and say hello to the guys.

"We stood there talking for a few minutes and I finally got around to asking them whose dog it was, and you know what? It didn't belong to any of them. They said that it had just always been there, and that it had waddled up to each one of them at some point and that's how the three of them had met. After that, they sort of saw that dog as their good-luck charm, so they didn't think they should send it away. None of 'em had any idea how that tag got there, either. I thought that was odd but I didn't want to push the subject and maybe get them mad at me, so I asked 'em how long they'd been coming downtown on Sundays. And you know what one of them said to me *then?* He looked at me and shook his head and said: 'Christ, boy! We come down here every day. We're in our eighties—everybody else we know's dead. What the hell else have we got to do?'

"I went home that day and cried myself to sleep. It was just terrible. Here I'd spent all this time thinking they were having a grand time, and all the while they were miserable. I didn't go by that corner much after that. It must've been five, six months later before I passed by there, and this time they were all gone. There was only that old hound dog, just as friendly as ever. I think it even looked *better* in some ways; more energetic, and its eyes weren't as bloodshot and droopy anymore. But it was just sitting there, scratching at that tag on its ear and waiting for the old guys to show up. It was still sitting there waiting when I left to go home and—"

And then Dad did something I'd never seen him do before; he dropped his head down and started crying. Even from where I was standing, I could see the way his body jerked and shuddered with the sobs.

Mom made a move to go to him but then thought better of it at the last moment. I wanted to call out "Give him a hug!" but I didn't. I was as stunned and confused as she must have been.

"Oh, God," said Dad, wiping at his eyes, but still the sobs kept coming. "I *hate* to get up in the mornings. You know? Some days I wish I didn't have to get up at all, that I'd never have to get up again, ever. Just lay there and stare at the ceiling until . . . I don't know what."

"Honey, what's going on?" Mom moved closer to him, but still would not touch him, as if she were afraid he might shatter into a thousand pieces.

"I wish I'd been a better soldier in the war, come home a hero like *Sergeant York* or something. But, no,

I gotta go and get all shot up and now I've got a bad hip and two legs that get all swoll-up on me until I can't hardly stand it hurts so much. I wish I'd been able to afford college, get me a degree in agriculture or something. We'd be on our own farm right now, one we *own*, and we'd be raising chickens, all of us. Instead we got this damn house that ain't even paid for yet and ain't gonna be anytime soon, and all I can do is drink until my hip or my legs don't hurt so much 'cause I can't afford the doctor bills anymore . . . then I yell at you and him and make everyone scared." He pulled in a deep breath full of snot and regret and wiped at his face again.

"I see the way he looks at me sometimes. He looks at me just like people used to look at those old guys on the corner when I was a kid. Like I'm some kinda joke. I don't want to be a joke to him, some worn-out old man who don't know nothing but factory work, and I don't want to be a bad husband to you. But every time I get up in the morning, every time I haul my fat ass out of bed, I think about them old guys. I can't help it. Because they might not be down on that corner anymore, but I *know*—as sure as I know that a man's hands weren't meant to be as scarred and calloused as mine are—I *know* that them old guys and that dog are still out there *somewhere*, and they're still sad and lonely and miserable and people still make fun of them and one day that's gonna be me, if it ain't already. An old, drunk joke of a factory worker that'll be forgot about an hour after he's dead. I know this. And when I die, that old hound dog's gonna show up on that corner again and sit there waiting for me. I'll sit there on them steps with it and wait for it to drag over the ghosts of other guys who bungled everything and—what the hell am I going on about? Listen to me, will you?

"Oh, Christ, honey, I'm so *sorry*. It's just I think about them guys and they way they were and I get so . . . scared."

Mom went to him now, kneeling beside him and taking him in her arms. "It's all right, honey, shhhh. There, there. It's all right."

"I love you. I don't much act like it most of the time, but I do."

"I know, shhh, c'mon."

Still, he wept, pressing his face into her shoulder. "I wish I'd given both of you a better life, that's all."

"You've given us a good life, and that's enough."

I couldn't watch any longer; I was an intruder, a spy, a voyeur, so I turned and left them there, a silhouette against a closed window, two people I now knew I'd never really known at all, a tableau frozen in the shadows: husband and wife.

God, how I wished that Beth and I would someday love each other like that.

I wasn't surprised to find myself crying as I got back into bed. I'd found out more about my parents in those few minutes than I would have ever found out if it'd been left up to me. What did their memories mean, anyway? Who cared about their hopes? I was young and had better things to busy myself with.

I wasn't the biggest fan of myself right then. I had never stopped to think that maybe it was important to them to share things like this with me, so that I might keep some small part of them alive after they were gone. *Here is one of my best moments, would you keep it safe for me? Here is the dumbest thing I ever did, remember it for me, please? This was your great-grandmother, try to keep her in your thoughts.*

It suddenly occurred to me that Mom hadn't told Dad that *I* loved him, too. Had she been too caught up in comforting him to remember? Did it just slip her mind or—

—or was she as uncertain about it as Dad seemed to be?

There was such stillness in that room, and it found its way into the center of my chest, whispering of a man's anger at seeing himself as being less than he really was; of a woman's need to give comfort even if it meant making herself vulnerable to that anger; of a young man's (really still a child in many ways) need to understand why he'd never seen them as being anything other than keepers and providers; and, most of all, in the stillness of the center, there in that house with its chronic angers, in that room, a final whisper from some dimly remembered poem about love's austere and lonely offices.

I told myself that I would find a way, a right time, a good moment to let him know that, yeah, I thought he acted like a son-of-a-bitch sometimes, but that I understood why a little better now, and that I loved him. Loved them both.

I drifted off to sleep to find myself on a downtown corner, and here was an old hound dog waddling up to meet me. I looked around to see if I could spot the little boy who would grow up to be my dad. I wanted to say hi, and to thank him.

* * *

Shortly after my nineteenth birthday, the Cedar Hill Healthcare Center fell into some financial difficulties—I never understood the specifics—and had to make some cutbacks in personnel. Luckily, Mabel wasn't among those who were laid off, but the woman with whom she often carpooled was among those let go. As a result, I began taking her to and from work, which was no burden; for one thing, I liked Mabel very much; for another, on those nights when she worked both the units and cafeteria, it was easier to just stay over at the house with Beth (the CHHC was only a fifteen minute drive from Beth's house, thirty from mine). Any excuse Beth and I could find to be alone (excepting for the Its, who soon learned that once that bedroom door was closed, it wasn't opening again anytime soon) was welcomed.

No, we weren't a couple—not publicly, anyway. Beth still went through relationships like most people went through tissues during allergy season, but during the frequent "breaks" in her love life, whenever we were alone, there was no such thing as "hands off." Even then I suspected that it was all going to break my heart in a major way sometime in the future, but when you're a teenager it's a lot easier to convince yourself that you're made of sterner stuff than you really are.

So I willingly became Beth's "fuck-buddy."

It wasn't just the sex—though I'd be lying if I didn't admit that was a factor—it was the *companionship*. I don't know if that's something a lot of people under thirty ever really grasp—it doesn't have to be the naked, sweating, rolling, groaning, shrieking do-me-do-me-do-me christ I'm-gonna-*come* routine all the time. Sometimes just sitting next to the person you love and watching a movie on television while their fingers brush lightly over the back of your hand is infinitely more satisfying, simply because they *get you*; they know that this twitch means one thing and that little shiver something else; they can tell by the way you clear your throat that you're about to laugh, or that when you stretch your neck to the left and no bones crack it means you're anxious about something: *companionship.*

Beth was splendid company. Even after she disappeared, the memory of those nights of doing nothing—watching television, listening to records, sorting through grocery store coupons, clipping one of the Its' toenails—made me smile.

And to a large extent, I have Mabel to thank for that—if I hadn't been the one driving her to and from work, I never would have truly understood that sometimes tenderness marks you far deeper than passion can ever dream.

Usually I'd get to the nursing home a few minutes before Mabel's shift ended and would wait in the cafeteria area, or chat with whomever was working the station while Mabel made her last rounds on the unit. The people there began to recognize me after a while, and by the time I turned twenty my presence there at the end of Mabel's shift was something of an evening staple; if I were even five minutes late, both eyebrows and questions would be raised: *You don't suppose he forgot, do you? It's just not like him to be late, is it? Doesn't seem right, not having him around at this hour, huh?*

Because I always used the same entrance and took the same route to Mabel's unit, I always passed the same doors. Most nights these stood open (a closed door, I came to find out, meant only one of two things: fast asleep, or dead and waiting for the funeral home to pick up the body) and I came to have "on-sight" relationships with some of the residents. You know the kind: pass the same person at roughly the same time often enough over the course of a day or a week or month and you both become something of a fixture in the other's life, even if you never speak or learn his name. *Nine-fifteen, time for Mr. Pickup to saunter by my door. I wonder if he's going to wear the leather jacket tonight or that gray windbreaker. Let's see, where is he? Ah, here he comes. Hmm. The windbreaker tonight. Good choice. Seems like he's in a good mood—maybe he got some earlier. Looks like a nice young man, though. Time to wave to him.*

The flip side to this was Mr. Pickup unintentionally made himself an expected part of the Door People's routine; the woman in 106 who blared *Later with Tom Snyder* from her television set just couldn't enjoy the second half of her program unless I stopped to hear her comment on how awful it was that they had to have so many gosh-darned commercials on these days; the two sisters in room 112 just *had* to know how the weather was tonight, and had I heard anything about tomorrow's forecast?; the silver-haired guy whose wheelchair was always parked near the vending machines would not—repeat, *not*—pop open his evening soda until I passed by so he could lift the can in my direction and say *"Salute, my boy!"*; and the two old farts in 120—who for some reason called me

"Captain Spaulding"—could have their evening ruined unless we ran through the same shtick:

> Old Fart #1: Here comes Captain Spaulding!
> Old Fart #2: The African explorer?
> Me: Did someone call me "Shnorer?"
> Them: We weren't talking to you!

Followed by uproarious laughter from them.

(Hey, I never said it was a *clever* shtick.)

One night I had the mother of all sinus headaches and passed by their room without so much as a glance. I heard one of them start the shtick—"Here comes Captain Spaulding!"—but was well past the room before his buddy could do his part. I stopped for a moment when a dribble of pain moved from between my eyes to the back of my throat, then turned back toward the water fountain that was only a few feet away from their room. I downed a couple of decongestants then figured, *What the hell, I'm here*, and poked my head around into their room.

They weren't looking at the door, nor were they looking at each other—in fact, they didn't seem to be *looking* at anything at all. They just stared. At an empty space where their laughter should have been ringing. At a place where a visiting child should have been sitting. At a lifetime of Maybe-Next-Year places they'd always meant to take the wife, but the old girl had gotten cancer too young and left this world before they could ever get away together.

There is a very thin scrim that keeps the ruined things behind the curtain of everyday life, and one of the weights that held that curtain in place had just been removed. Now, with no Captain Spaulding shtick, the edge of that curtain was fluttering, and something of infinite sadness and disappointment could be seen shifting: *Here we are, pal, two old sons-of-bitches at the end of our lives and no one else but each other to give a shit. It would've been nice to have our nightly laugh but that's gone now, too; just like our families, our good women, our strong young-man notions. It was nice while it lasted, though. Maybe they'll serve buttermilk pancakes tomorrow, huh?*

"Excuse me," I said.

They both started, blinked, then turned in my direction. The look on their faces suggested that something with three heads and a dick growing from its left nostril had just entered the room.

"I, uh . . . I was passing by and could have *sworn* someone in this room called me 'Shnorer.' Was that one of you gentlemen?"

It took them a moment.

It is him, right?

I believe so, yes.

Hey, the curtain fell back into place.

Damn good thing, too; I think tomorrow's poached eggs.

" 'Shnorer,' did you say?" asked Old Fart #1.

"Yes, I believe that's what I heard."

They looked at each other, then: *"We weren't talking to you!"*

Uproarious laughter. This time I actually joined in.

"Sounds like you got yerself a mighty nasty cold there, Captain."

"I do. I'm kinda dizzy and my ears are clogged."

"Have trouble sleeping?"

I nodded.

"Neither one of us can sleep worth a tinker's left nut, either."

They both smiled and told me I should take some tea with a little whiskey in it, and while I was at it could I sneak a little in for them? Maybe they could get one of them young nursing assistants a little tipsy and she'd give them an extra-long sponge bath.

I grinned and mimed tapping the edge of a cigar. "That's the most ridiculous thing I ever hoid."

That got a big laugh out of them, though I'm damned if I know why. I waved at them, sang a quick "Hooray-hooray-*hooray!*" and headed back down the hall. I made it a point after that to stop by their room every night and do the shtick until the night that door was closed and the names which I had never bothered to read were removed from the outside slots. I knew neither one of them slept worth a tinker's left nut, so that limited the options.

But, for that night, I felt better about myself and the world and my place in it. My sinuses, however, were having none of this fun and frolic and warm squishy happiness. I'd decided to give Mabel the keys and let her drive the car that night; the decongestants weren't helping, my chest felt like it had been filled with rubber cement, and I couldn't see clearly past five feet or so.

Which is why it took me a moment to locate the voice coming from another of the opened doors.

"You did the wrong routine," it said.

Here I go, stumbling around, looking for the speaker, banging my knee against one of the wall rails used by the patients who didn't get around so well on their own anymore.

"Hello?" I said.

"To your right, Baryshnikov."

I blinked, wiped my eyes, and found him.

Seventy, seventy-five, but he wore it so very well. Think of Burt Lancaster in *Atlantic City*. Class and style; shopworn and a bit craggy around the edges, but still commanding. If it hadn't been for the wheelchair and the gnarled branches that had once been his legs, I would've expected him to grab my collar and warn: *"Don't. Touch. The suit!"*

"Hello," I said. Then: "What did you mean, the wrong routine?"

"When you blew your cue back there and had to go back and cover your ass. Instead of trying to pick up the old routine where you'd left it writhing in a heap on the floor, you should've hit 'em with Groucho's 'Hello, I must be going' line."

"Hello, I must be going?"

He nodded. The light danced across his startlingly white hair. "Right. 'I cannot stay, I came to say, I must be going.'"

"Ah."

"Not a Marx Brothers fan?"

"*Big* Marx Brothers fan," I said, a bit defensively.

"That's good. You're young enough to be one of those Three Stooges people. That'd be a damn shame."

"Why?"

"Because there are only two types of people in this world: those who like the Stooges, and those who like the Marx Brothers."

"Buster Keaton was always my favorite, actually."

"He'd've been embarrassed, the way you were stumbling around out there. No grace. No style. No art."

I cleared my throat. "Well, thank you, James Agee, for that blistering review, but I came to say I must be going."

He clapped his hands loudly. "*There* you go! Not the most clever or smoothest transition back to the opening gag, but a damn good outing your first time. No doubt about it."

"Thanks. I think."

"You're welcome. Maybe. Hey, you got a minute?"

I checked my watch. "Actually, I'm here to pick up someone."

"Who? If it's your mom or grandpa or someone like that, they tend to discourage late-night roustabouting. Afraid if we actually have some fun it'll improve our dispositions and make us a bit more clearheaded, and then they'll be forced to deal with us like we possess honest-to-Pete personalities and feelings. Keepers gotta keep the kept kept, know what I'm saying? Ever had anyone talk to you like you don't have the brains God gave an ice cube? After a while you start to wonder if maybe they aren't right in addressing you like that because maybe, *maybe* you *have* taken up residence in Looney-Toons Junction and spend all your time discussing Heraclites's River with Elmer Fudd while out here in the happy world, they've been changing your diapers and drawing lewd grafitti on your butt with permanent markers. By the way, in case you lost track of what I was talking about before I wandered off the highway subject-wise, I'd just asked you who you were here to pick up. If I'm not being what you'd call a buttinsky. Too inquisitive. Nibby. Et cetera."

"Mabel," I said.

"Ah, our Angel of the Cafeteria and Catheters. I know her well, Horatio. Your mother? Aunt? Mistress—or are you a kept man? A heartless gigolo using her for your distasteful carnal pleasures while racking up charges on her credit card?"

"Your minute was up about thirty seconds ago."

"I'm sorry. I didn't realize you had such a jam-packed social calendar. How thoughtless of me. No wonder the Kremlin will return none of my calls. Can you set the clock on this damn thing?" He pointed to a brand-new Betamax unit that sat on top of his television. "It works just fine, I can record and all that, but I can't seem to set the clock."

"No problem." I'd been eyeing one of these for a while, but had held off buying because of the six-hundred-plus dollar price tag. But it would be nice to actually *record* movies and television shows to keep.

I set the clock for him.

"A wizard, that's what you are."

"I've been thinking about getting one of these."

He snorted a derisive laugh. "A gift from my daughter. She's in Los Angeles. She's in the entertainment business. These things are supposedly going to be all the rage in a few years. Thing is, for as much as it costs, you can't find all that many movies to play in it. There's a place over on Church Street that just opened, claims they have the biggest selection in the city—which amounts to being the most gifted ballerina in Hoboken, if you ask me, which I realize you didn't, but I'm old and lonely and like the sound of my own voice and, besides, you haven't exactly been taken hostage here, have you?"

"You in show business too?"

"Used to be." He extended his hand. "Name's Weis. Marty Weis. Friends call my 'Whitey' because of my hair. You can call me 'Mr. Weis.'"

"Nice to meet you, Mr. Weis. I think."

"Pleasure to meet you, too. Maybe. Hey—did you know that back in the heyday of vaudeville, Cedar Hill used to be one the biggest tour stops?"

I leaned against the door. 'Whitey' needed to talk to someone, I suddenly felt so sick I wasn't sure I'd be able to walk another ten feet, and after the near-miss with Old Farts #1 and #2 my guilt tank was already on 'F.' I wasn't going to take any chances.

"No," I said. "I didn't know that. I know it was once the boxing capital of the country."

"Back in the late thirties, early forties, you bet it was. It was the same thing with vaudeville. You know the Old Soldiers and Sailors Building?"

I shook my head.

"'Course not—you'd know it as the Auditorium Theatre."

"The one across from the Midland?"

"The very one. You ever get the chance, you ought to go in there and head down to the basement. There's a wall directly underneath the front of the stage that's covered in autographs from all the acts who played there. Houdini's autograph is there, so are the Three Keatons'. I've been there, I've seen it. There must be a thousand autographs on that wall.

Now that the place doesn't show movies or book acts anymore—"

"—not in about twenty years," I said.

"Thanks, I wasn't feeling enough like a fossil tonight." He shook his head. "It's a damn shame, all that history down there, all those names—some of *famous* people, too—just stuck down there in the dark where no one can see them."

"I never knew that."

"Not too many folks do, and the ones who are old enough *to* remember, can't anymore."

"Except you."

"Except me. I used to be a talent agent. The Double-Dubya. Whitey Weis. Midwest Talent and Entertainment. Handled Gypsy Rose Lee for about a month near the end of her career. Lot of other acts, too, but I doubt you'd know the names."

"Names that are on the wall under the stage at the Auditorium?"

"That's right. Thank you for setting my clock."

"What're you going to watch?"

"Watch? Hell, I'm not going to watch anything. You see what's on these days? There's a cop show, *Blue Hills* or *Blue Street* or—"

"*Hill Street Blues*?"

"That's the one. It might turn into something if they can ever hold the goddamn camera still, but otherwise—" He waved it away with a wince and a snort. "The blinking light was getting on my nerves. Thanks for setting the clock and listening to me prattle on. Now go. Away with you. Fair Mabel awaits. Just make sure you check the apple juice before drinking."

"Did I hear my name?"

We both turned and saw Mabel standing in the hallway. She smiled at me. "Is Whitey here giving you a hard time?"

"I was only extolling your innumerable virtues to this no-good hoodlum. What you see in the likes of him is beyond me. Why waste your feminine charms on hamburger when you've got all of this"—He gestured down at himself—"prime cut beef right under your nose?"

"This is Beth's guy," she said.

"*This* is him?" He rolled his chair closer, narrowing his eyes as he gave me the Double-Dubya once-over. "No accounting for taste. Well," he said, rolling his chair away, "as long as he's good to her."

"He is. He treats me well, too."

"He'd better. Make sure you have him set your clocks. Seems to be his most valuable asset."

I laughed. "I've enjoyed our time together, as well."

"That makes one of us." He winked at me. "Never mind me, son. I'm colorful. That's what happens when you live long enough. You get colorful."

"Strother Martin in *Butch Cassidy and the Sundance Kid*."

"Oh, good, he can quote throwaway lines from movie dialogue. Thank God I lived long enough to witness such a wonder. You realize, don't you, that the area in your brain you just pulled that little tidbit from used to hold your parents' anniversary date, right? 'Sorry, Mom and Dad, forgot today was your thirtieth but, hey, I can quote lines from William Goldman scripts! That makes up for a lifetime of my disappointing you at every turn, doesn't it?' For the love of all that's true and pure, Mabel, take him away before he launches into a recitation of the Steiger and Brando 'I-Coulda-Been-a-Contender' scene from *On the Waterfront*. I might weep openly."

Mabel slipped her arm through mine. "Good night, Whitey."

"Did you hear that?"

"What?" I said, enjoying the hell out of him.

"That was the sound of my death getting ten seconds closer because I'm *not* getting the sleep I need. An old man needs his sleep and I'm not getting mine. Now, let's see, *hmmmmm*—why might that be?"

"Good night, Mr. Weis."

"Are you still here?"

"I only came to say I must be going."

"On second thought, don't bother checking the apple juice. It'd serve you right if she got the containers mixed up."

Mabel giggled and pulled me away.

As we were walking toward the car I gave her my keys and told her why I wanted her to drive.

"I thought you were looking under the weather."

"I feel like I'm under the *ground*. Six feet under, to be precise."

In the car, I laid my head back against the seat and closed my eyes.

"Don't mind Whitey," she said. "He's a good one. Sharp as hell."

"I noticed. What's the deal with his legs?"

"Diabetes. It's pretty bad."

"That's terrible."

Mabel nodded. "Sure is. I guess he used to be a

dancer before he got into the talent agent business. He tell you all about the wall under the—"

"—stage at the Auditorium, yes. Is that true?"

"You know, it *is*. One of our supervisors has a cousin who used to work there when they showed movies. He's seen it."

"Huh."

"That would be something to see for yourself, though."

I turned my head and opened my eyes. There was something in her voice that sounded wrong. "Yeah, I suppose it would . . . be—is something wrong?"

She blinked, then fished a cigarette from her pocketbook. "Do you mind?"

"Go ahead. I can't smell anything anyway."

She lit up and inhaled so deeply I could almost hear the cancer cells cheering. "Had another meeting about the budget today."

"Bad news?"

"No. Looks like we've got another investor and will be able to hire back almost everyone who was laid off."

"That's *great*." I sat up and rubbed my eyes, wanting to give this my full attention. Both she and Beth had been nervous about what was going to happen should there be another budget cut. "Mabel?"

"Yeah, hon?"

"It *is* good news, right?"

She blinked, then, after a moment's consideration, nodded her head. "Oh, you bet it is. Sure. Only they want us to sign something."

"Like what?"

"I'm not sure. And that's what's bothering me. All we know is that it's called a 'confidentiality agreement' and we can't tell anyone about what it says."

"Have you seen it yet?"

"Lord, no—the paperwork won't come through for another week or two, but the director thought we should be warned. I asked him if he knew what it was all about and he said, 'Hey, if they want to give us X-millions of dollars to keep this place open for the next ten years, I'll have the cafeteria serve Billy Beer at every meal if that's what they want.'"

"A man of principles. Have to admire that."

"He's doing the best he can. Truth be told, a lot more of us should have been let go this last time, but he managed to convince the board to keep us." She looked at me and I could see there were tears in her eyes. "I haven't let on to you and Beth about how bad it's really been. I've been hanging on by a thread for a while now, financially. They could have let me go any time this past year, just walk in any day and—*kapow!*—no more job. Helluva thing to live with."

I squeezed her arm. "You never said anything."

"Why would I? Look at me, will you? I'm a sixty-one-year-old lesbian with no special someone in her life. I cook meals and clean bedpans and change diapers. I got a nursing degree but all that means to most doctors and administrators is that *they* don't have to be the ones to wipe the asses and write the reports and make sure the charts are in order—and when you get a two-fer like me, well, that's all the better. I can cook *and* mop up the mess they make after eating it."

"You're a great cook."

She grinned. "You're sweet for trying to change

the subject, but I'm an old gal and I'm scared and pissed off so just let me gripe for a bit."

"Okay."

She flicked some ashes out the window. "I didn't want to say anything to Beth about . . . about this—"

"—about the job?"

"No, something else." She squeezed my hand. "I'm gonna need you to help me tell her something. I got a call from the landlord a couple days ago. Some of the neighbors, they've been complaining about the Its. I guess one of their kids supposedly came home with fleas or lice—which God knows they couldn't have picked up at school or somewhere else, must be the old lezzie's animals—so they threatened to call the health department unless the landlord does something."

I had a terrible feeling I knew what was coming.

"We have to get rid of half of them," she said, her voice cracking. "Isn't that a pisser? Most of the poor things had no home to begin with, and now we gotta get rid of them to keep ours. I'd buy the house if I could afford it, but I can't, and there's been no rent increase in I don't know how long, and I'd never be able to find a house that size for what I'm paying—"

"—calm down, Mabel—"

"—and the landlord's a nice guy, he really is. He could've just been a bastard and told me to get rid of all of them but he didn't, he said we can keep four but four of them have to go and they have to be gone by the first of the month, so that means that sometime in the next ten days we have to choose which ones to get rid of—"

"—we'll take them to the Humane Society, it'll be—"

"—oh like hell we *will*. I mean"—she wiped a tear from her cheek—"I know they care for them as best they can, but after a certain amount of time they have no choice but to put them down. I can't do that. I can't hand them over to someone I know is going to have to kill them eventually. I have no idea how I'm going to tell Beth about this, I really don't . . ."

"You won't have to. I will."

"Would you? She'll hear it better, coming from you. She and I get along but . . . I'm not her mother. I wish I were, I love her like my own daughter, but she's always acted like I think I got stuck with her or something. I don't know . . ." She took a last drag from the cigarette and tossed it out the window. "Maybe something'll come up."

I had no idea what "something" she was referring to, or how it was going to "come up," or in connection with what.

"There ought to be a place," she said, "where they'd keep them healthy and happy for as long as they live, let them pass away naturally after a good life. Instead it's dump the old people here, dump the animals there; you wait for one to die, kill the other if they don't die soon enough. It isn't right, however you look at it, however you justify it. It's not right. There ought to be a place."

"I know," I said, my eyes closing as the decongestants kicked in. "I know."

"There really ought to."

"Mabel?"

"What is it, hon?"

"Why did you introduce me to Whitey as 'Beth's guy'? You know that we're not . . . well, she says that . . . I mean . . ."

"I love my niece, Gil, you know that, but sometimes she hasn't got the brains God gave an ice cube. You're her guy. She'll figure it out, eventually."

By the time we got back to the house what I thought was only a sinus headache brought on by a cold turned into a fever, then a 4 A.M. trip to the emergency room followed by a five-day stay in the hospital for pneumonia and dehydration. I never saw it coming.

What I remember of that first day or so was the cloud—that's the only thing I can call it. When I tried to open my eyes the lids would only lift halfway because there was a cloud pressing down on them. This cloud was a dull silver. It covered my entire face. I could feel it slipping through my lips and spreading down into my chest. It was hot and humid and felt like oil in my lungs.

I was sitting on a hillside, and it was raining. *God, how it was raining.* The wind was so strong that the rain was falling sideways.

I was sitting on a hillside, alone, watching as a ship of some sort sailed past in the distance. I thought perhaps I had friends on that ship, but they were leaving me behind.

And I was so angry.

So angry.

The anger was so powerful it made a soft buzzing noise inside. And whenever I dared peek out from under my too-heavy lids, I saw things hiding in the silver cloud made by the rain and mist.

Hunched things.

Silent things.

Things with bright red pinpoint eyes. I never saw their faces. I didn't think they had any. But their eyes told me enough. They were watching me. They had always been watching me. And someday they would step out of the cloud so I could see them. They would flip over the sky and tear out its tongue as they choked it to death. And I would be crushed by it. They would feed me to the dead animals who would claw down from their graves. They would claw down to get out because the sky had been flipped over. The world was upside down. The dead animals would rain from the sky, howling, speaking to me in human language. They would have red pinpoint eyes, too, and tell me ancient secrets. But they could see through the cloud. It was their home. Oil and silver were their skin, and their skin was hard. My skin was soft and pink. They chewed through it. With every bite I grew older, weaker, an old man with stick-thin arms and a shiny bald head. I couldn't breathe. I couldn't move. The silver was too hot. The oil was too thick.

I came out of the cloud. It was very dark in the room. A nurse stood over the bed, wiping the sweat from my face and neck and chest. She asked me if I would like some ice chips. She placed them in my mouth. They tasted like the autumn sky.

"Your fever's broken," she whispered to me, then gave me a shot. I closed my eyes. The cloud did not return. I was safe.

Safe enough.

* * *

My third day in the hospital, Beth came to see me, wearing the same outfit she'd worn the day she'd picked me up from the hospital when I was nine. Not the same *style* of outfit, mind you—the *same outfit*. Same halter top, same jeans, same belt, same everything. Yeah, the pants were a bit shorter around the ankles and the halter was a little tight here and there and might be showing some age but, damn, she still wore it well.

"I thought you might appreciate a little trip down memory lane."

"More like a face-first fall in the middle of amnesia boulevard. *Why* do you still have those things?"

"Because you said I was the most beautiful thing you'd ever seen that day."

"I was recovering from a gunshot wound. You could have been dressed like Minnie Pearl and I would have thought you were the hottest chick on Earth."

"'Chick.' Wow. Has a nostalgic ring to it. You're such a romantic."

"I love you."

"You'd better—do you know I can't feel the blood circulating in my waist because of these damn jeans? Who the fuck ever thought hip-huggers were sexy?"

"Guys who get to slide them off the hips of girls who wear them."

"You're one sick puppy. Speaking of puppies—" She sat on the edge of the bed and took one of my hands in hers. "Mabel told me about what happened. But it's okay, we found a place that will take them."

"Have you picked out who's going to go?"

"Not yet. We still have a week before we have to do

the deed. We decided you have a say in this, too, you know."

"I don't want to have to—"

"Each of us picks one to stay."

"But that leaves one—"

"Mabel picks the fourth. In fact, she promised me that she'd have it picked by the time I get home today."

"The rest go the Humane Society?"

"No. A place called . . . oh, what was it? Hang on." She dug into one of her pockets and removed a piece of wadded paper. Unfolding it, she smiled a "Me-and-My-Scattered-Brains" smile, then read: " 'Keepers.' It's a private organization, funded by donations and animal-loving rich people, I guess. They take your animals and care for them until a new home can be found. They don't put them to sleep, *ever*, even if they never find a new home."

"Just take them in and let them live out their lives naturally, huh?"

"Right."

"How'd you find out about them?"

"Someone who works at the nursing home with Mabel. She didn't find out all that much, but this is enough." She grabbed my hand and leaned in, smiling. "Isn't this *great*? I mean, don't get me wrong—I cried like hell when Mabel told me, and I'll cry like hell when we have to leave them, and I'll miss them . . . but it doesn't seem like it'll be so hard to live with afterward, y'know? Because I know they're going to be happy, they're going to be taken care of and loved and kept safe."

"There ought to be a place," I whispered.

"Huh?"

"Nothing. 'Keepers,' huh?"

"Yeah. Something about that name seemed familiar to me. How about you?"

I thought about it for a few seconds, then shook my head. "No. Yes. Maybe. I'm not sure."

Beth cocked her head. "Yeah, me too. It seems like it *should* ring a bell, but it doesn't, y'know?"

"Yeah, yeah I do." For some reason the color blue flashed through my mind, but its meaning—if indeed it even *had* any—was lost on me.

"Thanks for bringing me over to the emergency room," I said.

"You had a temperature of a hundred and four! We thought about turning off the stove and just using your forehead to heat the stew, but Mabel likes having you around. You *scared* us, you idiot! Did you know they put you on ice after you got here? I mean, they actually stripped off your clothes and put you in a tub full of ice to bring down your temperature. You were in brain-damage territory."

"That could explain a lot."

"I said *were*. You're safe now, so you can't use it as an excuse."

"Damn. It would've been a good one, too."

"Is that the resplendent Beth I see?" came a voice from the doorway. *Low* in the doorway. We looked over and down just as Marty Weis wheeled himself into the room. "A-ha! I've caught you in the act. Trying to thaw out Frosty the Snowman, I take it?"

" 'Frosty'?" I said.

"Word of your icy exploits have traveled all the way across the parking lot to our side of the tracks, Captain Spalding. I heard you awoke screaming for

Larry, Moe, and Curly to stop dancing on your pants, as you were still wearing them at the time."

"How did you get out?" said Beth between laughs.

"Yadda-yadda, Warden, as the late-great Lenny Bruce once said. *Shhh*—your aunt had a hand in my escape. Yadda-yadda. And if either of you tell me you don't know who Lenny Bruce was, I'll—"

"—weep openly?" I asked.

"'Scowl meaningfully,' was the phrase I'd meant to employ but—oh, all right, I *was* going to say 'weep openly.'"

"'A pro never forgets his good lines.'"

"*Magic*—you're quoting William Goldman again."

"May twenty-third."

Weis stared at me. *"What?"*

"My parents' anniversary. May twenty-third." I tapped my head; it still felt hot to me. "I can remember Goldman dialogue *and* important dates."

"The *miracles* I've witnessed in this lifetime. It humbles me. Truly. Or maybe it's only a hemorrhoid flare-up. Either way, it makes a definite impression." He rolled over to the bed and pulled a small box from under the blanket covering his legs. "A token of my esteem." He tossed it up into my lap.

I was about half afraid of the thing. "You're giving me a present?"

"I just paid for the gift-wrapping, but it's the thought that counts so let's not get all emotional— however if someone named 'Rico the Blade' comes looking for his 'lid,' say nothing of this conversation. I am a mule on the run."

"The considerate felon."

Beth shook her head. "You two ought to take this act on the road."

"Oh, my days on the road are long gone, Beautiful Bethany. Unless of course you're driving, then it's *Easy Rider* time."

"They both get blown away at the end of that movie."

"Yes, but it's to a Bob Dylan song, so that makes it symbolic and culturally significant. Perhaps Yukon Cornelius here could hum a few bars of 'Lay Lady, Lay' and we'll feel terribly important and meaningful as we pull into the Dairy Queen drive-thru. Lacks the sociological *pathos* of Fonda and Hopper biting the big one, but I always found that ending depressing, anyway. Ice cream is not depressing. Ice cream is yummy. Shotgun blasts to the chest are not. I hear they leave a slightly metallic aftertaste."

"Hey, I got an idea," said Beth, grabbing my hand and Weis's. "Let's do it. Let's have a road trip. The three of us and Mabel and the Its."

"The 'Its'?" said Weis. "Dare I ask?"

"No," I said. "Trust me."

"C'mon," Beth said. "We have to do this by next Thursday. Mabel can sign out Whitey here and he can ride along with us."

"I would ask where we're going," said Weis, "and what, exactly, the 'Its' are, but frankly I don't care. A road trip! Magnificent. If you're willing to get me out of that mausoleum for a day, I'll even go to Toledo—and I wouldn't wish *that* on Eichmann." He slapped his hands against his useless legs, and grinned from ear to ear. "I must go and choose an outfit from my

181

extensive wardrobe. One must always dress properly for a road trip."

"Just don't show up naked," said Beth.

"I would be dazzling in my raw manliness."

"You'd be an old man with no clothes stranded by the side of the road."

Weis considered this for a moment. "Ah, yes—but think of the attention I'd get." He gave me a thumbs-up. "See you soon, Mr. Freeze. Beware the Green Hornet."

"You mean the Caped Crusader," I said.

"Just making sure there's no brain damage. There isn't. What a tragedy."

Six days later all of us piled into Beth's U-boat of a station wagon along with four of the Its and took a drive. Beth drove and Mabel rode in the front with her, while I got to share the backseat with Mr. Weis and various of the Its who decided from time to time that the cargo area and Weis's folded-up wheelchair were just too boring. The temperature was well into the upper eighties and the air-conditioning didn't work so we had to make the drive with all the windows rolled down—much to the chagrin of Mr. Weis, who'd gone to a lot of trouble that morning to ensure his hair looked presentable.

"Jeez-Louise," he said, finally giving up trying to hold his white mane in place. "If I'd have known it was going to be like this, I'd've just wet my finger and jammed it in a light socket."

"It might have improved your disposition, as well," said Mabel. *Yelled*, actually. The sound of the wind blowing in through the windows made it impossible to talk at a normal volume; I don't think a word was said during the drive that wasn't delivered at three hundred decibels. Thank God I'd thought to bring along some aspirin.

The drive took forty minutes. The Keepers facility was located outside of Hebron, which meant having to drive through Cedar Hill, then Heath, past the Industrial Park, and making a turnoff near Lakewood High School that took you in a straight line for the better part of fifteen minutes. (By the time we actually arrived, I wasn't sure we were still in the same county.)

One of the Its got too excited and vomited on my pant leg. Twice.

"I see even our four-legged friends aren't immune to your considerable charms," said Mr. Weis.

"Watch out or I'll put him in your lap."

"I'll have you know that animals happen to adore me. Why, I handled an animal act back in the day—"

"Here." I picked up the It and dropped the animal in his lap. The dog licked his face, nuzzled his cheek, and puked on his shoulder.

"I shall have my revenge, dear boy."

"On the bright side, at least we have one clean set of clothes between us."

"I brought an extra set of clothes for both of you," Mabel called over her shoulder. "I had a feeling there might be some redecorating going on."

" 'Redecorating,' " said Mr. Weis. "What a tasteful way to put it."

Beth pulled a hand towel from her bag and handed it to me so I could clean off my shoes. The Its had once again gathered on or around the wheelchair in back and were craning their necks to stick their heads out the back window, which was opened a third of the way.

We pulled into a gas station and I helped Mr. Weis into his wheelchair so he could go into the restroom and change his shirt. According to the directions, we were only a mile or so away from the facility.

As I stood outside the restroom door waiting for Mr. Weis, I saw another station wagon drive past, this one heading back toward Hebron. There was a woman of about forty driving, and two young children riding in the backseat. A happy little dog was bouncing between the kids, sticking its head out the window, having a grand time. The children were laughing and the mother was smiling. I wondered if the dog was a new pet, and if they'd just gotten it from Keepers. I caught sight of Beth and Mabel (who'd also seen the children and the dog) and knew they were wondering the same thing. I hoped the children *had* just gotten their new pet from the same place we were about to deposit four more. Even if that weren't the case, I hoped Beth and Mabel thought it was; it would make leaving the four Its there easier for them.

Both of them had cried a little that morning as we loaded the dogs into the station wagon. They might as well have been abandoning newborn babies in trash cans, it hurt that much for them. Mr. Weis planned on treating everyone to an "extra-special" lunch after everything was finished, ". . . and maybe even a movie, if there's time." I thought that was a great idea. We'd all need to do something happy after this was done, regardless of how much Mabel and Beth insisted this wasn't going to upset them.

Mr. Weis rolled out in a crisp, clean white shirt, tossing his soiled one at me. "Easy on the starch next time, pal."

"Thanks for the Keaton book," I said. His gift to me had been a copy of Buster Keaton's autobiography, *My Wonderful World of Slapstick*.

"Ah, so you can read as well as launder clothes. Every day in every way, I find you more and more adequate." He winked at me and grinned. "Glad you liked it. If you want, I got Groucho's autobiography, as well. Might learn a few pointers about comic timing from it—God knows you could use some."

I helped him back into the car, folded up and replaced his wheelchair, then went into the men's room to change pants and clean myself up.

Onward.

The facility came into view about two minutes later.

It sat on the right side of the road, at the end of a long asphalt drive, directly in the middle of a wide expanse of blacktop like a passenger ship on a flat dark sea; Noah's Ark, Day 41. It was quite a large one-story building, made of limestone, concrete blocks, and metal. It could have been a city jail, or a building from an old prison compound suddenly displaced in the center of a field. There was no sign on the road telling you what the place was, if it was open, or why it was even here.

The asphalt drive branched off in two directions, and at least here there was sign telling you why: VIS-ITOR PARKING TO THE LEFT. The right-side parking lot was for SANCTIONED PERSONNEL ONLY, and was half-filled with about a dozen vans (some of which looked to be converted bread delivery trucks), each a dull tan color with only the word KEEPERS painted on the sides.

It took us a minute to find a parking space because the lot was quite full. What struck me was not that there were so many cars, but that so many of them were *expensive* cars, rich-people cars, cars driven by owners who were too important to be bothered performing a distasteful duty like the one we were here to discharge.

Beth parked, shut off the engine, then looked at Mabel. Neither of them said anything for a few moments which, in this heat, seemed two-and-a-half eternities long.

"I really don't mean to sound like I'm trying to take over or assume the role of cantankerous old fart," said Weis, "but it seems to me that this is the point where one of us should at least *pretend* we're going to get out of the car."

"In a minute," said Mabel, very softly, but underlined in steel.

Farther back, the Its sat still and silent, as if they knew why we were here.

"Maybe I should go check it out first," I said.

" 'Check it out'?" said Weis. " 'Check it out'? What are you, Edward G. Robinson in *Little Caesar*? We casing the joint for a heist? 'Check it out.' Lord save us from amateurs."

"I think that sounds like a good idea," Beth said. "We don't want to be wandering around with the dogs and have no idea where to put them."

Mabel nodded. "I don't think the dogs would like it if we dragged this out for too long."

I looked at Weis the same instant he looked at me. The dogs. They had said "the dogs."

I suppose in a way it must make it easier for a person to do something like this if they can remove their hearts from the event to some degree. Put your father in a nursing home, you suddenly stop referring to him as "Dad" and just as "him" when talking to the admissions nurse; "Dad" gives his identity a too-close proximity to your conscience, but "him," "him" is safe because it's nonspecific, "him" is a term applied to a Person You Don't Really Know, someone removed from you, someone you haven't spent your entire life around and who has helped determine the kind of person you've become. So "Dad" becomes "him," "Mom" becomes "her," and "the Its" become "the dogs."

Christ, I felt suddenly so sad. I suspected Weis did, too. When our gazes met I could see the signal flares going off behind his eyes: *Mayday, Mayday, we're sinking fast, jettison all unnecessary cargo immediately, Mayday, Mayday . . .*

I opened the door and started to climb out. "You wanna come along, Mr. Weis?"

"Thought you'd never ask."

I retrieved his wheelchair and got him situated, then leaned down by Beth's window. "I'll find out what we're supposed to do, where we take them and all of that."

"Thanks. It'll give us a couple of minutes to say good-bye."

"I figured."

She leaned out and kissed me. After all this time, her lips on mine still made my knees melt.

I grabbed the handles of Weis's chair and moved toward the building.

"Alone at last," he said.

"I didn't know you cared."

"No one ever does, it's part of my well-honed mystique."

I wasn't quite sure what to make of that so I left it alone. "Any thoughts on what movie you'd like to see later?"

"So long as it doesn't have Meryl Streep in it, I don't care. Don't get me wrong, she's a great actress and a looker, but she reminds me too much of my daughter. Have I mentioned that I'm a little irked at my daughter right now? I mean, I don't expect her to fly up here from L.A. every chance she gets, but I have trouble believing that someone can be so busy that they can't pick up a goddamn phone and call for five minutes once a week. I'm not asking to be the center of her life, you understand, but it gets boring as hell out here on the periphery sometimes. Was I raving there for a moment? Sorry."

"I'm sorry, too." And I was. He was actually pretty splendid company, once you got past the bluster and brouhaha.

The entrance to the building was surprisingly small—I almost couldn't maneuver the wheelchair through it—but once inside it seemed even larger that it appeared from the parking lot.

The entry area was probably about twenty feet wide and fifteen deep. To the right was a massive steel door with a single, darkened window at eye-level and a SANCTIONED PERSONNEL ONLY sign. It reminded me of the heavy iron door to that cell in every last Frankenstein movie where they imprison the monster and assure one another that it's strong enough to prevent the creature from escaping. Whatever lay beyond that door took up exactly half of the building. I figured that's where they probably kept the animal cages.

The wall facing us was concrete, about seven feet tall, and held three rows of eight cubbyholes, each big enough to hold a good-sized dog or cat; a fourth row, at knee-level, contained cubbies for the larger dogs—Saint Bernards, German shepherds, Dobermans, etc. Each cubby had a door of heavy iron bars attached to it. For the moment, all the cubbies were empty and their doors open. It looked like an automat after lunch rush; you could even see how the back wall of each swung open so whoever worked behind the scenes could retrieve the animals. A sign above stated that once an animal was placed inside, it became the responsibility of Keepers and would not be returned to the donor; it also warned that the locks were magnetized, so once a door was closed it could not be opened again from our side.

"Why do you suppose they do it that way?"

Mr. Weis shrugged. "My guess is it's a safety precaution. Folks wouldn't be bringing their animals here unless they absolutely *had* to. If you love a pet enough not to hand it over to those Nazis gas chambers at the Humane Society, then you love it enough to change your mind at the last minute, and that's not a good idea for you or the animal. My guess is a lot of folks have second thoughts once they see their pet behind those bars. This way, there's no going back."

Gary A. Braunbeck

"So they really only give you one chance to back out."

"Damn straight. Once it's in that cage, that's all she wrote."

The wall behind us sported a long shelf deep enough for a dog or cat to sit on and be groomed; there were combs, brushes, nail clippers, flea collars, bags of treats, and countless other goodies set out for people to use before leaving their animals. There was also a series of wooden lockboxes where you could leave a monetary donation; a sign over each box read: "Keepers is a privately funded, non-profit animal protection organization. Donations from the public, though not required, are nonetheless welcomed. All money goes toward the feeding and care of the animals. Keepers does not believe in destroying animals. Once they are with us, they are here for life, even if a new home is never found. Here they will remain happy. Here they will remain loved."

I read the sign again. "Seems almost too good to be true."

"Gift horse. Mouth. Looking into it. Bad idea. Get it?"

"Got it."

"Good." Then: "A Danny Kaye fan, as well. There's hope for you yet."

There was no wall to our left; instead, there was a massive and cavernous play area that extended so far back it looked like a study in forced perspective; swing sets for children, sandboxes, rows of folding chairs, picnic tables, music playing from unseen speakers, the smell of hot dogs and hamburgers . . .

if it weren't for the walls surrounding all of this and the ceiling of skylights, you'd swear you were in Moundbuilders Park on a summer afternoon.

And the animals were everywhere, dogs, cats, pigs, birds, rabbits, a couple of horses and cows, each fenced off in its own area (except the birds, who flew freely throughout) so that children and adults alike could pet them, either from outside the barrier or from within.

"Looks like a goddamn 4H convention," said Weis.

I thought it was cool. There were children playing on the swings, mothers sipping icy colas as they relaxed on the chairs or played with the dogs and cats. The animals themselves were clean and healthy and seemed quite happy. I caught glimpses of figures wearing tan jumpsuits with KEEPERS printed across their backs weaving through the pens and people, asking questions, making notes, handing out treats. All of them wore tan wool caps pulled down to cover the tops of their ears. Although it was comfortably cool in here—the air-filtration system must have cost a fortune, because you could barely smell any urine or feces or any other potently *animal* scents you would have expected—it wasn't cool enough for a cap of any kind.

A sign on the farthest wall proclaimed this to be the "Selection Area," and that we should take our time getting to know the animals before bearing them home with us. That was the actual phrase: "bearing them home." I don't know why that stuck in my mind. All of the signs contained odd little phrases like that, as if written by someone to whom English was a second language and so its most formal rules of usage were followed when composing the notices.

I wondered if the woman in the car and her two children had made a morning of it in here, playing with dozens of puppies and dogs before selecting the one that just seemed to love them so much they couldn't bear the thought of leaving without it.

Everywhere I looked there were women—well-dressed women, women who drove expensive cars and wore white gloves for afternoon tea and had a standing appointment with their hair stylist each week and whose children attended private schools—playing with a dog or cat or bunny, smiling as the animal wagged its tail or whiskers and licked a hand or face, and these women would grin from ear to ear saying, "How is Mama's little baby? Is Mama's little baby lonesome?" It was sweet.

"Beth and Mabel need to see this," I said to Mr. Weis. "I really think they'll feel a whole lot better knowing how this works."

"You don't suppose they've got an elephant stashed away somewhere, do you?" asked Weis. "I was expecting just cats and dogs, but *this*"—He made a sweeping gesture of the Selection Area—"is like a traveling zoo. I'm not trying to be a wet blanket or anything, so please let's not get into a discussion of my dreadful personality problems, but do you notice anything odd about the way the animals are behaving?"

"No."

"Of course not—*that* would require actual powers of observation, and since you're wearing mismatched socks, we can assume that's a lost cause. So allow me to assist you: Take another look. See that pen of cats over there? *Three times* now the same bird has landed on the fence within easy jumping distance, yet none of the cats have tried to get at the thing. None of them are even hissing at one another. Cats are territorial as hell, yet all of them are getting along just fine. None of the dogs are fighting or growling at each other. And despite all the noise and the kids and the movement, the horses don't look nervous. Ever spend time around horses? I love horses, hope I'll be one in my next life. Damn nervous animals most of the time, sudden movement and loud noises are no friends to their nerves."

"So the animals are well-behaved, so what?"

He looked at me as if I were drooling. "So it just doesn't seem *right* to me, that's all. *The Peaceable Kingdom*'s good in theory, but this is just *weird*, seeing it in practice like this. You don't suppose they drug the animals, do you?"

"I wouldn't think so. Would they be this active if they had sedatives in their system?"

"Hell—*I'm* on sedatives half the time and you don't see it slowing me down any, do you?"

"No, but then you're freakish."

"Pot. Kettle. Black. Fill in the blanks."

"Me. Go. Bring women and dogs."

"Here. Me. Wait. Air-conditioning. Bring adverbs when you return."

Beth and Mabel were very matter-of-fact as they placed the dogs into the cubbies and closed the doors, each of them trying for the other's sake to look strong, but I knew that on the inside they were crumbling. Mabel wrote out a generous check that she deposited in one of the boxes, and then I took her into the Selection Area. Beth said she wanted a moment alone. I wasn't going to deny either of them anything they wanted today.

Mr. Weis had gotten us a couple of sodas and hot dogs from one of the snack stands, and as we ate Mabel wandered through the Selection Area for about fifteen minutes, shaking her head in wonder, stopping occasionally to pet a dog or pick up a cat, and she tried to smile and be happy and enjoy it, and maybe she succeeded to some degree, but her mind and heart were still stuck in the barred cubbies—which had been emptied while my back was turned.

"That was fast," I said. If Mr. Weis heard me he gave no indication of it. I patted his shoulder and excused myself, wandering back out to the cubbies.

The steel door on the opposite wall was open just a crack. The breeze wafting through the crack wasn't just cool, it was outright cold. Could this be some sort of refrigeration area where they kept food for the animals?

I reached out to pull the door open farther and it swung out toward me.

Beth was standing there, shaking, her skin covered in goose bumps, holding a wrapped package the size of a shoe box. She looked dazed.

"Are you okay?"

She blinked, looked at me for a moment as if she had no idea who the hell I was or why I was bothering her, then came out, closed the door behind her, and said, "Yeah, I'm . . . I'm fine. Damn it's cold in there."

I began rubbing her arms. "I noticed. What's back there, anyway?"

She was looking at the empty cubbies where the Its had been a short while ago. "They don't waste any time, do they? That's good, you know? Get them out of sight as quick as possible. I doesn't hurt as much that way. That's important. For it not to hurt too much."

"Are you sure you're okay?"

She nodded her head, and even though she looked right into my eyes, her gaze was elsewhere. "I'm fine, I told you. Come on, let's round up the troops and blow this pop stand."

"What's in the package?"

"Huh?" She looked at the box in her hand. "Oh, something I need to mail out, no biggie."

I did not recognize the name of the person to whom it was addressed, but couldn't help noticing that the return address was the same.

"Beth?"

"Huh?"

"You sure you're okay?"

"Uh-huh." Wherever she was, she still wasn't all the way back yet, and I almost asked her if she'd snuck off into cold storage to fire up a joint, but then a burst of laughter from a couple of children in the Selection Area startled me and Beth sailed past to retrieve Mabel. I started to roll Mr. Weis out but he stopped me.

"Give me a minute, will you?"

"What's wrong?"

"It's all these *women*," he said. "Look at how they fawn over the dogs and cats. How they hold them like they've been the family pet for years. They're going out of their way to make the animals love them."

I looked, and he was right; it's one thing to pet an animal and play with it only briefly—most of the animals are happy for whatever little attention they get—but many of these women of the afternoon tea and white gloves were taking it three steps further: the more they played with the dogs and cats, the more their own tired beauty seemed to be revitalized, as if they were drawing a few moments of time-stolen youth back from the animals' energy and affection.

"There was a fellow I once knew," said Weis, "who was one of the *ugliest* men you'd ever laid eyes on— I mean, this guy had a face that would make a freight train take a dirt road. Used to get him work in horror movies all the time because he didn't need makeup. Thought he might go on to be the next Rondo Hatton. Anyway, every time I saw this guy, he was in the company of the most *beautiful* women—real jaw-dropping traffic-stoppers. Women who'd make Sophia Loren envious. One day I asked him what his secret was, and you know what he said to me?"

"If I yawn it's only in anticipation."

"Funny guy. He said, 'Regardless of how beautiful a woman is, there's always *someone* who's tired of her, who's glad to leave her. And they'll take any attention they can get, even if it's from a mug like me.'

"Look at these women here. I'm not talking about the younger ones with kids, but the others, the forty and forty-five crowd, the ones who're paying so much attention to the animals. They're all beautiful, and they're all here alone. You know why? Because someone is tired of them and was glad to leave them. Their husbands go off to the office, their kids go off to college, but they leave them alone, understand? They love their families, but their families always leave them in some way. Who've *they* got to leave? No one. So they come here. I've been sitting here listening, and every last one of them has at some point asked one of the attendants, 'Will they go to good homes?' But it's not out of concern for the animal, it's because they don't want this on their conscience. They have no intention of adopting one of them. It's the leaving that's the important part. It matters that they have someone to leave, so they leave behind this dog or that cat, some lonesome little animal who'd never leave them if they had the chance to give them their hearts."

Mr. Weis blinked, and for a few moments his eyes were every lonely journey I'd ever taken, every unloved place I'd ever visited, every sting of guilt I'd ever felt in my life; for that moment his eyes never focused on me, they brushed by once, softly, like a cattail or a ghost, then fell shyly toward the ground in some inner contemplation too sad to be touched by a tender thought or the delicate brush of another's care. You'd think God had forgotten his name.

So that's what lonely looks like, I thought. Mr. Weis caught my stare and for a moment looked humiliated; then he blinked and said, "I got snot hanging out of my nose or something?"

He was shaking so intensely I thought the arms would rattle right off his chair.

I touched his shoulder. "Why are you so upset?"

"Because!" he snapped. "Just . . . just because, that's all. Christ—five minutes once a week, is that too much to ask for?"

"Not at all."

He stared off at something only he could see. I let my gaze wander for a moment but stopped scanning when I saw something that seemed really, genuinely, seriously wrong.

In one of the pens sat a very chubby gray rabbit. Behind the rabbit was a large German shepherd. Next to it lay a cat. In front of the cat a duck wandered back and forth. A long, glistening snake slithered in, out, and around all of them, occasionally stopping to lift its head to flick its tongue at someone's nose. And perched on a pile of straw beside the entire scene was a gorgeous brown marsh hawk.

The animals stretched, touched and groomed one another, but made no sounds. Even the hawk was silent. This did not seem right to me. Considering what I knew of the various natures of the individual creatures in this pen, most of them should have tried to attack and kill the rest by now.

Then, almost as one, all of them looked right at me: *Something we can help you with, pal? Take a picture, it'll last longer.*

In theory, *The Peaceable Kingdom*; in actuality, an icy touch at the base of your spine—at the base of mine, anyway. This might be peaceful and happy and healthy, but something here was just . . . off. Definitely off.

Mr Weis tugged at my shirt and said: "How's that

new Spielberg movie sound to you, that one with what's-his-name from that space opera?"

"Raiders of the Lost Ark?"

"Supposed to be pretty slam-bang, from what I hear. I think maybe I could use a little slam-bang, how about you?"

"Sounds good." I didn't have the heart to tell him I'd already seen it and that it left me with the mother of all headaches but had at least cleared my sinuses quite nicely, thanks very much. I knew Beth hadn't seen it yet, which meant Mabel hadn't, either.

It was a blast. I found the movie even more obnoxious, contrived, and over-the-top than I had the first time but, damn, was it fun. It took Beth and Mabel a little while to get into the spirit of things, but once they did, they went all the way with it, clapping and cheering along with the rest of the audience, and by the time the Ark itself was about to be opened, it was almost like the bad parts of that day hadn't even happened; we were just four friends—scratch that— we were just a *family* out for a night of fun. Later we had a couple of loaded pies at Tammy's Pizza and played every song on the jukebox while Mr. Weis regaled us with endless anecdotes from his glory days. Only once, at the end of the evening as we were driving home, did I give that package another thought. I knew damn well that Beth hadn't had it with her when we left that morning, so the only place she could have gotten it was at the Keepers facility. In the cold storage area. But who'd given it to her, and why? And more to the point, why had she agreed to mail it out for them?

Mabel and I checked Mr. Weis back in that night. He hugged both of us before we left his room. The day had meant so much to him, it was so wonderful of us to take him along, did we think maybe we could do it again sometime soon? A movie and pizza again? He'd surely love that. I thought he was going to start crying. It was so out of character it seemed downright mawkish; as a result, I almost lost it myself, but Mabel—ever the graceful professional— assured him that we'd enjoyed his company, as well, and that, yes, we'd all do it again very soon. That seemed to please Mr. Weis—who gave me permission to call him Whitey from now on. I knew what that meant, and hugged him once more before we left.

Most of the truly significant moments of your life don't come with a blare of trumpets and roll of timpani. Half the time you're not even aware of their importance until well after they've tipped their hat to you on their way into the past. God knows most of the benchmark events of my life have only gained meaning through later reflection—*why didn't I realize this at the time?*—but that day was different. As we went into the house that evening, Beth squeezing my hand with a hard, damp strength of feeling that told me she wanted to make love until we couldn't breathe, I took a breath and filled myself with the night; the blackness above deep and comforting and nearly total, excepting a few distant stars that winked past the cold silver coin of the moon like children who'd succeeded in fooling "It" during a game of hide-and-seek. And I knew—with as much maturity and wisdom as I had within reach then, I *knew*—that something profound and irreversible had happened, that there would come a time decades from now when I would look back on this day, this night, this moment of her hand in mine as a smoky hint of autumn lingered under the summer night breeze, and I would be able to say with unbreakable certainty: *This was it, right here. You can see it on my face. This time, this breath, this moment.* It didn't matter that I had no idea *what* exactly had happened or why it was so important, but sometimes you get a feeling in your core that is so clear and strong it can't be anything but the truth in its most potent and undistilled form. Call it an epiphany if you want to be melodramatic, but I knew that this summer dimming into autumn as all summers must would be the last for me as I was *right now*; my youth was turning to look at me over its shoulder and smile farewell. Hope you enjoyed the ride, pal. It's been a real kick, but you're on your own now. Don't make love with your socks on, never cross against the light, and don't take any wooden nickels.

Right here. This moment.

This touch, this promise, this breath.

The last good night of my life.

A few weeks after our excursion to the Keepers facility, my father went into work drunk off his ass (which no one ever knew), fell into his press, and was killed instantly. When she hung up the phone after getting the news, my mother sat down as if every bone in her body had dissolved. She pretty much stayed like that for the next two months, with the exception of the funeral and a trip to the doctor for sedatives.

For my part, I wasn't surprised. Dad's drinking had gotten progressively worse over the last few years. It was only a matter of time before something terrible happened.

Don't misunderstand, I loved him quite a lot, and I cried for three days solid after his death, all too aware of the empty spaces in the house and my life and the world where he should have been but was no longer.

Beth and Mabel were there every step of the way; from going with me to identify his body (what was left of it) at the morgue until I guided Mom's hand to toss the dirt down on the coffin lid, they were there.

I walked out of the cemetery completely emptied of feeling. This was not the world I had grown used to. Dad wasn't here, so this was another planet, an alien landscape, something out of a book or fantasy film. In the real world Dad would be bitching about dinner being overdone or the rain-delayed ball game or how I wasn't doing anything with my life. Sure, he got on my nerves and embarrassed me sometimes and I don't know that I ever much liked him, but I *did* love him and now would never have the chance to make sure he understood the difference. I should have said something to him sooner, should have found him the morning after I overheard him talking to Mom and asked him to tell me about his Downtown Sundays as a child, and I should have listened, and I should have smiled, and I should have been able to recognize my duty within those austere and lonely offices to tell him that I understood, and that I loved him.

The luncheon afterward was organized by a group of volunteers from St. Francis de Sales (the parish to which all my family belonged but whose church none of us had stepped into for over a decade until this day); the ladies had set up tables and refreshment stands in the new cafeteria of the grade school located right next door to the church. I was tired, I was sad, and I was *hungry*, but I couldn't yet face the well-meaning friends and family members with their sincerely felt but empty-sounding platitudes, couldn't look at the bowls of potato salad and platters of lunch meat and trays of homemade brownies, couldn't stand the smell of the freshly brewed coffee, couldn't sit beside Mom and watch her try to eat while an army of mourners passed by the table, each of them compelled as if by holy proclamation to put a hand on her shoulder and then mine as they made their way over to the baked beans or that great-looking apple cobbler that was disappearing way too fast.

As we were driving back toward the church, Mabel mentioned in passing that she was out of cigarettes, and I grabbed the opportunity for a reprieve.

"Drop me off on the square," I said. "I'll run into the Arcade News Stand and buy you some."

The Arcade—a small, enclosed group of shops and restaurants that has been part of Cedar Hill since before I was born—was perhaps a ten-minute walk from St. Francis. I could get Mabel's smokes, then go over to Fifth and Main, cut up to Granville

Street, and be at the church before the first pot of coffee was empty. Everybody wins: Mabel gets her smokes, Mom gets a few minutes without my moping at her shoulder, and I get fifteen or twenty minutes alone.

No one argued with me about this, no one said my place was at the church, or that I was being selfish, or that it might seem thoughtless to other mourners in attendance. I loved all of them even more for this.

I was dropped off across the street from the Old Soldiers and Sailors Building. I stood there staring at the structure for a moment after they drove away. It seemed to me now that, thanks to Whitey, I shared a little-known secret with this place; down there, somewhere, stood a wall with the names of some of Vaudeville's Greatest written on it, and what was before to me just an old hulk of an abandoned theater now seemed so much grander. I wished I could have gone in and seen that wall. Maybe I'd come back and try sometime.

I went to the Arcade and got Mabel's smokes, but as I was getting ready to head on over to Fifth and Main I realized just *where* I was and what I had a chance to do.

On Downtown Sunday my dad went to the movies (either the Midland or the Old Soldiers and Sailors Building, they were right across the street from one another); then he'd get some candy or comic books afterward (the Arcade News Stand had been in the same place for fifty years); and then the old men sitting on the steps of the building on the corner.

Which meant the site of the old Farmer's Building and Loan.

Less than two blocks away.

Without realizing it, I had already walked two-thirds of the same route my dad had covered every Downtown Sunday when he was a child.

It wasn't exactly like following in his footsteps, and it wasn't as if he'd known I'd overheard him that night or would ever know now what I was about to do, but I'd just been given the chance to honor his memory by retracing his steps through one of his best memories.

How could I not walk over there?

It would be nice to say that I saw the square in a completely different light, much as I had the Old Soldiers and Sailors Building, but the truth was this area of Cedar Hill looked and felt just the same to me as it had any of the hundreds of times I'd walked these streets; tired-looking though dependable brick- and wood-fronted buildings, some with shingled roofs, some with aluminum, others—old warhorses who'd stood the test of time and the seasons and were damned proud of it so why change now—still sporting thick layers of tar paper over two-by-fours: the sturdy, inoffensive banality of a small Midwestern downtown. Nothing about its current state, nor the way it existed in my own childhood memories, made it special.

What *did* make it special was knowing that, back there, just over that way, fifty or sixty years ago, the child who would grow up to become my dad had come along this exact path, walked past many of these same storefronts, and had probably used the same crosswalk I was approaching.

Maybe this could serve as some small gesture of thanks.

I passed the Hallmark store, the shoe store beside it, and was moving toward the crosswalk when a man in his thirties who'd been walking ahead of me suddenly veered to the right and kicked a small cat that had been pacing him for a few yards. The cat wasn't being pushy or annoying, wasn't running figure-eights between his feet as he tried to move along, it was just walking beside him, minding whatever passed for its own fuzzy business, when this jerk, for no apparent reason, decided to swing around and drop-kick it into a doorway.

The cat reeled ass-over-teakettle, spitting out one of those uncanny, almost macabre screech-yowls of pain and fear that you can feel all the way in the back of your teeth, then hit the doorway with a solid *whump!* before spin-rolling back onto its stomach, legs splayed. It scrabbled its claws against the concrete but quickly found enough purchase to stand and shake some of the *What-the-hell-was-that-about?* from its stunned and wide-eyed face. It narrowed its eyes, licked a corner of its mouth, gave the tiniest of shudders, and then released a thin, dinky *meep* noise so full of confusion and physical hurt that I was ashamed to be a member of the human race in its presence. It looked up at me and blinked as if to ask: *Did I offend? Please don't hurt me. I'll give you rubbies.*

I walked toward it, slowly, then knelt down and held out my hand. The cat gave my fingers a per-functory sniff, then—in obvious pain—leaned forward to rub itself against my hand, the metal tag on its collar clicking against my watch band.

"Bad day?" I whispered to it.

Before the cat had a chance to answer I glanced up to see where Drop-Kick had disappeared to: he was turning down an alley between two buildings near the corner of the crosswalk. He'd never given the cat a second thought, just kicked the shit out of it to break up the dreary routine of his day and then kept going without so much as a backward glance.

It's good to be exposed to such naked, unself-conscious displays of compassion; it enriches one.

I never stopped to consider that something might go wrong (whatever part of my mind that governed rationality was still wandering around back at the cemetery); I just rose to my feet and followed him double-time into the alley.

He sauntered along, then stopped for a moment, stretched his back, and knelt down to re-tie one of his shoelaces.

That's when I took him.

I ran forward, pulled back my right leg at the last moment, did a half-pirouette, and threw everything I had into the kick; my foot connected solidly—*wham-o!*—with his ribs, knocking him back and down in a fast blur of flailing hands and other equally befuddled body parts. The side of his skull smacked against the alley floor and for a moment I thought he might have been knocked unconscious, but then he shook head, winced, and pressed both hands against his ribs, groaning.

I glowered over him. "Didn't anyone ever tell you that *hurts?*"

"Oh, man . . . *ow!*—what the fuck're you . . . oh, man. . . ."

I thought I heard the soft crackle of chipped bone scraping against chipped bone; I know that wasn't the case, but for that moment imagining that I *did* hear his damaged ribs whimpering under his skin filled me with a gleeful, nasty sort of satisfaction every person should feel once during their life, if only to know they never want to experience it again.

His face reddened under a fresh wave of pain, then he pulled in a deep breath and looked at me. "I'm gonna fuck you up, asshole." And he began to stagger to his feet.

The smart thing to do was run.

So, naturally, I just stood there.

He slipped, his back pressed against the wall, then he caught his balance and shoved forward with one of his hands; as he did this he looked quickly up and down the alley to make sure there weren't going to be any witnesses to the plague of biblical proportions he was about to unleash on my face; left, right . . . and then a slow double-take: *Huh? What the—?*

At both ends of the alley, sitting almost unnaturally still but with oh-so-attentive eyes, a group composed equally of dogs and cats of various sizes watched us with stark, unblinking interest. There must have been over a dozen animals in all.

Drop-Kick had almost fully pushed himself away from the wall when I shot out a foot and kicked his leg from underneath his bulk, sending him crashing ass-first to the ground one more time.

I stared at him, parted my hands before me—

Well?—then turned and walked out toward the crosswalk.

The animals at this end of the alley moved so I could pass, but none of them seemed in any hurry to leave.

At the corner, the injured cat—now moving a bit more steadily—came up to me and rubbed its face against my leg. I smiled at it, thought about just picking it up and taking it home with me, then looked up when I heard the signal click over to "Walk."

I stopped with one foot off the curb.

Across the street at the Farmer's Building and Loan, an old hound dog sat on the top concrete step staring directly at me.

I knew this wasn't the same hound dog from my dad's childhood, I did, really, but there was an odd moment between seeing it and allowing its presence to fully register when I thought, *Maybe . . . ?*

I shook it off but didn't move to cross the street.

I looked down at the cat by my leg. It blinked at me, seemed to outwardly sigh, then turned its head in the dog's direction.

From the top of the steps, the dog looked from me to the cat, and for the next few moments I just kept moving my gaze between them; the dog, the cat, the dog, moron with his leg cocked up in the air.

I pulled my foot back onto the curb just as the dog released a short, sharp bark. The cat, in response, moved its head up and down. They looked at each other once again, the dog licked its nose, and the cat blinked one eye.

Winked, rather.

The cat *winked* at the dog:

This meeting is concluded and the board has decided that rubbies were, indeed, the proper course of action under these circumstances . . .

The dog barked again, three times, much louder, and the cat released a long, high yowl, this one of the "Just-letting-you-know-I'm-here" variety.

When I looked at the cat now, I noticed for the first time the small blue plastic tag attached to the back of its ear.

In the back of my brain, something fumbled for a light switch and cleared its throat: *Ah-hem. Hello. Over here. Anybody?*

Where did I know this from?

Across the street, the hound dog lay down, its great floppy ears spreading out on either side of its head. I could not make out whether or not it also had a blue tag attached, but that thought fled with its tail between its legs as soon as I heard the guy back in the alley cry out.

The animals had moved into the alley and surrounded him. He was still ass-down against the wall, and a couple of the larger dogs—one of them a seriously grim-looking German shepherd—loomed on either side of his head, their noses so close to his ears I wondered if he could hear anything besides their wet, heavy breathing. The rest of the animals pressed near his sides and legs; every few seconds one of them would reach up and gently swat him with a paw, seemingly just to watch him jump or hear him yelp.

He saw me looking and said (not loudly, but with

great panic nonetheless): "Hey, buddy . . . no hard feelings, okay? Could you"—He jumped as the German shepherd, with a low snarl, nuzzled his face for an instant—"gimme some help here? Call the cops or the fuckin' pound or *Wild Kingdom* or someone?"

Though there was nothing overtly threatening in the way the animals stood, there was no doubt in my mind that this guy was going to be in a lot of painful trouble if they decided they didn't like him; at least half of them, as far as I could see, had a small blue plastic tag attached to the back of their ear.

Hello? Anybody home? (Tap-tap) *Is this thing on?*

The cat nudged my leg again, then growled. Not at me; at the animals in the alley.

I remember this next very clearly: The animals, as one, turned their heads to look at the cat, the cat gestured with its head toward the hound dog across the street, and as soon as the animals' attention was on the dog, it rose from the steps and crossed the street to take its place on my other side.

It sat there for a moment, then yawned, shook itself, and licked my hand.

The animals in the alley focused their full attention on me. If they'd had arms, those arms would have been parted before them, silently asking: *Well?*

Life gives you many odd and marvelous gifts on a daily basis, if you take the effort to notice: the tinny, distant chords of music from an approaching ice-cream truck; the geometrically perfect formation held by a gaggle of geese as they fly overhead; being the first person in the morning to see the streetlights turn off; scanning through radio stations on a car radio and suddenly coming across a favorite, back-then song you haven't heard or thought of in twenty years; the sound made by your teeth as they bite into a fresh apple; the scent of newly baked bread or pastries wafting from the door of a bakery; the way an attractive woman passing you on the street holds eye contact a few moments longer than is really needed . . . gifts. Common enough, but strange and wonderful when you catch them.

And then there are rare moments when the odd, strange, and marvelous gifts decide to tag-team your ass: getting a phone call from a person you've only just thought of after many years, and finding that they'd only just now thought of you, as well, and figured what the hell; finding an old photograph that you had convinced yourself long ago you'd *imagined* as having existed; knowing exactly, precisely what someone is going to do or say several minutes before they do; or finding yourself in the middle of a downtown square one afternoon with a dozen animals silently asking if they should let this guy walk away unharmed or not, it's your call.

Gifts wonderful and strange and not to be questioned too much when they're bestowed upon you.

I almost laughed from the craziness of it, then simultaneously shook my head and waved my hands forward in a quick gesture of dismissal: He's not worth it.

I turned to go. The hound dog and cat where nowhere to be seen.

When I looked back down the alley not three seconds later, Drop-Kick was completely alone. The animals had vanished as silently and as quickly and totally as they'd appeared.

He looked at me with an unreadable expression on his face.

For some reason I had the sense Dad had just said *You're welcome* to me.

I shrugged at Drop-Kick and walked off toward St. Francis de Sales where my widowed mother waited among the mourners for her son to return and Mabel was probably chewing through the back of a chair because she still didn't have her smokes.

Just as some mistakes are too monstrous for remorse, some moments of wonder are too sublime for anyone who wasn't there to understand. I never told anyone about what happened that afternoon; it was mine, only mine, and would always remain so.

Beth and Mabel stayed at our house for a couple of days until things started to settle, but despite all good intentions we started getting on each other's nerves. There are, in my opinion, three stages to helping the grief-stricken: 1) *Is there anything we can do?*; 2) *What else do you need?*; and 3) *Christ, what is it* now?

We were skirting dangerously close to stage three when Beth pulled me aside one night and said we needed to talk. Mabel was in the living room teaching Mom to play pinochle, so we decided to sneak out for something to eat. We ended up at the A&W Drive-In where a roller-skating waitress brought us a tray of root beers, hot dogs, and onion rings. There was something comforting in the way that plastic tray hung on the side of the car window, something of the old days, high school weekends, all-night record parties, dancing with your girlfriend in the autumn moonlight, maybe stealing a kiss in the lilac shadows.

"How are you feeling?" she asked.

"Like maybe you want to smother me in my sleep but are too polite to say so."

She smiled. "For as big as that house is, it has sure seemed cramped the last day or so, hasn't it?"

"Yeah, I guess." I took a bite from the steaming hot dog. It tasted like the end of all summers.

"I think Mabel and I should go back home tonight."

"I figured as much."

"Are you mad?"

"No, not really. I mean, *no*, not at all. I understand."

"It's just . . . you and your mom need some time alone. We've done all we can but we're just getting in the way." Which was true; I'd lost count of how many times I'd nearly walked in on one of them in the bathroom or opened the refrigerator to find my last bottle of Pepsi had been drunk by someone else.

"Can I call you if I need you?"

"Of course. Any time, you know that. And you're still going to give Mabel rides to and from work, right?"

"Right."

"So it's not like we're never going to see each other ever again."

There was something she wasn't telling me and I said as much.

"I wanted to ask you something," she said, not looking at me. "You remember all the stories I told you about my mother? How she was this famous stage actress?"

"Let me guess—you were lying?"

"Wow. You figured that out on your own and everything—*of course* I was lying. My mother is an

214

old barfly who'd screw a crippled walrus if it bought her a drink. The last Mabel or I heard, she was living in a flop house in Kansas City with some biker. That doesn't matter—the thing is, I always sort of wanted to try my hand at being an actress. I did some plays in high school and I wasn't bad—"

"—you never told me you were in any plays. I would've come to see you if—"

"—I didn't want to embarrass myself in front of you, all right? But things are a lot different now. I want to do something else in my life, something different, something . . . I don't know . . . more. Welsh Hills Players are having tryouts for *Pippin* next week and I thought I'd give it a shot."

"That sounds *great!*" I said, turning toward her and taking her hand. "*Man,* I bet you'll have fun."

"The thing is, there might be a lot of rehearsals, which means a lot of evenings where we won't get to see each other, and I don't want that to be a problem."

I shrugged. "I don't see why it should. I could even come and watch you rehearse, if you wouldn't mind."

"God, no. Just promise you won't laugh at me."

"I won't. Or if I do, I'll go outside where no one can see me." I leaned over and kissed her. "What brought on this sudden desire to return to the stage?"

"The way your dad died."

I stared at her. Ever since the night of the call I had tried not to think about the manner in which he'd died. Dad operated a massive punch-press. It had all but cut him in half when he'd fallen in. I knew that everyone said he'd died instantly, but what the hell does that mean, really? If he'd lived long enough to see those teeth grind down a second time, it was too long. It had to have been agonizing, the pain and fear. Laying there with your guts oozing out, watching as this massive roof of iron teeth came down at you.

"I don't understand."

She squeezed my hand. "Remember how you told me he'd wanted to raise chickens for a living, be a farmer? I kept wondering if that was the last thing that went through his mind when he died: 'I should have raised chickens like I wanted to.' And it made me so damned *sad*. To die knowing that you were never really happy, feeling like maybe you'd wasted your life and no one would give a damn or remember you."

"Please stop," I said.

"What is it?"

I was starting to cry again and didn't want to. I'd wondered the very same things. Maybe if he'd gone ahead and tried his hand at farming, he would have been happier, would have felt that his life was worthwhile, wouldn't have started drinking so much.

"Just . . . don't talk about Dad anymore right now, okay?"

She reached up and wiped a tear away from my eye. "Okay."

We sat in awkward silence for a few moments, then—for some reason, maybe because it was the first non-Dad related thing to pop into my head—I asked her something that had been on my mind, off

216

and on, for a while: "What was in that package you mailed?"

She tilted her head and blinked. "What package? When?"

"The day we took the dogs out. You went in that back room and you had a package when you came out."

She gave a slight shake of her head. "I don't know what you're . . . are you sure I had something?"

"Yes."

She thought about it for a moment, then shrugged. "Sorry. Parts of that day are fuzzy. I was pretty upset."

There was something she wasn't telling me, and I knew it.

Of course, since we hadn't so much as kissed over the past few weeks, it wasn't hard to figure out.

"So, who is he?"

"Who?"

"The guy you're dating? Someone who's trying out for the show, as well?"

She sipped her root beer and shook her head. "I don't want to talk about him with you. I don't like talking about other guys with you, okay?"

"Okay . . . ?"

"I'm sorry I brought up your dad, but I just don't want to reach the end of my life and have only regrets. Does that make sense? Acting is something I've always wanted to pursue, so I'm going to. And don't you worry—I've got no illusions about going to Broadway or being in the movies. Community theater is the ticket for me."

Gary A. Braunbeck

"And I can come watch you rehearse?"

"And you can come watch me rehearse."

I couldn't come watch her rehearse; the director—a pretentiously flamboyant small-town ar-*teest* who was so enamored of his own incomparable brilliance it was everything he could do not to fuck himself twenty-four hours a day—wouldn't allow it. Beth got the female lead and was scheduled to rehearse four nights a week, then—as opening night loomed closer—every weeknight and Saturday evenings, as well.

I took a part-time janitorial job to fill the evenings. I liked janitorial work; you were alone, it was quiet, no one was breathing down your neck, and at the end of the shift you could actually *see* what your labors had accomplished: a disaster area was now rebuilt and tidy, things shone where before they looked lightly sheened in rust, the smell of the bathroom was pleasant and clean, nothing crunched underfoot as you walked across the carpet, the windows now glistened. Let's hear it for the bad-ass with his mop bucket and Windex.

I finished each night in plenty of time to take Mabel to work. On nights when I knew Beth's rehearsal would run late, I stopped in and talked with Whitey so he could update my growing list of character flaws. At home, I took care of dinner and laundry and paying the bills and making sure that Mom didn't discover where I'd hidden the rest of her medicine; after the first time I caught her trying to take a triple dose of sedatives—"Oh, hon, I didn't think it would hurt anything, I've just been real jumpy" (which I didn't buy for a second)—I made it a point to get one of those pill trays and fill only one compartment at a time with only the prescribed doses. I did this three times a day. I wanted to trust her, wanted to believe that she'd never try taking more than she was supposed to . . . but I didn't.

I started to understand why Mabel sometimes seemed so depressed at the end of her shift; despite telling yourself you were doing this for someone's good, you felt somewhat like a captor.

The week Beth's show was to open, I picked up Mabel after I got off work, as usual. She said hello and asked me how my night had been, then sat staring out the window, nervous and tense, chewing at her thumbnail. I asked her if everything was all right and she mumbled something that was supposed to be in the affirmative, then returned to silence for most of the ride. As the nursing home came into view, she cleared her throat and said: "You won't have to do this anymore after tonight."

"I don't mind, Mabel, really." She'd been doing this a lot lately, telling me how bad she felt about imposing on my time, how she'd just find another nurse to ride with; for a while that's endearing, then it just starts to offend. I did not want anything bad to come between us. "You don't have to find someone to ride with, I—"

"Oh, no, it's not that at all." She smiled at me, a full, cheek-to-cheek smile that should have been radiant but instead seemed an affectation. "I'm buying a new car tomorrow morning. Got it all picked out, have the down payment, the whole nine yards."

I pulled into our usual parking space, killed the engine, and looked at the building. The Cedar Hill

Healthcare Center no longer looked like the same place; two new additions (a larger and more up-to-date Physical Therapy unit, as well as a second—and nicer—visiting area) gave the place an almost regal, ersatz-exclusive appearance, and a third addition—what would be a friendlier employee break area, complete with a bunk room for those working double shifts—was nearing completion. Whoever had taken over the place was making serious changes.

"The new owners must have *some* capital behind them," I said.

"You have no idea." Her smile wavered for a moment, then came back just as bright and twice as phony as before. "Beth wants the station wagon for God only knows what reason, so we're going to get that fixed up, and I'll have my own car. Do you know this is the first time in my life that I'll have a car that's all mine? The very first time. It's nice to able to afford new things, better things. For the first time in my life I don't go to bed worrying about having enough to pay the bills at the end of the month. You have no idea how good that feels to an old gal like me. So I figure I deserve a new car. You can come over and see it. Maybe I'll even drive *you* around." Cheerful words, mundane words, words you hear in various combinations every day from various people; someone's getting a new car, independence, go where they want when they want . . . nothing special in these words.

Except that her inflections were all wrong. I don't want this to sound histrionic, because there was nothing overtly dramatic about it; it's just that as I'd come to know what Beth was feeling through her body language and silences, I'd come to know Mabel's moods through her speech patterns, her tones and inflections and pauses, and that evening they were *wrong*; her tone would rise where it should have lowered, she'd stretch out syllables for no reason, her volume would sometimes go from a normal conversational level to a near-shout to a conspiratorial whisper in the same phrase, once even in the same word. A stranger meeting her for the first time would assume that she was just a little tense and distracted; I knew that something dire was going on and she wasn't talking about it, and it was going to end badly. I had seen this happen enough with Mom to know when someone was about to implode.

"Okay, Mabel, c'mon. It's *me*, okay? What's the matter?"

She lit a cigarette and rolled down the window. "There shouldn't be anything wrong. I don't know why I'm acting like this. You get to be my age, you learn to live with things that bug the shit out of you; you learn not to look a gift horse in the mouth."

"Did you just skip to the end of this conversation or did I miss something?"

"Huh?" She looked at me, blinked, and shook a small but at least genuine smile onto her face. "I, uh . . . I'm sorry. I guess I drifted off for a minute."

"What gift horse? What're you talking about?"

She pulled in another drag, let the smoke curl in front of her face for a moment, then exhaled. "It's been so great since they took over, it really has. We've got new uniforms, extra help, better food, the working atmosphere has never been so good, and the *money* . . . Lord, I'm making almost twice what I was making this time last year, and that's on top of the great bonus we got for—" Her eyes flashed a quick *oh-shit* and she left the sentence unfinished.

"The bonus you got for . . . ?" I prompted, then it came to me: "The confidentiality agreement. Is that it?"

"I really can't. I just"—She reached over and took my hand—"really can't talk about it. The way I figure it, I'm just about a year away from having everything paid off and being able to afford a house—not just rent a nicer one, but *buy* one. Do you know I've never owned a home? Isn't that a pisser? It would be nice to spend the third act of my life in my own home. And if I don't screw up, if I do what I agreed to and keep this job, then I can have all that. Is that so bad? Does that make me callous? Is it such a terrible thing to want an actual home and peace of mind? Christ, I've spent so much of my life worrying over one thing or another that by the time I took a real breath it was halfway over."

"No one's saying you haven't worked hard for everything, it's just—"

"—and I'm not going to find anyone, you know." This followed by a phlegm-filled, bitter, ugly little laugh. "Sure, if I lived in San Francisco or Los Angeles or someplace like that, someplace where they don't look down on you because you're gay, I might stand a chance. But look at me—I'm an *old* gal. Whatever chance I had for a great romance in my life has long past, so if I'm going to be the lovable old-maid aunt, why can't I at least be comfortable and content? Dammit, I've *helped* people, you know? I've cared for them when no one else wanted to—and not just because it was my job, understand. I did it because I wanted what was best for them. All of them. This is no different, really. Is it?"

Look up "bemused" in the dictionary and you'll find a picture of my face at that moment. "What the hell is wrong, Mabel? Why are you talking like this?"

She squeezed my hand and opened the car door. "I have no idea. They say the mind is the first thing to go."

I held on to her; I wasn't going to let this drop. "What aren't you telling me?"

"What I'm not supposed to. Maybe I'll be able to explain it someday, but not now. I don't know. I keep my word. I've always kept my word, that's important. For right now will you just answer a question?"

"Sure thing."

"Am I a bad person?"

"God, no! You're one of the finest people I've ever met. Why would you even ask—"

She pulled away from me and closed the door. "I've got a ride for later. I'm going straight to the dealership when I get off. Come by later this week and see the new car. I'll drive us to Beth's opening night."

I watched her go inside, then started the car and drove away. I was almost home when I jerked the wheel around, made an illegal U-turn, and went back. Maybe Whitey would still be up and could tell me something. Even if he wasn't up, I'd shake his ass awake. I figured I was owed one genuinely rude interruption.

I parked in my usual spot and started to go through the back entrance.

It was locked. Not only that, but it now required a card-key to open. Something made a whirring mechanical noise over my head and I looked up in time to see a security camera pirouette on its wall-mount and point at me.

I did what we've all done at one time or another—made a goofy face and waved. A few moments later one of the regular shift nurses—Arlene—appeared at the door and used her card-key to open it. "Let me guess—Mabel forgot something?"

"Maybe I just wanted to flirt with you." Arlene was sixty if she was a day.

"Maybe if I was twenty years younger I'd drag you into the linen closet and make you do more than flirt." She opened the door wider and let me in. "But my husband wouldn't like it."

"It's the thought that counts," I said, moving past her.

"Mabel's in the break room having coffee. Come get me when you need to leave and I'll let you out."

I pointed at the new lock. "Has there been much of this? I mean the new security?"

"They're turning this place into something out of that *2001* movie, I swear. You need card-keys to move between units now, and every hall has its own camera and a microphone so we can hear if anyone calls out for help. You'd think we were guarding the gold at Fort Knox. There're even three more full-time security guards, two inside and one covering the grounds for each shift. We're getting to be quite the place, we are."

"I don't have to worry about being stopped or something, do I?"

"No," she said, reaching into her pocket and removing a plastic credit-card-looking thing at the end of a dark ribbon. "Just make sure you wear this where it can be seen." She draped the visitor's pass over my neck. "You have to wear one of these at night—even a fixture like you."

" 'Fixture.' Oooh. I love it when you talk like an interior decorator. Tell me about *accouterments* next. Whisper about them slowly."

"You are the most *evil* boy, aren't you?"

"I get a lot of complaints about that, yes."

"Who said I was complaining?" And with that Arlene led me to the unit and left me to my own devices. The break room was in the hall opposite the one leading to Whitey's room, so it didn't exactly take a lot of sneaking and skulking to get to his room—though I was anxiously aware that I was on camera now.

I passed the room which had been the former home of the Captain Spalding Brothers and slowed. The new occupant—who for the moment had the room to herself—was sitting in her wheelchair, asleep in front of a color television displaying a muted re-run of *The Waltons*. There was a vibrantly green potted plant on the windowsill, several books stuffed between a set of hand-carved cherry-wood bookends, themselves shaped like books; an antique Tiffany lamp whose stained-glass shade glowed softly from the 40-watt bulb underneath, diffuse sunlight warming church windows. A patchwork quilt lay neatly folded at the foot of her bed, while the head was covered in an assortment of small, colorful pillows. There were framed photographs hanging on the wall next to her bed; a black and white wedding picture, so faded around the edges it looked like something glimpsed through a fog; several color photographs of the same cat and dog taken years apart, the cat going from a bright-eyed gray-furred kitten to something that looked like an overused feather duster with a rheumy gaze, the dog journeying from its days as a square-bodied bundle of muscles and legs to an arthritic bundle atop an old throw rug that, like the animal lying on it, had seen better days. I wondered if the animals were still alive, and then why there were no pictures of children and grandchildren anywhere to be seen. Everything about the room and the woman sleeping in the chair whispered of weariness, of too much quiet, not enough voices and visitors. A lamp, a quilt, some books, a television, and frozen moments from memory framed on the walls; this is what her life had come down to. I wondered if any of those books were poetry collections, if perhaps it contained any Browning, if she had certain well-thumbed pages marked for easy finding or knew them by heart; did she ever fall asleep repeating snippets of sonnets in her mind as she looked at the frozen moments from her life?

> *My heart is very tired, my strength is low,*
> *My hands are full of blossoms plucked before,*
> *Held dead within them till myself shall die.*

I knew Whitey would kick my ass up between my shoulders if he knew I was thinking these things. ("Know what your name would have been if you'd've been born an Indian? 'Dark Cloud.' Trust me on this. They wouldn't have had to worry about having their land stolen by the White Man and then being systematically slaughtered, no. You would've *depressed* them to death!")

I smiled at the thought, wished this sleeping woman pleasant dreams and a happy day to come (I also couldn't help but smile at the bumper sticker someone had pasted to the back of her wheelchair: I ACCELERATE FOR FUZZY BUNNIES), then headed on down to Whitey's room.

His door was closed.

I stood there staring at the thing, my poised fist frozen in mid-knock.

Maybe this was part of the new security measures, keeping the doors closed at night—but then why hadn't Miss Acceleration's door been closed, as well? No, this wasn't what it appeared to be, it couldn't be, I wouldn't accept it, wouldn't allow it. Whitey might not be in the best shape, but it had only been three days since I'd last seen him (he wasn't very talkative and insisted he wasn't feeling well, though I suspected he was just depressed and wanted to be left alone) and I refused to believe that anything had happened to him. Mabel would have told me. I knocked, then waited for him to shout something insulting.

Nothing.

I grabbed the door handle and began to open it when the rest of it finally registered: his nameplate had been removed from its slot in the wall next to the door, the clipboard that held his chart was no longer hanging on its hook underneath his name, and the lights in the room were off. Whitey always kept the bathroom light on at night so he didn't have to stumble through the dark to take a leak.

If I don't turn on the light, everything will be fine, I thought. *Right now it's dark and you're not looking at anything that confirms what you're trying not to think about, so for this moment, in the dark, Whitey's here and sleeping and everything's the way it was the last time you were here.*

The smart thing to do was not turn on the light. I'd lost too many people recently. Dad was chewed up and dead and gone, Mom might as well be dead for all the joy she found in her day-to-day existence, and I'd seen so little of Beth for the last six weeks she might as well have been in Guatemala with the Peace Corps. I would not allow another person to slip away from me. And the best way to ensure that would be to do the smart thing, and the smart thing was not to turn on the light.

I turned on the light.

Two beds, both empty. No television, no video tape machine, no pictures, no books in precarious stacks; nothing in the closets but hangers, nothing in the restroom except an unused roll of toilet paper, a full soap dispenser, and a tub and sink that were desert-dry.

I stood in the empty room shaking my head while something in the middle of my chest tried to snap through my rib cage. This was not—repeat *not*—happening. Maybe I'd gone into the wrong room, it could happen. So there I was back out in the hall checking the room number and it was the right number but that didn't mean anything, Whitey was always bitching about how little space he had in there so maybe they'd just moved him to another room, a bigger room, one big enough to hold all of his stuff and leave space for his ego, left side first, I went down the left side of the hall first, checking and double-checking the names next to the doors and Whitey's wasn't among them, so now it up the right side, double- and triple-checking the names and it wasn't there, either; I reached the end of the hall and went left toward the break room because Mabel was there and she'd know, she could tell me what was going on—

—unless she didn't know, unless something happened earlier today and the detritus had already been cached away and no one had told her—

—the door to the break room stood half-opened. I started to push my way inside when I heard Mabel say, "It's probably for the best," but there was something in her voice that told me she was simply parroting a practiced response, that she didn't really believe what she was saying but wanted whomever she was talking with to think she did. Then a male voice replied, "It's always for the best, it's important you remember that." Then I had the door open and was standing there long enough to see that the man she was speaking to was dressed in an expensive gray suit with white shirt and blue tie and wore a bowler hat on his head that was pulled down to cover the top half of his ears—then he noticed me.

"This area is for sanctioned personnel only," he said. His face and voice were both granite.

I reached down and fumbled at the thing hanging around my neck. "I've got a visitor's pass."

"That doesn't matter—you shouldn't be in here. What's your name?"

Mabel's face drained of color the second I answered his question but I figured it was more out of concern that she was about to get into trouble. I decided to play it safe and act as if I didn't know her, like I was just some schlub off the street who couldn't find his butt with both hands, a floodlight, and a seven-man search party.

"I'm sorry if I've interrupted anything but I was looking for . . . for my uncle, Marty Weis?" I pointed over my shoulder, looking directly at Mabel. "His room's empty, ma'am. Has he been moved to another unit?"

Mabel released a breath and said to Bowler-Hat, "I'll take care of this," then walked over and gestured for me to move toward the nurse's desk. As we walked down the hall she slapped an iron clamp that looked like her hand on my elbow. "How the *hell* did you get in?"

I looked back to see Bowler-Hat standing outside the break room, watching her escort me out. "Arlene let me in, she said—"

"—she shouldn't have let you in. Unless it's an emergency, there are now no visitors allowed after eight-thirty."

"I'm sorry, Ma—uh, ma'am, I didn't know." She shot a quick thank-you glance at me when I said "ma'am." "Where is he?"

"Mr. Weis is no longer with us," she said, a little too loudly. She pulled me past the nurse's desk toward the hallway where I'd entered; her entire body was rigid and we were moving a little too fast.

"Please tell me what happened."

"Mr. Weis is no longer with us, sir. You can call the Admissions office after nine tomorrow morning."

We turned down the hall and moved toward the door. After a few steps Mabel looked back over her shoulder, then doubled her pace, yanking me along. Her grip on my arm tightened.

"That *hurts*," I whispered.

"Jesus, I wish you hadn't told him your name."

"So what? Big deal—what's he going to do, issue an APB?"

Mabel swiped her card-key as she none-too-gently spun me around and began to push the door open with my back. "Listen, you know I love you, right?"

"What the—aren't you worried about him hearing you?"

"He didn't follow us and this hall isn't monitored. You know I love you, right?"

"Yeah . . . ?"

"And you know I don't say or do anything without a damn good reason, right?"

"Yeah . . . ?"

"Good." She blinked, then gave a weak, unreadable smile. "You need to leave right now and go home and not come around here or the house for a little while, a couple of weeks, at least, okay?"

"Where's Marty? He didn't . . . didn't—"

"—Mr. Weis is no longer with us. That's all I can tell you." Then she silently mouthed the words *He's fine* while slowly shaking her head. "Please do this for me, will you? Go home and stay away for a couple of weeks."

"But . . . but what's . . . I mean—"

"Do it for me, please?" This wasn't just out of concern for her job—there was hard, raw, genuine fear

231

in her voice. Before I could say anything else she pushed me outside, closed and locked the door, then spun around and returned to the unit, not giving me so much as a brief backward glance. I was just some schlub off the street.

Back home in the kitchen I put all of Mom's morning medications in their compartment and then went to bed, where I lay weeping for another hour or so before there was a soft knock on my door and Mom stuck her head inside.

"Is everything all right?"

"Fine," I said in the same clipped, melodramatic way we've all said it when we're upset and don't want to say *Everything is awful and I just want to die so leave me the hell alone, please.*

She held the collar of her tattered blue housecoat closed as she looked out in the hall toward the stairs. "Well, try to keep it down, will you? Your dad will be upset something terrible if he comes home and finds you this way."

I stared at her; she stood silhouetted in the doorway like some wisp of a dream that lingers in the eyes for a moment upon waking. "I'm sorry."

"You don't need to apologize, hon, it's all right. We just don't want to upset him. He works so hard."

"I know."

She started to close the door, then said: "Is it time for my medicine?"

"Not yet, you take it in the morning."

"Well, it *is* the morning. It's after midnight, isn't it?"

"Go back to bed, Mom. Take it when you get up again."

"Are you sure?"

"Yes."

"You're a good boy, you know that?"

"Thanks, Mom."

She looked at me for a few more moments, then closed the door.

After another half hour I got up and put on my headphones and listened to records until a little past eight-thirty. The songs—some of them were old even back then—wove a curious kind of safety cocoon; this one came out when I was in sixth grade; this one was playing the first time I told so-and-so that I liked her in the eighth grade and she didn't laugh at me—didn't *kiss* me, either, but at least didn't laugh; and this one, this one I always listened to by myself because it struck at something deep inside me that I didn't want anyone else to know about because they might make fun of it or find a way to use it against me when they were mad or just feeling mean and needed to take it out on someone.

Around nine I took off the headphones and called the Cedar Hill Healthcare Center, asking to speak to someone in Admissions. As soon as they answered I gave them the same bullshit story about being Marty Weis's nephew and how I'd tried to visit him last night, cha-cha-cha. It wasn't hard to sound scared and confused.

"Mr. Weis is no longer with us," said the Admissions person.

"I *know* that, ma'am, I was just wondering if you could tell me where he's gone."

"Mr. Weis was checked out of our facility two days ago." *Was checked out*, not *Checked himself out*.

"Can you tell me who checked him out? Was it his daughter from Los Angeles?"

"I can't give out that information, sir, and no forwarding address was provided."

This went on for about ten minutes, I was transferred to three different people, all of whom gave me the same story, word for word: *Mr. Weis is no longer with us.*

I hung up while being transferred yet again, paced my room for a few minutes, then lay back down on my bed and listened to some more music.

Then I fell asleep, and dreamed of Mom standing over her medicine in the kitchen.

I jolted awake, snapping up my head so fast I heard the bones in my neck crack and felt a sharp stab of pain.

Something had happened.

Something was wrong.

I had no idea *how* I knew this, but the feeling was too strong to be ignored.

Yanking off the headphones, I headed downstairs. If I remembered filling the compartment and replacing the lids on the bottles, then I must have put the meds back in their hiding place as I usually did; even half-awake, your body more times than not will remember certain physical routines even if your brain doesn't.

She was sitting at the table, face-down, her nose pressed against the Local section of *The Cedar Hill Ally*. One hand was still clutching the newspaper, the other held the cup of now-cold coffee she'd taken the pills with.

The radio was tuned to the local classical music station. It was playing something from some opera, Mom being the opera fan.

On the counter, five bottles of prescription medications sat where I'd left them last night. The "Morning" compartment was unopened, as were all the bottles except one—the sedatives; that bottle lay on its side, displaying the depth of the nothing it contained.

Oh, hon, I didn't think it would hurt anything, I've just been real jumpy.

I knew she was dead before I even touched her. I sat there, holding her hand and saying over and over again: "You rest now, Mom, you've earned it. You rest now, Mom . . ."

I wondered what song I'd been listening to when she'd died. I wondered if she'd tried calling up to me but I didn't hear her because of the headphones. I wondered if she'd died thinking that her life had been wasted and no one would remember her. ". . . you've earned it. You can rest now. . . ."

I wondered if her hands had ever held blossoms.

I made the necessary calls, I waited with her body until the coroner's wagon and police arrived; I answered all their questions, let the police collect the items they requested, and agreed to come down to the station later that day and let them take my prints. ("A formality," said the officer. "It will help us make a determination.") After they left, I called Criss Brothers Funeral Home and told them what happened and, yes, I could come over in a little while and make the arrangements; then it was only a matter of gathering together all the necessary papers (insurance information, etc., which Mom kept in the same metal filing box with everything relating to Dad's death), calling what few relatives Mom still had in the area, and going about the rest of the awful business.

A lot of the next several days is something of a blur, so I'll skip around and just hit the high points, if you don't mind: her death was ruled accidental, I was not charged with gross negligence or anything else, her doctor was quick to mention her depression and confused state of mind, and the fact that she'd lost her husband only four weeks before confirmed for everyone that the entire incident was a terrible tragedy. Her obituary ran three short paragraphs and read more like a job resume than the summation of a life. Her remains were cremated (she'd been very specific about this for as long as I'd been alive) and placed in the finest urn Criss Brothers had to offer. There was a brief and bleak memorial service held in the chapel at the funeral home with about thirteen people, myself included, in attendance. When all was said and done, I was left sole owner of an empty, paid-for house, and had a respectable amount of money left from their insurance policies. At twenty-one, I was "set" for a good while, provided I used my resources intelligently.

The memorial service was held the Friday morning Beth's show was scheduled to open. The night before she called at eight-thirty from a phone at the theater. I hung up as soon as I heard her voice. Less than a minute later the phone rang again and I let the answering machine pick up.

"Listen," she said, "we're taking a dinner break. The dress rehearsal was a disaster and we're running through the whole thing again at ten. We need to talk and—God! I just heard how stupid that sounds. I'm so sorry about your mom, I really am, and so is Mabel. Did you get the flowers we sent? I'd really like to come to the service tomorrow morning. I would've called sooner but I've been trying to work up the nerve to—"

I picked up the receiver. "I love you, Beth, and we should be together, and you know it. I feel so *alone* right now, and I could just . . . never mind. I don't think I want to talk right now."

"Then don't say anything, just listen for a minute, okay?

"Happiness scares the hell out of me, it always has. I mean, it's great at the time but I know it's never going to last. I didn't come to live with Mabel right away, you know. Mom tried palming me off on other relatives for a long time, and I'd stay with them for a couple of weeks, a month maybe, but eventually they'd always send me back because I was in the way, or didn't get along with their cat, or made them nervous or whatever. It didn't matter how hard I tried, how I concentrated on changing myself, remaking myself so they'd like me better and want to keep me, it was never good enough. This went on for a few years, and after the first couple of times I learned how to adapt, okay? I wasn't going to be in any place for very long, so I found a way to make fast friends. Mostly boys. If I put out, they didn't treat me like I was some kind of dog. And I'd spent

Gary A. Braunbeck

so long being treated that way I started to believe that's what I was—I still do, sometimes. But you spread your legs for them and you're the most beautiful girl in the world, even if it's just for one night. I knew it was okay to enjoy their company and stuff and not care about the consequences because I wasn't going to be around long enough for anything I said or did to matter. I learned to trust happiness only if it was temporary, because then it's okay when it ends. You can always find another quick fix in the next place.

"Then Mabel took me in and that was that. I stayed. And that meant having to trust I'd be happy for the long run, but the long run wasn't in my repertoire so I just kept acting like I was going to be moving on any day now. But I didn't. I stayed. Then one day I meet the cutest little boy in the world while I'm in the hospital and even though he's only nine he acts like he's thirty and I know that he's going to be something really great when he grows into himself. And he was, and I loved him—I *still* love him, even though he can't see what a great person he is. I got . . . I got *comfortable*, all right? And I always associated 'comfortable' with bored, because I always wanted things to be *new*, do you understand? I hate that about myself, but things are only interesting to me when they're new—*that's* when I feel the most alive. So anytime I'd start feeling bored, I'd see someone else for a week or so and *that* was new, I made myself new with them, and it was exciting and unpredictable and when it ended, when I'd get back in sync with you, *we* were new again. I've just been so used to re-making myself for so long that I couldn't stop.

"I know that doesn't justify what I've done—what I've been doing—and I'm not trying to make excuses, right? I just wanted to give you an explanation because I *do* love you and I've hurt you so much and you didn't deserve it and if there's anything I can do, any way to make it good again, to fix things, to make you feel less alone—"

"—are you done?"

A soft breath, a softer swallow. "Yes."

I looked at the room in which I was sitting, at the furniture and the small bits of dust here and there and the faded pictures on the mantel and decided that I couldn't remain here. This was an alien shelter in an alien world where outside the walls people you thought you knew were just stacks of carbon hiding behind the scrim of humanity you put in front of them so you wouldn't have to deal with what they really were.

"I'm sorry you got bored with me. And I'm sorry there's no way this can ever be fixed. I can't be your friend anymore. I love you . . . I love you too much in another way for that, so I can't be your friend anymore and that makes me sad. Please don't come to the service tomorrow, and please don't ever call me again. I hope the show goes well. Break a leg."

I hung up. She did not call back.

I spent the next two weeks making all the necessary arrangements to leave Cedar Hill, stopping only long enough to eat or sleep, neither of which I did in any great quantity. *Pippin* received decent reviews, especially for Beth.

I gave notice at work. I stored most of the furniture and all of the keepsakes. I hired a cleaning crew to come in and scrub the place from top to bottom. I hosed down the outside until the aluminum siding shone. I had a landscaper come in and fix the lawn, adding flowers and plants out front and a pair of small trees in the backyard. Both Mom and Dad had often remarked how they'd wished we had more shade back there.

One of the offices I cleaned nights was a downtown real estate firm. I showed up an hour early on one of my last nights and spoke with the manager, who was all too happy to help make arrangements to put the house on the market. I gave her all the necessary information on the house, as well as the bank account number where the funds were to be deposited, and told her I would call with my new address as soon as I was settled. We made copies of the keys, signed some forms, and shook hands.

I decided to go down to Kansas and visit my grandmother for a while. She was old and not in the best of health and had cried for an hour on the phone when I called to tell her about her daughter's accidental death. She had neither the strength nor the money to make the trip to Ohio for the service. I wanted to be around her for as long as she might still be alive; I wanted to be around someone who'd known my mother as a child and could tell me things about her that I'd never known. Dad's mother never entered into the picture; she never liked me and I never liked her, so there would be no love lost between us.

Two nights before I planned to leave, I was sitting in the middle of the emptied living room reading an excellent biography of the late blues guitarist Roy Buchanan when it suddenly occurred to me that I never knew what Mom's or Dad's favorite song was. I have no idea where the thought came from, but once it entered my head it would not leave, and soon—after polishing off half a twelve-pack of Blatz (Dad's beer of choice)—I started to cry. It seemed to me that someone should have cared enough to ask either of them if they even had a favorite song and, if they did, should have cared enough to remember what it was. So I focused on that until my head felt like it was going to implode.

The ringing of the phone jarred something back into place, and as soon as I answered, the first thing out of my mouth was, " 'Kiss an Angel Good Morning.' Mom's favorite song was—"

On the other end, someone burst into sobs.

I shook myself back into the moment at hand and said, "Hello? I'm sorry about—who is this?"

Beth spluttered out my name, then said: "I'm s-s-sorry, I know y-you said not to call but s-s-something's happened and I . . . *ohgod* . . . please come over. I can't ask anyone else t-to—"

I was sitting up straight, every nerve in my body twitching. "What's wrong? What happened?"

". . . gotta . . . gotta do something with the animals now, I d-d-don't know what I'm supposed to . . . She said everything was okay, I *asked* her, you know? 'Everything's fine now,' that's what she said. . . ."

Forget the lies and feelings of betrayal and the anger and rage and pain and jealousy and everything else; when someone you love calls you in the middle of the night in hysterics, you tell your pride to screw itself and go to them without another thought.

I pulled up in front of house and knew right away something wasn't right. For one thing, it looked as if every light in the place was on; Beth and especially Mabel were frugal as hell when it came to utilities—neither one of them would have left that many lights burning; for another thing, the U-boat was gone and Mabel's new car (a tan Toyota Tercel, a very smart and sensible car) sat in the driveway; it was well past two A.M. and Mabel should have been at work. The third thing I discovered when I went to knock on the door.

The house was unlocked.

This was not the worst neighborhood in Cedar Hill, but you wouldn't live here on "Renter's Row" unless you absolutely *had* to.

I entered and closed the door behind me. I called out for Beth and, getting no answer, Mabel.

Nothing.

I took a deep breath, my heart triphammering, and immediately began to cough and sneeze. It smelled like the place hadn't been cleaned in days; everything was sopped in the stench of animal shit and old urine mixed with the musty scent of shed fur and . . . something else. Something meaty and rotten. It was so overpowering I ran into the bathroom and threw up.

Breathing through my mouth, I checked the kitchen and backyard, then Beth's room.

She was gone, and so were all the Its.

Finally I knocked on Mabel's bedroom door;

when there was no answer I began to open it and saw a piece of paper that had been taped there but had fallen to the floor. I picked up and unfolded the note. It was from Beth:

I couldn't stay here any longer. I hadn't been home in a couple of days. She must have done it while I was gone. I'm like you now. I've lost every-one. I'm so sorry for everything. There ought to be a place for people like us. I hope you can forgive me someday. This is why I don't trust happiness. It's better to leave and re-make yourself. It's always been the best thing. I love you. Always remember that.

I opened the bedroom door and—
(If I don't turn on the light, everything will be fine.)
—turned on the light.

The first thing I saw were all the pink- and rust-colored feathers scattered around the room, on the floor, sticking to the walls and curtains and light fix-tures, but as I stepped closer to the mess on the bed I realized that the feathers had once been white. The dull buzz of flies sounded in my ears. The carpeting grew more and more damp the nearer I came to the bed. There were probably a thousand other smells and splotches and sights but the closer I moved toward the bed, the more my peripheral vision faded out until I could see only through a small, frozen, iris-out circle.

The upper half of the mattress and headboard were splattered in blood speckled with chunks of bone and mangled tissue. She'd dressed for work before lying down and placing the feather pillows over her face. After that it was a simple matter of pulling the pistol out of the drawer in her nightstand, pushing and prodding into the pillows until she could feel the barrel's position through them, or maybe she'd already had the gun in her hand before she lay down, or maybe—

—one of the stained feathers dislodged from the overhead light and brushed against my shoulder on its way down.

The gun lay on the floor near the bed. I wasn't about to touch it or anything else in the room. My chest was so tight I thought my lungs were going to collapse. Something was strangling me from within. My vision blurred because of something in my eyes. I reached up to wipe it away but made the mistake of moving at the same time. I stumbled over my own feet and fell onto the bed. I heard the muted splash as I hit the soaked remains of the pillows and the body underneath. I felt heavy tepid liquid slopping between my fingers and soaking into my shirt. It was all over me. I panicked and tried to push away but only managed to slip and fall face-first into the worst of it. I scrabbled around like a crab on a beach, tangling myself in gore-saturated sheets and wet feathers until, at last, I managed to grip the edge of the headboard and pull myself up. I lurched around, trying to wipe the blood from my eyes until I bumped into the dresser. I looked up and saw myself in the mirror and almost lost it. At least I didn't scream. Not once. As much as I wanted to just throw back my head and let fly with a howl to bring down the house, I didn't. I backed away from the bloody thing in the reflection, blinked, and saw what was on the floor by the other side of the bed.

Patients' files.

I'd watched Mabel and the other nurses at the home make notations in enough of these things to recognize one on sight. What the hell had she been doing, bringing these home with her? One was enough to get her fired, but she must have had a couple dozen piled there. Blood pooled over the top file and ran down the sides of the others like fudge on a sundae. A thin stapled stack of papers lay off to the side of the pile. It too was bloodied, but words could still be seen peeking through the smears here and there. I knelt down and leaned close. It looked to be some kind of contract. I saw the word **AGREEMENT** in bold-face type; the rest of the upper line was hidden behind a small slop of blood. I moved closer. I made out Mabel's name, and the words "in strictest confidence hereby agree" and knew what I was looking at. I scanned down the rest of the page, stopped, and came back to some words about a third of the way down the page I had seen on my first pass but hadn't let register.

between Keepers and

I heard the echo of her voice from the last time we'd had a real conversation: *And if I don't screw up, if I do what I agreed to and keep this job, then I can have all that. Is that so bad? Does that make me callous? Is it such a terrible thing to want an actual home and peace of mind?*

"What the hell did you agree to?" I asked the silence of the dead room.

Am I a bad person?

A dial clicked numbers in the correct sequence and all the tumblers fell into place and a door opened and something awful stepped out to make itself partially known.

. . . gotta do something with the animals now, Beth had said.

I don't remember if I closed the door behind me when I ran out of the house, nor do I know if anyone saw me leave, but since the police never showed up on my doorstep after that night I have to assume that I was not seen—or that if I was, no one cared. Around here, you were not your brother's or sister's keeper.

Around here, you were not your brother's or sister's . . .

. . . you were not your brother's . . .

. . . you were not your . . .

. . . YOU WERE NOT . . .

. . . I closed my eyes and took several deep breaths. *(Cutting things off a little soon there, aren't you, pal?)*

I smoothed out the issue of *Modoc* flat on my lap, then opened to the last page once again.

. . . YOU WERE NOT YOUR BROTHER'S OR SISTER'S KEEPER.

I began to tear it in half, then thought better of it.

"You can't force me to remember the rest of the night," I said.

I opened to a random page.

WOULDN'T TAKE ANY BETS ON THAT ONE IF I WERE YOU, GIL.

This time I did rip it in half, then threw the sections onto the barn floor and ground them in to the hay, mud, and stink with the heel of my shoe.

"That was *mine*," said Carson from the far end of the barn.

"I'll buy you another one."

"That's okay. I won't need it."

I faced my nephew and said, "Carson, you need to tell me what's going on, all right? I read the comic, and Long-Lost didn't tell me anything I didn't already know."

"That's 'cause you wouldn't let him."

I blinked. "What do you mean by that?"

He sighed, then rubbed the back of his neck. "I think it's good that you said you like swans, UncGil."

"What the fuck do swans have to do with any of this?"

Carson stared at me for a moment. "Don't you know what it is that makes them special?"

I stormed over and grabbed him by the shoulders. "To hell with swans, Carson. And fuck *Modoc*, all right? Look at me. I'm *scared*, Carson, do you understand?"

"I know. I'm sorry." He looked on the verge of tears. "But I gotta tell you something, okay?"

"All right."

He threw himself against me and squeezed so hard I thought he was going to dislocate part of my back.

"I love you, UncGil. You took good care of me. I'm gonna miss you."

"You're going to—whoa, there, wait a second." I pushed him back and looked into his eyes. "You're not going to miss me, you're not *going* anywhere."

He nodded his head, silver tears spilling down his face. "Long-Lost says it's time."

My breath caught in my chest. "Time for what?"

"For you to know the first part of his story." Carson walked over and bent down, picking up the comic book—which was now whole again.

"Here you go, UncGil. It's just on the first page this time."

"How do you know this?"

He shrugged. "The Great Scrim, it . . . I dunno . . . it kind of is pulled real *tight* here—you know, like when you wrap a sandwich too tight in plastic wrap? It kinda tears in places? Well, because this is where the Magic Zoo is, the Great Scrim is real tight like that, and it tears in a couple of places. And Long-Lost, he can make things happen where the tear is." He opened to the first page and offered the comic to me. "I can't read what it says, only you can."

I did not take it from his hands—I wasn't about to *touch* the goddamned thing. Instead, I leaned down to read:

DO YOU REMEMBER THE DREAM YOU HAD WHEN YOU CAUGHT PNEUMONIA, GIL? THE RAIN, THE SILVER CLOUD MADE BY THE MIST? YOU WERE SITTING ON A HILLSIDE, WATCHING A BOAT SAIL AWAY, AND YOU KNEW YOU HAD FRIENDS ABOARD THAT BOAT? OF COURSE YOU REMEMBER IT, *I* SENT IT TO YOU.

THAT'S WHAT HAPPENED TO ME, GIL. BUT MAYBE YOU NEED TO A QUICK BIBLE LES-SON. TRY THIS: "AND NOAH WAS SIX HUN-DRED YEARS OLD WHEN THE FLOOD OF WATERS WAS UPON THE EARTH.

"AND NOAH WENT IN, AND HIS SONS,

AND HIS WIFE, AND HIS SONS' WIVES
WITH HIM, INTO THE ARK, BECAUSE OF THE
WATERS OF THE FLOOD.

"THERE WENT IN TWO AND TWO UNTO
NOAH INTO THE ARK, THE MALE AND THE
FEMALE, AS GOD HAD COMMANDED NOAH.

"OF CLEAN BEASTS, AND OF BEASTS THAT
ARE NOT CLEAN, AND OF FOWLS, AND OF
EVERY THING THAT CREEPETH UPON THE
EARTH,

"AND IT CAME TO PASS AFTER SEVEN
DAYS, THAT THE WATERS OF THE FLOOD
WERE UPON THE EARTH.

IN THE SIX HUNDREDTH YEAR OF NOAH'S
LIFE, IN THE SECOND MONTH, THE SEVEN-
TEENTH DAY OF THE MONTH, THE SAME
DAY WERE ALL THE FOUNTAINS OF THE
GREAT DEEP BROKEN UP, AND THE WIN-
DOWS OF HEAVEN WERE OPENED.

"AND THE RAIN WAS UPON THE EARTH
FORTY DAYS AND FORTY NIGHTS.

"IN THE SELF-SAME DAY ENTERED NOAH,
AND SHEM, AND HAM, AND JAPHETH, THE
SONS OF NOAH, AND NOAH'S WIFE, AND
THE THREE WIVES OF HIS SONS WITH
THEM, INTO THE ARK;

"THEY, AND EVERY BEAST AFTER HIS
KIND, AND ALL THE CATTLE AFTER THEIR
KIND, AND EVERY CREEPING THING THAT
CREEPETH UPON THE EARTH AFTER HIS
KIND, AND EVERY FOWL AFTER HIS KIND,
EVERY BIRD OF EVERY SORT.

"*AND THEY WENT IN UNTO NOAH INTO THE ARK, TWO AND TWO OF ALL FLESH, WHEREIN IS THE BREATH OF LIFE.*

"*AND THEY THAT WENT IN, WENT IN MALE AND FEMALE OF ALL FLESH, AS GOD HAD COMMANDED HIM: AND THE LORD SHUT HIM IN.*

"*AND THE FLOOD WAS FORTY DAYS UPON THE EARTH; AND THE WATERS INCREASED, AND BARE UP THE ARK, AND IT WAS LIFT UP ABOVE THE EARTH.*"

... EVER TAKE A LOOK AT THAT STORY AND ASK YOURSELF, WHAT'S WRONG WITH THIS PICTURE? AFTER ALL, GIL, WEREN'T THERE MORE ANIMALS ABOARD THE ARK THAN HUMAN BEINGS? BUT WE'LL GET BACK TO THAT...

ALL YOU NEED TO KNOW IS THAT GOD JUMPED THE GUN A LITTLE BIT. NOT EVERY ANIMAL MADE IT ONTO THE ARK, BECAUSE NOT EVERY ANIMAL HAD A MATE.

TAKE ME, FOR INSTANCE.

I WAS THE FIRST ANIMAL, ALL OTHERS SPRUNG FROM ME ... YET WHEN IT CAME TIME FOR THE RAINY-DAY CRUISE, I WAS LEFT BEHIND! DO YOU KNOW HOW MUCH THAT HURT MY FEELINGS, GIL? DO YOU HAVE ANY IDEA HOW ANGRY I WAS? HOW ANGRY I STILL AM?

SO I WENT AWAY. WHEN GOD DESTROYED THE WORLD, HE OVERLOOKED SOMETHING ... THAT ONLY ONE WORLD AT A TIME CAN BE DESTROYED. HE WAS SO

BUSY PISSING ALL OVER THIS ONE, HE
DIDN'T EVEN NOTICE THAT I SLIPPED OVER
INTO ONE OF THE OTHER ONES, WHICH I
MADE MY KINGDOM. I'VE HAD TO START ALL
OVER FROM SCRATCH, GIL, BUT THINGS ARE
COMING ALONG NICELY.

SO NICELY, IN FACT, THAT I'M READY TO
ADD AN ADDITION, SO TO SPEAK.

AND I THINK YOUR WORLD WILL DO JUST
FINE.

OF COURSE, I'VE HAD TO HIRE SOME ... I
GUESS YOU'D CALL THEM MOVERS.

OR KEEPERS.

A ROSE BY ANY OTHER NAME, BLAH-BLAH-
BLAH.

I DON'T KNOW HOW LONG THIS WILL
TAKE, GIL—RAW MATERIAL BEING SO DIF-
FICULT TO COME BY—BUT THINGS ARE
WELL UNDER WAY. THE TEAR IN THE GREAT
SCRIM IS GETTING WIDER EVERY DAY. NICE
TO KNOW I STILL HAVE A FEW TRICKS UP
MY SLEEVE IN THE MEANTIME.

WHICH REMINDS ME—YOU MIGHT WANT
TO SAY GOOD-BYE TO YOUR "NEPHEW" NOW.

Carson dropped the comic book.

He was shuddering; from the top of his head to
the bottoms of his feet, he was shuddering as if in
the grips of a grand-mal seizure.

"Jesus—*Carson! What's wrong?*"

I moved toward him but he screamed and waved
me back.

Outside the barn, I could hear the roaring of lions,

251

the trumpeting of elephants, the growling of bears, the barking of dogs, the screams of loons. The walls shook as the animals began pressing against them from outside, clawing at the wood.

In the back of the barn, a massive shadow moved as Carson's scale model of Long-Lost took its first few tentative steps.

Carson screamed again.

He collapsed to his knees as his face began tearing in half, he felt it—*I* felt it, felt every sensation chewing through his body and there was nothing I could do—felt the fire burning through his nose as he struggled to his feet and stumbled away from me, hoping that it was all over now, please let it be over, please let this be the last of it, but then his face began swelling around forehead and nose, swelling like a goddamn balloon, so he looked away, looked down at his hand and saw it pulsating through layers of dried mud, felt the cold thing crawling between his shoulders again, eyes twitching, and then his face split apart like someone tearing a biscuit in half, only there was no steam, just blood, spraying, spattering, *geysering* around, and he tried to look behind him and see the animals as they clawed against the walls of the barn, tried to see *me*, tried to see if UncGil was still there, but the pain was killing him because the cold thing shuddered down between his shoulders and began to push through, snapping his shoulder blades like they were thin pieces of bark, and he screamed, screamed and whirled and slammed himself into the wall trying to stop the pain, trying to stop the thing from getting out, but he stunned himself for a moment and slid down to the floor, leaving a wide, dark smear behind him, howling as the first thing sawed through his back and fluttered to life, he was on his hands and knees now, waiting, trying to breathe, breathe deep, and now, *OHGOD* now the second one was tearing through, making a sound like a plastic bag melting on a fire, pushing through, unfurling, and he could see them now because their span must have been at least fifteen feet, and he threw his head back to cry out, but he couldn't make any more human sounds, so he screamed, screamed so loud and long that his eyes bulged out and his face turned a dark blue and then his scream turned into the wail of an angry bird of prey as his body jerked back into a standing position, his arms locking bent, his hands clenching, every muscle in his body on fire; writhing, shifting, bones snapping, he shrieked in the cage of the barn as his chest puffed out through his shirt and covered in thick layers of brown feathers and the flesh dropped from his body like peelings from an orange and he tried to move his arms, tried to grab something, then he jerked around from the waist and his arms dropped off, brittle branches from a burned tree, and he yowled again, louder than before, wishing that the pain would end and just let him die, then he fell back on his great wings and looked up into my face, into my eyes, and for a moment I thought I heard his voice whispering, *I'm as much a part of you as you are of me*, and then something snapped below his waist; snapped, wriggled, pushed up.

With one last shriek he jerked back as the spasm took hold of him, pushing the corded claws up through his groin.

And I stood facing a huge brown marsh hawk that

stood nearly as tall as I did. It flexed its wings, then shook itself, spraying the walls with ribbons of meat and liquid that had once been my nephew.

I looked into its red marble eyes, then began backing toward the door.

The gigantic hawk that had once been my nephew stomped through the barn, its massive wings unfurling, making splinters out of the stall doors and rafters.

I turned and ran.

Outside, animals had gathered off to the side to watch.

Rhino, elephant, manticore, bear, gryphon, lion, centaur, cat, swan, and so many others I couldn't see their features.

They had no interest in me.

They were watching the barn behind me as its roof splintered outward.

I heard a roar, and a screech, and the vibrations of something very, very large working its limbs back into life.

I ran across the field, not looking back, cutting myself on tree branches when the light of the moon was obscured by massive wings.

Somehow, I made it to my car and managed to get back on the road without killing anyone.

It never once occurred to me to go anywhere else but home.

Above me, the shadows of giant wings seemed to guide my path.

Or watch to make certain I didn't try deviating from it.

III

The Valley of
Love and
Delight

ONE

I pulled up in front of my house, killed the engine, and ran inside, slamming the door closed behind me and locking it.

The sound of massive, pumping wings flew over the house. The force of the downdraft from them shattered a couple of windows.

I leaned against the door, shaking.

Jesus Christ, what now?

It wasn't long before I had the answer.

A pair of bright headlight beams cut a path through the darkness. I pulled back the curtain to see a large tan vehicle shaped like an old bread-delivery truck crawl past my house, its driver sweeping the street with a handheld searchlight. The truck came to a stop and the driver killed all lights. It took my vision a moment to adjust afterward—the light had shone directly in my face at one point—and by the time I could focus clearly the driver was out of the truck and looking in my yard. It was already dark so I wondered how he could see.

He adjusted a strap on something he'd just put on his face, then reached up and hit a switch between his eyes. It wasn't actually between his eyes, of course, but that's how it looked. I caught a flash of a small green light glowing where the bridge of his nose should be and realized that he'd just donned and activated a pair of night-vision goggles. I wondered if they were Starlight technology like the scopes soldiers used in Vietnam. I wondered how expensive they were and how Cedar Hill Animal Control could afford such high-tech gear.

An SUV came around the corner, its headlights shining on high, enabling me to both see the driver and read the name on the side of the truck.

Neither came as a surprise.

He was impeccably dressed, expensive suit, tie, bowler hat on his head.

The side of the truck read: KEEPERS.

Still, my legs began to buckle, my chest felt tight, and my heart once again tried to squirt through my ribs; my breath came up short as I pressed my back against the wall and slid to the floor, a hand over my mouth.

I held my breath, listening to his footsteps as Magritte-Man made his way up the walk, then to one side of the front porch before turning around and going back to his truck; I continued holding it until the sound of his engine faded into cricket-song and streetlight buzz. When I finally allowed myself to exhale, everything inside me became miasma and dissipated into the twilight.

—grabbing my shirt through the bars of the cage and

pulling me toward him, blood seeping into the cotton of
my shirt as I lifted the bowler and showed him that it was
undamaged, looking into my eyes, lips squirming in a
mockery of communication because his vocal cords had
been cut out long ago, sounds that were a burlesque of
language, but there was something there, something that
drew him to me or me to him, and he turned his head ever
so slightly to the right and pulled me closer to the bars—

—I shook my head and pulled away from the wall.
A thin layer of perspiration covered my face, neck,
chest, and hands; my arms were shaking, and for a
moment I feared I was going to vomit. This last, at
least, proved to be a false alarm.

Pressing a hand against the front door, I eased myself onto my sponge-like feet and dragged in a few
deep breaths to steady my nerves and my balance.
Grabbing my shirt through the bars of the cage? Where
the hell had *that* come from? I never get my memories mixed up in that way, one bleeding over into the
other until the seams couldn't be spotted.

(Are you sure about that one, pal?)

Christ.

Rubbing my eyes, I made my way into the downstairs guest bedroom before I even knew where I was
going or why. Ever notice how there are times when
your body's memory and will operate independ-
ently from your own? Synapses take a detour and
you're left wondering, *Why am I here? / Doing this? /*
Looking for . . . what?

I reached for the light switch but at the last moment my body's will took over again and wouldn't
let me turn it on. This room had to remain dark; I'd

have to rely on the light spilling in from the other room to see things.

I moved the bed several feet to the right, then yanked away the cheap throw-rug that lay underneath to reveal the area of flooring that had been torn up and then replaced with a 3 × 3 trapdoor—an addition the plumbers suggested in the event that the new pipes running underneath needed to be accessed during an emergency. A padlock held the door firmly closed. I retrieved my keys from their hook by the front door and flipped through until I found the one for the padlock, opened it, but did not pull up the door. Not yet.

Trying to look as casual as possible, I made my way through the downstairs, turning off a few more lights but not enough to slide everything into darkness; the light over the sink in the kitchen, the table lamp in the living room, and my desk lamp remained on. They would give me plenty of light for what I needed to do.

I went into the linen closet for the second time that day, pulling out all of the hand towels and wash rags on the top shelf, then reaching back and flopping my hand around until I felt the curved brass handle on a wooden box; pulling it out and setting it on the floor of the closet, I turned the dials on the combination lock until the lid popped up with a soft click. I hadn't opened this thing in years, hadn't really wanted to, but now I had to. My body's will commanded me.

The 7.65mm *Deutsche Werk* semiautomatic pistol looked just as it had when Mom gave it to me after Dad's funeral, along with his medals. He'd taken this gun from a dead SS officer in Austria near the end of World War Two. He'd kept it cleaned and oiled and had insisted on firing it at least once a year to make sure it was still in good working order. When I was much younger and still thought of guns as something powerful and romantically alien, Dad would sometimes let me fire it in the air at midnight on New Year's Eve. The gun was small but its recoil packed a wallop. Dad used to laugh every year when the thing'd knock me on my ass after I fired.

I jacked back the slide to make sure it was empty, then loaded the clip, chambered a round, set the safety, and shoved it into the back of my pants. (I've always hated movies where some guy shoves a gun into the front of his pants to hold it in place; sneeze, trip, or bump into something and it's hi-diddle-dee-dee, the eunuch's life for me. I hadn't been with a woman for a very long time, but it seemed a good idea to keep the package attached, just in case. It's the little fantasies that keep us going.)

From inside the lid of the box I removed the serrated SS dagger in its ankle-sheath and strapped it on. After double-checking to make sure it was securely in place, I reached under the closet's lower shelf, shoved aside a few mid-sized storage boxes, and pulled out the one weapon that hadn't come from my father: a Mossberg 500 pistol-grip, pump-action twelve-gauge shotgun. I took down the box of shells and fed it until it was full, then pumped a load into the chamber, stood up, and kicked the closet door closed behind me. I still wasn't sure why I felt compelled to arm myself like a road-company Robert

DeNiro in the penultimate reel of *Taxi Driver*, but my body told me I'd know soon enough.

A few moments later I was back at the front door, peering through the window.

Magritte-Man was back with at least two others of his ilk. The three of them stood, all bowlers and dapperness, on the sidewalk, night goggles at the ready. I stood up straight and looked right at them. I wasn't sure they'd seen me, so I waved at them.

Magritte-Man returned the gesture, but neither he nor the others made a move toward the house. At least there wouldn't have to be any sneaking around now, dim light or no.

They might—mark that—*might know about the crawl-space, but not the trapdoor.*

I started back toward the guest bedroom, moving the shotgun from one hand to the other and shaking each empty hand in turn because my fingers had gone numb.

Not you, I thought, hoping some small part of the universe would scatter the thought Magritte-Man's way. *She will not go with you.*

I will not allow that.

I will bury her here.

You won't get your hands on her, not you, not you, not you . . .

I'd kill all of us before I let that happen.

Two

I put the Mossberg on a small table just inside the guest bedroom and knelt to open the trapdoor. This was the first time I'd used it since having it installed, and I was surprised by the thin cloud of sawdust that blew into my face. Coughing, I waved the cloud away, blinked until my eyes were clear, and started to drop my legs into the opening.

Something outside slammed against the side of the house with enough force to shake the floor and cause the Mossberg to nearly fall off the edge of the table.

I scrambled to my feet, grabbing the shotgun as I ran toward the living room. Whatever slammed against the house had raised some dust of its own, because a dissipating smog of sandy debris was swirling against the window. It wasn't until I was just a foot or so away from the window that I realized it wasn't dust at all.

Crouching, I pulled back one side of the curtain to take a look.

It was a cavernous silver mist—so thick in places it was nearly impossible to make out the shape of Magritte-Man's truck in the street—that churned as if caught in a strong wind. But there *was* no wind. There hadn't even been any humidity. The old joke might say that if you don't like the weather in Ohio just wait a minute, and sometimes it sure seems that way, but barring any sort of significant meteorological aberration, no way in hell could a mist this heavy and wide-spread form in a matter of . . . I quickly played in reverse everything that had happened since I'd loaded the shotgun . . . *ninety seconds?*

I looked out the window again. At the rate this was going, the mist would turn into heavy fog in no time.

Ninety seconds.

Dropping the curtain back into place, I moved through the living room toward the back door. The mist couldn't be a natural phenomenon; yes, the weather here can make some extreme swings from time to time, but not like this, not a mist-bordering-on-fog that looks like it followed the tail of a major storm in summer, not in less than two minutes. So it stood to reason (didn't it?) that Magritte-Man and his droogies had to have created it. It had only been two minutes, so whatever they were using to generate the mist couldn't have worked up enough vapor to encircle the entire house—hell, even if they had more than one means of creating the mist (dry ice, a fog machine maybe?), there still hadn't been enough time.

(There you again, pal—trying to create logical reasons for stuff that you know damned well—)

Up yours.

I threw open the back door and stepped onto the porch, the Mossberg pointing out from my hip.

The mist formed a semi-solid wall that spread out to create a barrier around the yard and rose so far into the evening sky it was impossible to see where it ended and the October clouds began. I leaned over the porch railing to see just how far the barrier extended; at both the far left and right edges of the house it curved so sharply and so abruptly it actually formed corners before continuing.

It was surrounding the house.

I felt a damp chill and exhaled; my breath became silver vapor as soon as it hit the air and billowed in front of my face, faintly glowing. From deep inside, the mist shimmered with silver light—nothing bright or blinding, but enough to illuminate the yard and the outside of the house.

Moving down the steps I looked from side to side for some sign of the others. I caught a glimpse of one of them when a pair of thin red beams cast by their night goggles glided across the mist from about ten yards to my left. Mossberg at the ready, I ran toward the spot from which the beams had come; just as I hit the mist the handle-grip of the shotgun punched into my ribs, causing me to cry out as I tumbled backward from the force of the impact.

It took a few seconds for my torso to stop throbbing and the breath to find its way back into my lungs. What the fuck had I slammed into? Rolling onto my side, I picked up the Mossberg and checked to make sure the gun and knife were still in place, then got to my feet and looked around for who- or whatever had hit me. As far as I could tell, I was alone in the yard—whose boundaries were rapidly shrinking against the encroaching mist. In a few minutes it would be all the way up to the back porch.

I turned back toward the spot where I'd remembered seeing the beams and moved closer to it, slowly this time. I knew this was probably the wrong thing to do—after all, the back door was unlocked and stood wide open (*Why not just send out written invitations?* I thought)—but I had to let them know I wasn't going down without a fight.

I heard a dog bark from outside the barrier, another one howled in response, then the song of an unseen nightbird was answered by the yowls of a stray neighborhood cat.

The mist was playing with me; whenever I moved forward, it retreated, expanding the boundaries; if I moved back, it would advance, swallowing more of the yard. I did this three times, moving backward and forward to make sure I wasn't imagining it, and I wasn't; the mist moved in the opposite of my direction each time. Finally, I remained still, as did it.

Flexing the fingers of my left hand, I reached up; a small area of the barrier pulled away from the tips of my fingers. I folded my fingers into my palm and watched the area begin to fill in, and that's when I came up with my right hand still fisted around the shotgun's handle-grip and punched at it.

I heard the bones break well before the pain had a chance to register, but by then I was down on one knee and whimpering, my right hand cradled against my chest. As far as I could tell, I had broken my fourth and fifth metacarpals. A jagged, bloody scrape lay across the width of my hand, made thin and black in places by my swollen knuckles. *Jesus!* It had been like pummeling my fist against a slab of granite. I could still feel the vibration of the impact all the way up into my shoulder and neck.

Struggling to my feet, I grabbed the Mossberg with my left hand because my right was useless for the moment. The mist remained stationary, churning, forming surreal shapes.

I wondered if my neighbors had noticed what was surrounding my house. Were any of them watching right now, their curiosity piqued, or was this mist engulfing the entire block? It had to have occurred to at least *one* person that this wasn't normal, right? (Assuming that black mastiffs hadn't been disassembling people around here, as well.)

This was Cedar Hill, and in Cedar Hill if anything not normal or even mildly interesting happens, well, then, you call the police or the trusty news team at Channel 7 and get a mobile unit right over. If they'd dispatch a crew to cover the opening of a new electronics store one county away, they'd sure as hell send someone to a local neighborhood to cover the appearance of an intensely localized weather anomaly.

Never count on the help of others when you most need it. Take my word on this. I wasn't about to assume that any of my neighbors had called or were *going* to call anyone to report this. So I did the only thing I knew for a fact would get someone on the phone to the news or police; I rose to my feet, lifted the Mossberg over my head using only my left hand, pointed it into the air, and fired.

The force of the blast wrenched my left arm backward and tore the handle-grip from my grasp. The shotgun flew back and landed in the grass about five feet away; I half-spun around, my shoulder screaming, nearly losing my balance. Almost none of this had to do with the physical effects of firing the weapon—some of it, yes, you can't fire a scattergun with only one hand and not get jolted down to your marrow—but more than anything, it was the *sound* of the shot.

Under the best and most controlled of circumstances a gunshot is deafening, but it seemed as if this one had gone off in the center of my skull; it hadn't just been a noise or an explosion—it was a pulverizing force that ripped the air from inside me and jammed an invisible ice pick into each side of my head. I stumbled around in half-circles pressing my hands against my ears (I had done this before, I *knew* that I had held my ears like this before, that there had been pain and panic then, as well . . . but where and when and *why?*) while stomping my feet and working my jaw in order to create some kind of pressure and *please God* make one or both of my ears pop—but nothing helped. At one point the pain and weight became so great I thought I was going to pass out, then a soft hiss began to issue from the base of my brainpan, someone letting the air out of a bicycle tire, and I pulled my hands away and felt the cool air enter my ears with a soft *whoosh*. I shook my head once, then twice to see if I could jar anything into functioning, but there was only a thick, gluey numbness; I didn't hear so much as *feel* the hissing, which was rapidly giving way to a deep, disturbing thrum. I blinked, turned slowly around, saw the shotgun lying in the grass, and made a beeline for the thing. It was vital I have something to focus on besides the disorienting pressure in my head, and the Mossberg would do just fine. Looking up to where the mist met the clouds, I prayed that the blast hadn't blown out my eardrums and rendered me permanently deaf. I shook my head once more as I swung down and grabbed the shotgun with my good hand, and as I returned to a fully upright position there was hiss and a buzz and a pop and something that sounded like a sheet being torn into shreds by a pair of teeth, then a moment of nauseating dizziness and then . . . sound. I could at least discern (if not actually *hear*) sound again. Not much, just the echo of a dog's bark coming from somewhere deep under the Atlantic Ocean, but it was there, and I could recognize it, and that meant that the damage wasn't (*thank you thank you thank you*) permanent. Despite the circumstances, I smiled as I made my way up the back steps and into the kitchen. It was only as I was locking the door and shoving the kitchen table up against it that I allowed myself to acknowledge what I hadn't wanted to admit while out there: the noise and force of the blast had been so fantastically intensified—so brutally magnified—because they had been contained.

The mist wasn't just surrounding the house, it was *encasing* it.

I thought, This must be how a pheasant under glass feels.

Then a remembered voice: *You might say they're not from around here.* But who'd said that, and when? Where? Like with holding my ears, I *should have* known, but . . .

(You're getting awfully close to not leaving me with any choice here, pal.)

I looked out the window over the sink. The mist roiled forward, stopping only a few feet from the bottom step of the back porch. Two thin red beams danced across a part of the wall, then one of Magritte-Man's cronies stepped through and simply stood there. The glow from his night goggles made him look almost comical. He gave a quick nod of his head to affirm that he could see me. I flipped him the bird with my right middle finger and immediately shrieked from the pain. I had to do something about my broken hand and I had to do it now or I didn't stand a chance. Bowler (I now chose to think of him and the others by this name) waved a hand to get my attention, then made an odd gesture. I stared at him, shook my head, and he repeated the gesture, albeit a bit more exaggeratedly.

The front of the house.

He was telling me I should go look at something in front of the house.

Fuck you, Bowler, I thought. *I'll go take a look when I'm damned good and ready.*

I stumbled into the bathroom and threw open the door on the upright cabinet where I keep all breed of crap—extension cords, old lighters, duct tape, loose tools, lighter fluid, a little of this and a lot more of that . . . and medical supplies. I removed everything I would need: bandages—both the elastic and gauze variety—as well as gauze pads, medical tape, hydrogen peroxide, and a couple of old finger-splints I'd hung on to after getting my left hand caught in a car door about a year ago. I laid out everything on the sink's counter and took a deep breath.

Do it now, before you turn chickenshit.

I gripped the broken fingers with my left hand, released the breath I'd been holding, clenched my teeth, then simultaneously pressed down and pulled out.

The *snap!* made by the bones as they popped back into place seemed even louder than the shotgun blast; the pain shot up my arm right and hammered directly between my eyes. I dropped to one knee, grabbing the edge of the sink with my left hand to keep from hitting the floor, and tried to hold in the scream.

From under the house, the dog howled as if she'd felt it, as well.

"I'm st-still here, g-girl," I whispered, trying to pull myself up. I was hit by a wave of pain, dizziness, and nausea, and fell to the floor.

(You're not going anywhere for a minute or two, pal, so now it's my turn.)

I couldn't fight him; not now.

Hell, I could barely move.

(You left the house right after you found Mabel's body, remember?)

If you say so.

(You figured Beth had taken the rest of the Its to the Keepers' facility.)

271

That sounds about right, sure.

(So that's where you went.)

Whatever.

(This ringing any bells yet?)

If it was, do you think I'd admit it to you?

(Fine, we'll do it the hard way, then.

Even though it was cooler than usual, the humidity was high that night, and every street you

THREE

drove along was alive with a thin layer of mist that skirled across the beams of your headlights. You were driving through a sea of cotton. A deer darted across the road at one point, followed a few seconds later by two rabbits. Whichever road or street you took, there was always some kind of animal in your peripheral vision; a dog, a cat, a raccoon moving through the bushes and shadows on the curb.

The facility was harder to find at night; the road wasn't lit at all, and the moon was hiding behind thick stationary clouds as if it were afraid or ashamed to allow its light to reveal too much.

You passed the building and had to turn around. You killed your headlights before turning up the asphalt drive, then pulled over into the shadows. You were going to have to walk the rest of the way.

Have you ever in your life been so anxiously aware of the silences in the night or the sound of your own breathing? Creeping up the drive like some thief casing a target house and nearly jumping out of your skin when a skunk waddled across the drive on its way from one patch of trees to the other. The area around the building was lighted by a sole sodium-vapor light at the edge of the visitors' parking lot. You spotted Beth's U-boat parked at the farthest end. On the other side of the building, Keepers' vans formed the long, segmented shadow-shape of a giant serpent in slumber.

You started toward the entrance doors when another car turned onto the driveway. Because you were still covered in Mabel's blood (oddly enough, cleaning up before leaving the house never entered your mind), the last thing you needed was to be seen like this. You leapt aside, cowering behind a trash Dumpster as the new-looking Mercedes drove up and parked in front of the entrance.

A man and a woman got out and opened the back doors. The man removed and unfolded a wheelchair while his wife helped a much older and frail-looking woman out of the backseat; once she was situated in the chair, the man reached into the car, removed a pet carrier, and the three of them went inside.

As soon as they were through the doors you ran across the lot toward the U-boat to see if Beth and the remaining Its were still there. Maybe she'd gotten here, parked, then froze as the shock of Mabel's suicide finally hit. You'd find her sitting there, hands gripping the steering wheel so tightly their knuckles would be white.

It was empty.

You took a deep breath and tried unsuccessfully to steady your shaking hands. You thought about the day everyone had piled into the car and brought the other Its out here, the way Whitey had gotten so emotional about the leaving women, how Mabel walked through the selection area in a semi-catatonic daze, and the way you'd found Beth coming out of the room behind the large steel door.

Remember how you suddenly wished that you smoked? A cigarette would've helped right then, the feel of it between your fingers, the aroma of the tobacco as it was ignited by the flame, the first deep inhalation . . . oh, yeah. That would have been nice. Mom liked to smoke. Dad preferred a pipe. You missed them terribly. You missed Whitey and Beth and Mabel, missed the world you'd once known and had taken for granted.

You heard car doors slam, and then you slunk over to the front of the building in time to see the Mercedes' taillights receding; the driver didn't even signal or slow as the car reached the road, he just tore out of there with a squeal of tires and burst of exhaust and a sudden, violent leftward skid that he quickly corrected before gunning the engine and speeding away.

Wiping blood and perspiration from your face, you took another deep breath and stepped inside.

An old cat sat in one of the top cages; it was the only animal here, and you were the only person. You stared at the cat and it, in turn, showed its interest in you by yawning.

You knew this animal—*recognized* it, anyway—but couldn't place it. It wasn't one of the Its but, still . . . where had you seen this disenchanted arthritic bundle of fur and teeth before?

The selection area was dark and closed off by a collapsible, barred security door.

That left only the large steel door on the right.

You peered through its window but could see nothing, then realized this was intentional, that a person could only see through from the other side. You reached down and grabbed the handle. It never occurred to you that this door might be locked; if that *had* been the case, you might be a much different and happier man now, but it was unlocked and swung open with only a minimum of effort and besides, pal, I'm not doing this to play "What-If?" with you.

The cold draft from behind the door seemed less severe than before, but that was probably because the night itself was cooler and so the contrast in temperatures wasn't as drastic.

You stood there pondering meteorological conundrums for a few more seconds, anything to not step in and hear that door clunk shut. If you'd followed baseball, you might have reviewed stats for the season. You could have counted the freckles on the back of your hand. Or recited all the lyrics to "American Pie" until the Chevy reached the levy only to find it dry.

"Do it, you fucking coward," you whispered to yourself.

Three seconds later you stood on the other side listening to the door clunk shut behind you. The sound reverberated with the same cold, metallic finality a lifer must hear every night when the prison bars electronically screech into their magnetized locks.

Once the door has been closed, the animal cannot be retrieved from outside.

You were in a dim corridor whose sides were delineated by a string of ankle-level safety lights that stretched its entire length, then bent around a corner roughly a hundred feet away. The walls on either side were vaguely familiar. You could easily see the boards that had been used as forms for the concrete because several of them had warped before the concrete had set properly; they looked like ghosts trapped in the walls, stuck forever between this world and the one they came from and now wished they had never tried to leave.

Remember where you saw this before? That afternoon in the sub-basement of the hospital? On your way to the Keepers' lab? Of course you don't—or *won't*. If you did, then I wouldn't be pestering you with all this, would I?

It doesn't matter. Here you are, in the facility, and you have to find Beth. She was in here somewhere, she *had* to be, there was nowhere else she could have gone, so you followed the lights until you turned a corner and slammed your shin against something left haphazardly in the middle of the floor.

A wheelchair.

Bending over to rub your leg, you saw the bright bumper sticker attached to the back of the chair: I ACCELERATE FOR FUZZY BUNNIES.

Then you thought of *The Waltons* with the sound muted, of a handmade quilt neatly folded at the foot of a bed, of a book of poetry and some lines from Browning and faded photographs on a wall and—

—and knew now why you'd recognized the cat.

You wondered if Miss Acceleration's file was one of those lying on the floor beside Mabel's bed, and if Whitey's was among them, as well.

The dial clicked, another set of tumblers fell into place, and you moved on.

The air back here was slightly warmer but much more damp and smelled of a farm: wet straw, urine and feces, moist fur . . . But there were other, more disparate smells mixed among them: freshly laundered sheets, antiseptics, talcum or baby powder (you never could tell the difference between the two, could you?), and an eye-watering assortment of medicinal odors—cough syrup, rubbing alcohol, iodine, Mercurochrome, gauze and bandages. What was it you assumed then? That this was the area used for ministering to animals who were ill or hurt at the time they were dropped off.

Except there were no animal sounds; no dogs barking, no cats hissing, no birds chirping or pigs snorting, nothing. Even this late at night there should have been a *few* animals awake and making their discomfort or hunger known, but the only sounds were the hum of a hidden generator, the steady exhalation of the air-conditioning, and your own footsteps. You were so anxious about the silence you failed to notice the metal lip rising out of the floor ahead and tripped on the damn thing.

Stepping up and grabbing the rail to regain your balance, you discovered that this section of floor was raised and covered in a long strip of rubber tread. The railing extended the rest of its length on both sides; an automated walkway, one of those moving sidewalks used at malls and airports. To the left was a large red button with which to activate the motor.

You chose to move under your own power; the

lack of noise might be disturbing, but at least it wouldn't betray your presence.

As soon as you took your first step a light blinked on to the right and a dog leapt at you. Crying out, you jumped to the other side of the walkway, lost your balance, and landed on your knees. Crossing your arms in front of your face, you took a deep breath and readied yourself for the thing to sink its teeth into your arm.

But nothing happened.

You looked up and saw that the light was from a 12-inch television screen—the dog was nothing more than an image from a home movie.

Screens activated by your weight on the tread lined the walls on both sides of the walkway, displaying videos and photographs of dogs, cats, birds, horses, and countless other animals, all of the images underscored by soft music piped through unseen speakers: it took a moment, but you at last recognized the music as Aaron Copland's *Appalachian Spring Suite*.

You stood up and continued moving down the walkway, looking from one side to the other as the show continued.

Each video or photo of an animal was displayed for perhaps ten seconds before cross-fading into a video or photograph of a person, then the person's image cross-faded into a photo or tape of someone else, and this someone else cross-faded into another animal. Once the sequence played through, the screen went black and the words "To Be Loved" appeared before everything started again. The screens on the left ran through a similar sequence, only this began with a person, went to an animal, then another animal before coming back to a person, ending with the words "To Have a Place."

You came to the end of the walkway and stepped down to the floor.

Before you was a set of large swinging metal doors. Over the entrance was a bronze plaque with the words "THERE IS A REASON IN NATURE FOR SOMETHING TO EXIST RATHER THAN NOT." You stared at the words for a few moments before pushing open the doors to reveal a long hallway with more concrete walls, lighted intermittently with bare bulbs cradled in bell-shaped cages of wire dangling from the ceiling. This, too, was known to you (from the hospital's sub-basement), but you couldn't place it just then. But that's okay—you've got me for that, pal.

Back here the smell of a farmyard was just as potent, but stronger still were scents distinctly, unmistakably human: sweat and strong body odor unsuccessfully masked by perfumes and aftershaves.

Aware of barred doors on either side up ahead, you moved forward and caught a glimpse of a framed painting hanging on the wall to my right: René Magritte's *The Son of Man*. Written on a square placard underneath it were the words "To BE HUMAN." On the wall across from it hung an almost exact duplicate of the painting, only this time instead of an apple there was a dove in front of the man's face, and a small light trained on it from above highlighted the dove; the placard underneath this had a simple one-word statement on it: "OR?"

You could still hear the richness of Copland's masterpiece through unseen speakers; the sound quality grew clearer and fuller the farther you moved down the corridor.

On the left was a large cage with an ox standing inside. It was skin and bones and covered in whip scars, some of them so fresh they were still seeping. Its eyes were a milky red and its lolling tongue was yellow. It stood on trembling legs streaked with dried liquid shit that had squittered from its diseased bowels, not making a sound, turning its head toward you as if asking for help. Its scalp had been peeled away to reveal the skull underneath, a series of red "Xs" decorating the surface.

Something large, wide, and unpleasant-smelling lay sleeping in the shadows of the cage across from the ox. You began stepping over to see if you could get a better look at it, then decided you didn't want to know.

Each cage was separated from its neighbor by about two feet of wall space, and in the center of that space was another 12-inch monitor displaying the same bizarre series of home movies you'd seen in the corridor. You wondered why caged animals would want to watch home movies. Did whoever designed this area think the animals would understand what they were seeing?

The next cage—cell, cubby, whatever, like it makes a difference—was empty, but the one directly across from it was occupied by Miss Acceleration.

The sight of her in that cage hit the "pause" button on your entire somatic nervous system; you couldn't have moved at that moment if someone had been emptying an AK-47 at your head.

The monitor next to her cage showed the image of a dog jumping around for no other reason than it was happy to be outside in the sunshine.

She was sitting in well-stuffed leather easy chair with her handmade quilt spread across her lap and covering her legs. She held a small book in her hands and was gently rocking herself forward and back, forward and back, forward and back, her faced pinched with intense concentration, as if remaining still would bring some terrible curse from Heaven down upon her head. The framed photographs from her room at the nursing home decorated the wall behind her.

You gripped the bars and tried to open the door but it seemed welded in place.

Once the door has been closed, the animal cannot be retrieved from outside.

She looked up at you, smiled, and said: "It's all right. Everything's all right now. Yes." Forward and back, forward and back.

You swallowed once, very loudly, and then asked: "Do you know where you are?"

"I'm home," she said, her voice cracking on the second word as if it were the most beautiful thing she'd ever spoken. "I mean, I'll be going there soon."

You started to speak again, but then remembered the new security measures at the nursing home. Were you being watched? Were you on camera this moment? Just because you couldn't see any cameras didn't mean they weren't there; and if there were cameras, there were microphones, as well.

But if you were being watched, if they knew you were trespassing, why hadn't any of them shown up to stop you?

"Listen," you said to Miss Acceleration, "I've got to find somebody, and as soon as I do, we're going to get you out of here. Do you understand?"

"Is it time for my programs yet? I do so hate to miss them." Forward and back, forward and back, staring at me. "Are you my son?"

"No."

"Are you sure? You look an awful lot like him."

"I'm sure."

"It doesn't matter. Everything's all right now. I'll be there soon." And with that, she closed her eyes and continued rocking.

If you saw her out in the world she would have been just another old woman, the type who usually holds up the line in a grocery store, or is waiting for a bus that's always running late and so wants to strike up a conversation in the meantime; one of those meticulous old gals who knows and cares about the exact type of gift you're supposed to give on a particular anniversary, who has so many interesting stories to tell but no one to listen to them because you don't want to bother with a dry, old, used-up little bit of carbon whose hands are arthritic claws covered in liver spots and grotesque, plump purple veins; you would have looked at her and seen only another humorously annoying old woman counting out exact change as if it were a holy chore assigned to her from above. And you wouldn't have stopped to think that underneath this monumental punchline of dying cells, wrinkled skin, and fading memories there existed someone who'd always been, but now was rarely seen as, a real human being; one with hurts and hopes and lonely places in their life they filled as best they could by standing in the line at the grocery store, or chatting with strangers at bus stops, or endlessly bending the driver's ear while counting out exact change. You would never see her as ever having been in love, or dancing with her favorite beau to music from the Glenn Miller Orchestra, young and vibrant, with a laugh that rang like crystal and a long, promising, full life ahead of her. You would never wonder or care if she often cried alone at night, or how many times she'd offered her heart only to have it crushed and spat upon, or if her children remembered to call her on the weekend or visit at Christmas. Maybe there was a Great Love who lay slumbering in some graveyard and she was the only person who took the time to replace the wilting flowers with fresh blossoms—you might have imagined that, maybe, and then smiled at the sad, sentimental absurdity of this image from a fairy tale: *There once was an old woman who lived in the past where someday all of us will be.*

At that moment you wanted to know everything about her and her life, every detail no matter how extraneous or trivial. You did not want to walk away from her because she might be gone when you came back; they collected them fast around here.

A sound a few yards away startled you and you looked in its direction.

Someone had coughed.

"Don't worry," you said to Miss Acceleration. "I'll come back for you. I promise."

She continued chatting as you walked away: "I think a bunny would be nice, don't you? A big, round, fluffy gray bunny with great floppy ears. Yes, I think a bunny would be *so* nice. . . ."

You blinked back something in your eyes, swallowed against something vile roiling up from your stomach into the back of your throat, wiped some more blood from your hands onto the sides of your pants, and found the next occupied cage.

Behind these bars a little boy with massive facial deformities lay on a cot, his lower body covered by a sheet. From the ceiling there extended down a pencil-thick cable that spread out at the bottom like the wires inside an umbrella, each one attached to one of the matchbox-sized rectangles implanted in his skull. The skin of his exposed scalp was crusty and red where it fused with the metal. He jerked underneath the sheet as if in the midst of a seizure, arms and legs twitching as the silver matchboxes sparked and faded in a precisely-timed sequence. His eyes were held closed by two heavy strips of medical tape and fresh, glistening stitches formed a "W" across his face from temples to cheeks, meeting above the bridge of his nose. A clear plastic tube ran from one of his nostrils into a large glass jar set on a metal table beside the cot; with each jerk, dark viscous liquid crawled through the tube and oozed into the jar. With each sequence of sparks he bit down hard on his lower lip, breaking the skin and dribbling blood down the side of his face. His skin was red and glistened with sweat and every time he convulsed, he jerked back his head to expose the pinkish-white scar across his neck.

 . . . *when there are this many, they cut out their vocal cords . . .*

285

You kept moving; movement was good, movement reinforced the illusion of an assured destination and a guaranteed way out once you reached it, and you needed to believe that you were going to get out of this.

You passed beaten, bandaged dogs of every shape and size, kittens and cats who had been kicked nearly into pulp or whose fur had been doused in gasoline and set aflame; they lay very still, taking shallow breaths as tubes fed them both oxygen and liquid protein.

The monitors in the wall showed happy pictures, happy families with their happy pets having happy times.

A deep aluminum bathtub sat in the center of the next cage. The steady *drip-drip-drip* of water from the faucet echoed like faraway gunshots. Something splashed around, pounded one reverberating boom of thunder against the side, then rose partway above the lip; it was a woman—or had been, once—with red hair, mottled and discolored skin, and a neck that had been slashed several times in different places with a straight-edge razor; she looked at you through bulbous piscine eyes and brushed a wet strand of hair from her forehead. Then the slashes on her neck opened moistly, blowing air bubbles before contracting again.

Gills. She had gills.

You made some kind of a sound, soft and pitiful and child-like, that crawled out of your throat as if it were afraid of the light, and then you backed away, hands pushed out as if holding closed some invisible door.

Your legs felt weighted down by iron boots. You did not so much walk as shuffle along, periodically looking down at the floor to make sure the earth wasn't about to split open and swallow you.

Next was a teenaged boy with dozens of membranous man-of-war tentacles slobbering out all over his body in phosphorescent clusters; in the cage beside him was a shaven goat whose front legs were far too thick and ended in a clump of five toes; across from the goat was a plump Down's syndrome girl of uncertain age with a jutting facial cleft whose body was sprouting thick green feathers; in the cage beside her, a bear was grooming its fur not with claws but a model's thin, creamy-skinned, delicate hands; then came a little boy with an impossibly thin neck who smoothly rotated his head so his too-long and thin tongue could snap at the midges swarming around the light; and, finally, a middle-aged woman who might have once been pretty, before the split lip, broken nose, and two black eyes: she squatted on sludgy, misshapen legs that bent outward at incomprehensible angles. Most of her weight seemed to rest on her gelatinous, flat webbed feet. She looked at you first with confusion, then longing, and, at last, a resigned sort of pity.

You staggered backward, pressing yourself against the bars of the cage behind you in order to keep from collapsing to the floor. You closed your eyes, shuddering, then looked farther down the corridor to where a curved brass railing disappeared into a stairway under the floor.

"You *don't* want to go down there. Trust me when I say this to you."

Gary A. Braunbeck

You spun around and saw him standing—
standing!—in the middle of the cage, half-hidden in
shadows. You could see his face, part of his exposed
chest, and a moist, leathery-looking towel wrapped
around his waist. You'd never seen him fully upright
before; he seemed so tall.

"Whitey!"

"Captain Spaulding," he replied. "Decided to do
some more exploring, did you? Hooray-hooray-
hooray."

You gripped the bars. "Jesus Christ, Whitey, what
the hell is this place?"

"Be it ever so humble, there's no place—goodness
gracious me, what a mess you are. Been waltzing
with fresh carcasses through a slaughterhouse? I
trust it was a Strauss—one should never waltz to
anything but." He blinked, then made a disapproving *tsk-tsk*. "You are not at all presentable, dear
boy—not that you were a breathtaking heartthrob to
begin with, but the importance of good grooming
and careful hygiene cannot be overrated. Soap and
water are our *friends*. You may quote me on that."

"Whitey, for chrissakes! *What is this place?*"

"Hark—what's this I see? My goodness, the pro-
gramming schedule around here never gets boring,
I'll give 'em that. You ought to take a look at the
screen there, Captain. Required viewing."

The scene on the monitor changed from the home
movies of before to a close-up of an asphalt alley
floor. The camera seemed to be hand-held because
the image jerked and shook but, after a moment,
things settled down and the camera did a slow turn
to the right. The face of a border collie filled the

screen. The silver tag hanging from its collar caught a glint of sunlight and threw a bright spot into the lens, but then the camera turned forward once more, catching a fast glimpse of the top of a cat's head, tilted upward a few degrees, and focused on something in the distance.

It took a second for you to realize what you were looking at.

A man with his back to the camera was running down the alley toward another man who looked as if he were doubled over in pain or looking for something because he was kneeling. Then the running man pulled back his leg, did a half-pirouette, and kicked the kneeling man in the ribs.

You stood there outside Whitey's cage and watched a film of yourself attacking Drop-Kick that afternoon after Dad's funeral.

"Didn't think you had it in you to do a Bruce Lee like that," said Whitey. "You have good form, by the way."

The scene had been filmed from two different angles, one from each end of the alley. What struck you as odd about it—aside from its existing in the first place—was the angle from which it had all been filmed; it was very low to the ground, as if the camera operator had been lying on their stomach so as to—

—*no*.

You remembered how the face of the collie had filled the screen. You remembered how the animals had sat so unnaturally still that afternoon. How the sunlight glittered off the tags hanging from some of their collars.

This had been filmed with the cameras held at about collar height.

"Technology's a wonderful thing, isn't it?" said Whitey. "A camera no bigger than a tag on a collar. Been around for a while, from what I hear. I mean, just look at *that*."

The alley scene was gone, but the camera remained just as jerky as it had been before. A shadow passed over the lens, leaving a smear in its trail. This kept happening for several seconds until, at last, the blurry image of a face could be seen forming. The face bounced up and down, as if it were looking down into the lens of the camera it was carrying while trying to clean something off the lens and—

—"Oh, *no*," you said.

Your thumb passed over the lens one more time and you then were looking into the face of your fifteen-year-old self. You were crying like a baby, lips moving, forming words that could not be heard but you didn't need to hear them, you knew damn well what you'd said to that poor cat as you stood there by the trash cans in back of Beckman's Market.

The image of your bawling face was very clear, indeed; you'd wiped more blood from the tag on its collar than you'd thought.

You shook your head. "I never was able to make out its name."

The image faded back into the home movies of before.

"You got a good heart, Captain," said Whitey. "That counts for something in the end. Or so goes the rumor." He jerked his head down and to the left once, twice, three times, then made a chuffing sound as he kicked at the thick layer of straw covering most of the floor. "They've been aware of you for a long time now, Captain. They're very good at keeping track of folks who interest them.

"To answer your question about what this place is: It's sort of their version of Ellis Island—and don't ask me—" He chuffed once again, shaking his head. "—who 'they' are because you have to know at this point and, besides, a pro never wastes time repeating a gag that everyone in the peanut gallery has heard a dozen times. But I digress. Do me a favor— there's a bag hanging on the wall to your right. Be a splendid fellow and get it for me, will you?"

You grabbed the canvas pouch by its strap and lifted it from the hook on the wall. "Who are they, Whitey?"

He laughed. "You might say they're not from around here."

You held the pouch through the bars. It must have weighed ten pounds. "What *is* this?"

"Dinner," he said, moving forward into the light.

His arms were gone, that was the first thing that registered; in their place were two large clumps of ugly knotted scar tissue that protruded from his shoulders like the padding under a vaudevillian's oversized coat.

Then you acknowledged the whole of him and went numb. All you could hear was the blood surging through your temples and the echo of Whitey's voice from another time, another world.

I love horses. Hope to be one in my next life.

He was almost halfway there.

His head had been shaved except for a hand-sized,

Gary A. Braunbeck

Mohawk-like patch directly in the middle; the rest of his exposed, scabrous scalp was implanted with the same silver matchboxes you'd seen on the others, only these weren't hooked up to any electrical wires dangling from the ceiling. His now-massive torso was lacquered in thousands of short brittle hairs that grew more dense as they neared his waist. His neck was twice as long and twice as thick as it should have been, glistening with sweat and frothy streaks of lathered mucus.

Before you could snap out of your stupor, Whitey cantered forward, dipped down, craned his neck, and slipped the handle of the pouch around the back of his head, all the time singing the words to the *Mr. Ed* theme.

"Oh, a horse is a horse, of course of course . . ."

From somewhere nearby a low, thrumming groan began to take form, rolling across the floor, slowly growing in volume and power.

"Nothing like room service," said Whitey, then shoved his face deep into the pouch and spun around as the thrum grew louder and stronger.

The heavy white mane flowed from the center of his head all the way down his dense, ashen, solid back. His spine was thick as a forearm; with every move its powerful muscles stretched and quaked and rippled. His gaskins and hocks were mostly concealed by the leather towel—which wasn't a towel at all but something organic, something sentient, a living mass that pulsed and breathed as it made itself a part of his flesh—but the rest of his legs were clearly visible; the hard cannons, the steel-like tendons, the pasterns and fetlocks and, worst of all, the burnished, astonishing, impossible hooves. Moving in stops and starts as he fed, hooves scraping through the straw and clopping loudly against the cement floor, his mane fanning out like a column of bleached flames, Whitey continued to shake his head and chuff.

"*. . . an no one can talk to a horse, of course . . .*"

The thrum whip-cracked like the snap of a bone and became an eruption, bouncing off the walls, resonating up and down the corridor, spiraling overhead, within and without, a ripped-raw, berserk, frenzied, lunatic siren of a sound with enough power behind it to throttle you to the floor, legs scrabbling to push yourself backward, far back, away from the harrowing shriek, and you began to cover your ears but each time the sound tripled in volume and force, there was no stopping it, no blocking it out, it engulfed everything but you couldn't think of anything else to do so you ground the heels of your hands against your ears and held them there, throwing yourself totally into the rattling cacophony as something shredded deep in your throat and you realized the sound was even closer than before because it was coming out of you, had been coming from you this whole time, but you didn't care, couldn't move, and wouldn't stop screaming, screaming, screaming.

Whitey pulled his face from the bag and clopped forward to kick a hoof against the bars.

"*Will* you stop that irksome racket? Stop it right now! *Stop it!*"

You pressed the knuckles of your fist into your mouth and bit down, choking off the noise; whether the blood you tasted was your own or Mabel's, you couldn't tell.

"That's better," said Whitey, cantering around the cage. "Hysterics are so unbecoming. Downright distasteful, if you ask me. I personally feel diminished by your behavior and think you should"—he shook his head and chuffed, spraying gummy globs of oat-flaked spit—"apologize at once."

You pulled your fist away and whispered, "I'm sorry."

"You damned well ought to be. Is that any way to behave when you visit a sick friend? I think not. Sincerely."

"Please, *please* tell me what's happening."

"No begging, if you please. Hey—would you like to see a trick? Ask me what two plus two equals, go on—oh, never mind, you're a terrible audience. I'll do it myself." He cleared his throat and said, "Whitey Weis, the renowned Double-Dubya, here's your question—quiet in the studio, please. For a handful of sugar cubes, tell us . . . What's two plus two?" He extended his left leg and scraped his hoof against the cement four times. "Listen to that applause, folks, isn't he amazing?" He trotted forward, pressing his face against the bars and looking down at you. "Did you like that? Please say you did, it's my best one."

You could only nod your head.

If the heart makes no sound when it shatters, then the mind is even quieter when it begins to collapse.

Whitey's head jerked down and to the right once, twice, three times; he held it like that for a moment, then a shudder ran down his sides and he stamped a hoof down against the floor; when he turned his face toward you again his eyes were still and his expression pensive. "Look at me, kiddo."

"What?"

"Watch that tone. Mind telling me why you had to come here?"

You pulled in a ragged, snot-filled breath and wiped your eyes. "I'm trying to find Beth."

"Your fair lady-love? Stands about yea-high with one of the ten greatest smiles in the history of history itself? The gal you've been in love with your whole life but who doesn't really share your feelings? Or if she does, she's too scared to act on them. *That* Beth?

"She was here earlier. She told me about Mabel, the poor old girl. Not that you'll understand or even believe me, but I wept when I heard the news. Mabel was one of the good ones, and there are so very few of them left in the world as the days go by."

You stumbled to your feet. "Where did she go?" You pointed to the right. "Did she go down there? Down those stairs? Is that why I can't find her?"

Whitey stretched one leg forward, bent the other back at the knee, and leaned low. "If I say 'yes,' you're going to *go down there*, aren't you?" He shook his head in the slight, subtle, human manner, then gave a disapproving whistle. "I don't know, kiddo. I was serious when I said you don't want to do that. You have to be pretty desperate to get *this* far, but down there ... once you hit the bottom of those stairs, there's no coming back as you once were."

You slammed a fist against the bars. *"Goddammit,* Whitey! For once in your miserable life would you give someone a straight answer?"

He smiled at "miserable," then bent even closer. "How very interesting that you chose that word. Tell me: do you have any idea what it's like to be one of the forgotten, the discarded, the unloved or the damaged? Can you even for a second imagine how it feels to reach a point in your life where the only promise a new day brings is one of more loneliness? And don't you *dare* piss and moan to me about the pain of puberty or adolescent angst—those are *hangnails* compared to what I'm talking about.

"Think about this: a child is born retarded or deformed and knows only the mockery of other children and the embarrassment of its parents; a woman who's worked for years, worked without complaint or much thought for herself, who's struggled and sacrificed to build a good home for her family in the hopes they'll love her as much as she loves them, this woman is rewarded with what?—the disrespect of her children and bruises inflicted on her by a husband whose own life hasn't gone exactly as he'd planned, so he has to take his aggravation out on *someone*. Do you think that makes her feel like her life's labors have been worthwhile?

"Consider people like you, people who grew up in this town, people in their twenties and thirties who were born into this best of all possible worlds to find only poverty, abuse, or sickness waiting to greet them; they grow up afraid, cold, hungry, full of resentment and despair because from the moment of their first breath everything was already ruined for them—what reason do they have to hope for anything? They wander around with no real sense of purpose, going from job to job, place to place, person to person, nothing and no one lasting for very long, so once again they're left with only their thoughts and a gnawing emptiness and a heart that was born broken. Where can they go to feel wanted?

"And then there are the old farts like me, bone-bags who eventually become a burden to their families and a joke of what they once were or dreamed they'd become. We are asked to pack the whole of our life's remaining acquisitions into a single bag or box, along with a dusty photo album or two, then are driven to a colorless room and left to sit and stare at a television that gets lousy reception, or old pictures on the wall that some bozo thinks will make us feel all warm and fuzzy and *not* remind us that we've outlived our friends, our usefulness, even the place we once held in our childrens' lives . . . so there we remain, sitting, staring, wishing for a visitor or someplace to go, just some little variation in the routine that's slowly depressing us to death. But there's never any variation, so our bodies continue to deteriorate and our skin turns into tissue paper as we fill our noses and lungs with the smell of approaching oblivion. Are any of us with our sadnesses, our deformities, our bruises, broken hearts, declining health, the whole index of personal miseries—are we somehow *undeserving* of consideration? A five-minute call once a week, a kind word or affectionate smile, an understanding touch? What effort does that take? When exactly were we deemed unworthy? Who decided this?"

He was getting more and more agitated as he

spoke, shifting his weight from leg to leg, stamping his hooves against the floor or kicking them against the bars, continually shaking his head as if to break apart the thoughts and scatter the pieces from his head, chuffing and snorting to disgorge the bitter taste of the words in his mouth.

Up and down the corridor, the occupants of the various cages began to stir and move toward their barred doors. Their voices and growls and peeps wove a soft, murmuring cloth of sound that spread out between the cages like a picnic blanket over green summer grass.

"Well, guess what, kiddo," said Whitey. "There *is* a place for us. A way to be loved. A way home. Not just us, not just people, but any living thing whose existence becomes intolerable. Are you paying attention? There may be a quiz later."

The music was being turned up in small increments. Whitey craned his horse's neck up and to the side. "Almost time."

"For what?"

A smile. "You'll see soon enough."

There was a loud buzz, followed by an ever louder metallic click.

"Whitey, what's going—"

"—wait for it. It'll come around again in a minute or two." He winked. "A pro knows when 'Places' is being called." Then he cleared his throat again and said, a bit too loudly: "Shall I tell him?"

The murmuring blanket whispered agreement. Whitey cantered around his cage, his head thrown back. "Yes, yes, *yes!*" He stopped, shook himself from head to hooves, then clopped to the bars. "Human beings running the show, kiddo, was a mistake. Got that? Wasn't supposed to happen like this.

"See, way back when before there was a 'when' to go back to, when the world was new, there were only the animals, but they weren't animals as we know them now, nuh-uh: they were capable of abstract thought and speech and all the other qualities we now call 'anthropomorphic.' And they were happy, and they gave thanks to their creator—the First Animal, the one from which they all sprang into being.

"But creating the world and the galaxy around it and the universe around the galaxy and all that snazzy razzamatazz, well . . . it wears out A Divine Being. It's anybody's guess what specific whatchamacallit El Heffe was in the process of creating when He screwed the pooch—that's just one those Great Mysteries that we have to live with, but, again, I digress.

"What happened was: God blinked. Can't really blame Him, He'd been working without a break for six days and you can only stare at something for so long before you can't see it anymore . . . so He blinked, looked away for a moment, and just left this new thing He'd been working on laying around, unfinished.

"During the Big Blink, as I like to call it, certain cells in this whosee-whatsit super-dingus mutated while others fused together, creating metazoans and—*whammo!*—the DNA dominoes fell into sequence and the double helix did its ninth configuration dance and by the time the Almighty Anybody checked back, an amusing accident called evolution had taken place: here stood Man, effulgent and curious and all starkers, scratching his ass and looking for a good place to build the first mall.

"So He let Man hang around for a while to see what would happen, and *of course* it didn't work out, but by the point in the show where the whole Forty Days and Forty Nights production number was to go on, Man had convinced the animals that they couldn't survive without him. Know how he did that? He whipped, beat, humiliated, starved, and worked them until they were so weary and sad they stopped using speech and abstract thought. With each new generation, they'd become more silent and simple-minded and had no choice *but* to depend on Man. So God wrote a reprise called Noah—not just because He didn't much cotton to the idea of expunging this interesting accident called Man, but because, by then, the 'beasts of the field' were too stupid to know it was time to pair up and save their collective hide."

Another loud buzz, followed by another click. Whitey craned his neck once more, shaking off foam. "Shit, I got all caught up in things and lost track—was that the second or third time?"

"Second."

"Okay, got one more to go."

Every synapse in your brain was firing at you to get the fuck out of there but you couldn't; you had to hear the rest of this—if for no other reason than because he still might tell you where Beth had gone.

Appalachian Spring was reaching its most famous

movement, and from up and down the corridor, human voices and animal sounds began to merge . . .

. . . and *sing:*

" 'Tis the gift to be simple,
'Tis the gift to be free,
'Tis the gift to come down where we ought to be,
And when we find ourselves in the place just right,
It will be in the valley of love and delight . . ."

It was impossible to tell which voices were wholly human and which were wholly not; and then you thought: *Maybe that's the point.*

"I'm hogging the spotlight, friends," shouted Whitey. "Let's not be shy here, come on, get in on the fun!"

A woman's voice called out: "There was a beast no one remembered, alone of its kind, who did not have a mate . . ."

Another voice, this of a child: ". . . and it was left behind in the storm that day . . ."

They started coming rapidly after that, maybe human, maybe not, maybe something in between, but their words rang clear and high:

". . . but it found a place of safety, another world just beyond the great scrim of this world, and there it waited, and when the rains stopped and the sun shone once again, God asked this creature if it was lonely and it said 'Yes . . .' "

". . . so God shared with it one of the secrets of Creation . . ."

". . . and with this secret, the creature was able to use part of itself to create another like itself . . ."

". . . and they were called the Keepers . . ."

". . . and God gave the Keepers a Task, and sent them out into the world, the world of the First Animal, to create their own kingdom, separate from that of Man . . ."

"Figuring it out, kiddo?" asked Whitey.

"*Ohgod. . . .*"

"I think it's sinking in," he called down the corridor. A third click, followed a third buzz.

Whitey did a quick canter-dance around his cage, chuffed, shook off some foam, then said (in a dead-on impersonation of Bert Lahr as The Cowardly Lion): "Lemme at 'em, lemme at 'em—it's showtime, folks!"

From the bottom of the railed stairway someone or something screamed.

An alarm began screeching a staccato squawk.

Bright security lights snapped on, mercilessly illuminating everything beneath.

And the cage doors opened.

Blinking against the too-bright lights, you turned to run but the corridor behind you was already filling with those you'd passed before; the ox, the goat, the teenaged man-of-war, the coelacanth woman and bear and all the rest; they slid, rolled, scooted, flopped, walked, and crawled toward you. Bringing up the rear, hunched over because it was still getting used to walking upright, the dark sleeping thing from the cage across from the ox loped and stumbled forward, slick flesh stretched so tightly over its skull and face it looked as if it might tear at any moment. There was something of the wolf about it, or so you thought, but by then you'd turned and started to run toward the hidden stairs only to find the way blocked by a dapper gentleman who tipped his bowler hat in your direction.

Behind him stood four other well-dressed men with their bowlers pulled down to cover the tops of their ears. And you knew why: the tags. They were hiding the blue tags stapled to the backs of their ears. Whitey had one, the ox had one, the goat, the boy on the cot, everyone and everything had a blue tag stapled in the same place.

Whitey stepped out of his cage, whispered "Follow my lead, kiddo, or you're toast burnt on both sides before your time," and nudged you with his scar-knotted shoulders until you were backed against one of the opened doors. He winked once more and stood in front of you.

"See, kiddo, the thing is, the First Animal, he's figured out a way to reclaim this world, but he can't do it in one big, grand swoop like God did; no, he's got to do it a little bit at a time, piece by piece, with whatever materials the Keepers can gather. *Raw* materials, you might call 'em.

"The procedure takes a while, and it hurts like hell, but it's getting there. Bugs in the system. Kinks to work out. Luckily, there's no short supply of miserable, lonely people who wished they'd been born as anything else but what they are."

He leaned forward, breathing hot, moist breath into your face, breath that smelled of the fields, the sky. "Once the balance has been sufficiently offset again, once there are more animals than people— like it was supposed to be—then the First Animal can step through the scrim and restore this world to its natural order. Maybe by then God will have admitted to the fuck-up."

Around you, the others were crowding close.

Too close.

"We had an agreement," said Whitey to the figures and things surrounding you. "I already fulfilled my part, I gave you a possible candidate and she was brought here tonight. So *he* walks out unharmed, right?"

The first man in the bowler spread his hands benevolently and gave a nod, then snapped his fingers. The four other bowler-men moved forward.

Two were empty-handed.

One carried a package wrapped in brown paper with an address written across the top.

The other carried a syringe.

Whitey turned toward you and offered a sad smile. "Won't see you again after this, Captain. It's been a real pleasure. You're a better man than you think you are. Work on your timing. And that fear of bathing."

"What are they going to do to me?"

"Nothing harmful. *You* didn't come here voluntarily, so they have to let you leave."

For a moment you couldn't find your voice, and during that moment two of the Keepers grabbed your arms and pulled them behind you; the one with the syringe took the plastic cover from the needle, steadied your head with his free hand, and slipped the needle into a vein in your neck, sinking the plunger.

The image on the monitor changed; again you were looking at the same downtown corner where you'd encountered Drop-Kick, but this time the film was older, grainier, black-and-white. The face of an old man filled the screen as he petted the dog from whose point of view this had been filmed. Then another old man's face came into frame, then that of a third. Finally, the dog whipped its head around and started running toward a young boy crossing toward it from the other side of the street. The boy had a comic book tucked under one arm. He was holding a bag of scraps from a restaurant. He offered the dog something from the bag. The dog looked up and the boy who would grow up to become your dad smiled down at it. It was the most wonderful smile you'd ever seen.

This was him.

As a boy.

Smiling, with scraps in hand.

Overhead, the squawking alarm sounded in time to the music, one of the figures began whispering something in your ear, and the things assembled in the corridor sang a lullaby while your brain and body melted into something light and shiny and unbound:

"When true simplicity is gained,
To bow and to bend we will not be ashamed
To turn, turn, will be our delight
Till by turning, turning, we come round right. . . ."

You dreamed you were a man who believed no one loved or cared about him. Your hands were scarred from a lifetime of hard labor. You had once dreamed of raising chickens for a living, but the war and your injuries and family demanded otherwise. Now all of it was gone, and you stood alone in a dark hallway. A thin mist swirled around your feet and began to rise, and when this mist filled the room, it was light again. A man stepped out of the light and fog and tipped his bowler. He asked you what you wanted to be. "An eagle," you said. "Eagles are free and admired. Eagles are loved and respected." He said that was good, because an eagle is what you were supposed to have been in the first place. He asked if you knew someone else who might like to be something else. You said yes and told him a name.

We're putting things right for Long-Lost, he said as he pointed the way. *It's taking longer than we'd planned, but we're getting there.*

Then he took you to a place where they changed your body and gave you feathers and flight. It hurt, but it was worth it.

You were loved. Admired. Your heart knew no pain or sorrow. The sky had no place for such things.

You rolled over and opened your eyes. You were back in your house. On the floor. Your clothes were fresh and clean; your skin was creamy and smelled of soap. You wondered if you'd come home drunk. Mom and Dad would be very upset with you. But they were dead, weren't they? Yes. That was right. They were gone and the house was yours. Only you were leaving soon, weren't you?

You tried to sit up but your limbs were rubber, so you stayed on the floor.

It seemed to you that there was someone else you should say good-bye to, but you couldn't think of anyone. That bugged you. You didn't have so many friends that you would forget one. That was rude. Thoughtless. You weren't that geeky little four-eyed dweeb anymore; you had friends. Didn't you?

Did you have a girlfriend? It seemed to you that you did, but you couldn't picture her face or remember her name.

Foggy dream remnants, that's what it had to be; foggy dream remnants. You lay back down on the floor and closed your eyes.

You dreamed that you were a dog sitting out in the rain. You were tied to a post. Your sides hurt because you'd been beaten because you had soiled the carpeting. It wasn't your fault—there had been no one home to let you out. But now you were in the rain and it was cold and you wanted to be lying near the hearth in front of the sweet-smelling fire inside. They beat you a lot, even when you didn't soil things. You wished they wouldn't do that. You loved them and wanted them to love you. But some people can't love a dog. The rain beat down very hard. Mist rose up from the ground. A nicely dressed man came out of the mist and tipped his bowler hat to you. He asked if you were lonely and you said yes. You were surprised that you could talk; you'd never done it before. The man said it was because you'd been made to forget that you could. He asked you what you wanted.

"To be human," you said, speaking clearly and with ease. "So I can know how they feel and why they put me out in the rain."

"*Come*," he said, freeing you from the post. "*And remember to think as much as you want and say whatever you wish. Things have been mixed up for a while, but we're putting them right.*"

You trotted beside him—the pain in your sides slowed your progress, but he was patient and kind—and you asked, "How?"

He stopped and pointed back toward the house. "*Someday*, he said, "*all of these people will be as you were, and all of you*"—he knelt down and stroked your back—"*will be as they are. Then things will be right again. As right as we can make them.*"

"Can I have a family?" you ask.

"Yes," he said. "Long-Lost would like that. He needs someone to claim and protect one of his . . . I guess you'd call them 'angels.' So you shall have a sister when your parents are no more, and no one—including you—will question this reality. To the world, you will have always had a sister. Your sister will have a son. He will love you very much. And he will have a gift. He will be one of those who will help lift the Great Scrim so that Long-Lost can step through." Then he shrugged. "Sometimes, a god has to be sneaky.

"You may remember all of this, or you may not. We'll see. But it will come to pass, whether your memory serves you or not."

He took you to a place where they made you human. You could dance and laugh. You could hold delicate objects in your hands.

You could speak of your love to others.

You could know the glory of a kiss.

And no animal would you treat with thoughtlessness or cruelty. The world to come had no place for such things.

You woke in the morning, gathered your bags, and went to Kansas. You stayed with your grandmother for nearly a year, until the night she said she was tired and went upstairs and lay down to sleep for the last time. You cried at her funeral but were comforted by the knowledge that her last months had been full and rich. You loved her and had often told her so. She never knew a day without an embrace or a kiss on the cheek. She had gone upstairs that last night still laughing at a joke you'd told her. Some ghost of that smile remained on her face when you found her the next morning.

You stopped drinking and sleeping around after she was gone. She had always worried that you were hurting myself. Maybe she was right. This seemed the best way to honor her memory, and that of your parents. You would try to live the rest of your life as well as possible.

The real estate firm in Cedar Hill sold the house for a very good price and both you and your sister made a lot of money on the deal. Your sister was especially grateful, having just had a baby and her husband having just abandoned her.

After a few years, you moved back to Cedar Hill. Home is home. Even if no one's there waiting for you.

You decided to drive back, make a little vacation out of it, stop and see the sights along the way, however long it took.

The morning you were packing up your things to leave, a delivery van from some company called

Hicks Worldwide pulled up in front of your apartment. The driver got out and walked over to where you stood next to your car. He greeted you by name.

"I believe you have a package for me," he said, smiling like a happy puppy.

You blinked a few times, then opened your trunk, moved aside a few bags, and found the parcel all the way in the back. You did not recognize the name of the addressee. You handed it to him without a word. He thanked you, climbed into his van, and drove away.

You came back to Cedar Hill and used some of the money to start your own small business. It was a moderate enough success that you opened another store in Columbus.

Somewhere in there, your sister became ill and died. You became Carson's legal guardian.

You love your nephew very much. He's very special. A gift, some might say.

You went back to a few old haunts. Barney's Saloon was gone, replaced now by some store called Marie's Hosiery. It looked like a nice shop.

The Old Soldiers and Sailors building had been torn down; left in its place was an empty lot. You seemed to remember something about a wall of signatures having been in there, but couldn't quite bring the thought all the way into the light.

You kept planning for something, but could never quite remember what, only that you had to arrange certain things in your house a certain way.

It seemed for the best.

You went on dates, bought them dinner, took them to plays or movies, even made breakfast for a few of them. None of the women ever seemed interested in anything long-term and you couldn't find it in you to be hurt or offended.

Life went on, as it will whether you want it to or not. You saw yourself as neither a bad man nor a good one; you just Were.

Then one day while driving home you saw an old man get killed while chasing his hat. You stopped to watch him die. You answered questions from the police. You came home and found a dog on your lawn.

A package arrived.

Someone called about your nephew.

You found him in an old barn at the Magic Zoo.

He changed.

Guided you back home.

Visitors came.

That brings us all up to date, pal. Now, was *that*

FOUR

so hard?)

Maybe not for you.

(Yeah, but at least now you can't bullshit yourself into thinking it happened any other way. Good-bye to all the happy pills the doctors have given to you.)

You waiting for me to thank you?

(Like the hero always says at the end of the movie, My Work Here is Done. Doesn't mean shit to me whether you thank me or not.)

Pulling myself up into something like a standing position once again, I cleaned the blood and disinfected the wound as best I could, applied the gauze pads, put the splints in place with some of the medical tape, then tightly wrapped my hand in the elastic bandage; I was able to move only my thumb and index finger without much pain, the rest of my hand was swollen and useless. I looked down at the Mossberg. I had seven shots left in it and a full clip in the pistol. Sixteen shots altogether. Assuming that I was able to retrieve the shotgun if I dropped it again.

I bent my right thumb and index finger several times to make sure they were still working. Satisfied they weren't going to lock up on me, I sat down on the closed toilet lid and balanced the Mossberg on my lap. I slipped my right index finger over the trigger and situated my thumb in the proper position on the handle-grip; my other three fingers I arranged as best I could, making sure that the right side of my middle finger was parallel to the underside of the trigger-guard, then I used half the roll of duct tape to bind my hand to the shotgun. No way was this going to come out of my hand or be taken away from me.

That done, I tore one of the remaining gauze pads in two and wadded up the halves to use as ear plugs—if I had to fire again, I wanted some protection against the noise.

After that, I opened the cabinet over the sink where my storage habits are a little more traditional; cough syrup, aspirin, throat lozenges, and . . . where was it?

There.

The same accident that had necessitated the finger splints last year had also brought with it a prescription for painkillers, most of which I still had left. God bless codeine.

I popped the lid off the plastic bottle and tossed two of the tablets into my mouth, then twisted down so I could drink some water from the tap. All better now (or telling myself I was, anyway), I put the bottle in my pants pocket, ran my good hand through my hair, and looked at my reflection in the mirror. If I saw this fellow on the street, I'd cross to the other side and run like hell.

I turned away and started toward the front of the house.

There was something going on there that Bowler wanted me to see.

The mist was pressing against the remaining windows. I wondered how much longer it would be content to do that before deciding to just smash through the glass—and if I doubted it had the ability to change into something solid, I had only to look at the wreckage of my right hand.

I opened the front door and leveled the shotgun.

About nine of them stood scattered around the front yard, arms folded across their chests, bowlers perfectly straight, goggles shooting out thin red beams that in places formed "X"s when they crisscrossed with those from another Bowler's. Something about their stances suggested they were waiting for something important to happen.

On the periphery of the thrumming in my ears I began to hear . . . music. Muffled at first, until someone turned up the volume and the bass began to register in my bones; then a harsh, nasal voice began singing words, something about soldiers, tin soldiers, yes: tin soldiers and Nixon—

Ohio.

Someone was playing Crosby, Stills, Nash, and Young's "Ohio."

Three Bowlers who'd been standing beyond my field of vision emerged from the mist and started toward the porch. Their movements were deliberate and exact; dancers executing a carefully choreographed ballet routine. One of them wore an absurd wig of long, straight blonde hair beneath his hat. Another

Gary A. Braunbeck

carried a boom-box from which the song was blaring. I leveled the Mossberg and took a step forward, taking care to make sure the screen door didn't close behind me.

The first Bowler held up a white placard like those used in old vaudeville acts; written on it were the words: THE DOUBLE-DUBYA PLAYERS PRESENT. Then he backed away, bowing his head and parting his arms, taking the boom-box from the second one's hand.

The second one, using overblown, melodramatic gestures, clutched at his chest and dropped to his knees, then fell face-first against the ground. The third Bowler went down on one knee, arms parted at his sides like a Celebrant blessing the Hosts at Mass; the long straight hair of his wig caught on a breeze I couldn't feel and blew slightly to the right.

The others began to applaud, but then Magritte-Man came stomping forward like a petulant child, wildly waving his hands in the air, silencing them. He grabbed the two performers and wordlessly moved them into different positions.

That's not exactly correct. He moved them back into the *same* positions, only this time facing away from me, frozen in tableau except for the hair of the wig, which now blew to my left.

I couldn't move.

They'd recreated the Kent State scene almost perfectly. After all, this *was* the angle from which I'd seen it. From behind.

The song reached its final chorus as Magritte-Man stepped back, examined his players, then threw his arms in the air and bobbed his head with great enthusiasm. The Bowlers already scattered throughout the yard broke into loud and enthusiastic applause, a few even placing fingers in their mouths to whistle.

As "Ohio" ended, Magritte-Man tapped his players on their shoulders and the three of them joined hands to take a bow; first for the overjoyed audience in the yard, then, turning around and clasping hands again, for me.

Behind them, the mist swirled and churned, forming the faces of countless animals; dogs, cats, horses, pigs, cows, swans, bears, and more. Some of them were of species so foreign or exotic they could be seen only in zoos or the pages of *National Geographic.*

Each of these mist-animals cried out in their own primal language, as if to echo the sentiments of the audience and express their pleasure with this evening's entertainment. The players turned and bowed to the spectators once again. The applause swelled, heads nodded in admiration, red beams danced and bounced through the glowing silver gloom.

As the applause began to die down, Magritte-Man turned to face me, holding another white placard. He smiled, then pulled the placard away to reveal yet another underneath, only where the previous one had been blank, this one had a word written in large black letters:

RING

He tossed it aside to reveal the next:

ANY

317

Then the next:

BELLS?

"How did you know?" I shouted, my voice creating heavy ripples of gummy pain inside my skull. *"How the fuck could you know? It's been thirty goddamn years since—"*

He tossed aside the BELLS? placard to unveil a new one, then another, then another and another, until he'd said what he wanted to say:

YOU KNOW DAMN
WELL WHO
TOLD US
ABOUT IT

I was shaking so violently I thought my internal organs were going to drop out through the legs of my pants. "No riddles—*who told you?*"

Another card:

GUESS.

But I didn't have to. I'd known the answer since WELL.

I moved forward another step. The Mossberg felt like it had fused to my hand, flesh and steel becoming the organic tissue of a new limb.

"Tell me," I said to him. "I want you to say it. I want to hear your voice, if you've got one. If it's going to be like this, I want for us to have spoken once as civilized men." I aimed directly at his chest. "So you tell me what—"

He pointed at the Mossberg, then waved his other hand to draw the Bowlers' attention, as well; as he did this, he moved up to the second step and stood less than two feet away from the business end of the shotgun.

The Bowlers clustered nearer the porch, some leaning their heads to the left, others to the right, all of them evidently fascinated by what they saw.

Magritte-Man pointed to his right hand, then to mine, and that's when I figured out he was drawing their attention to what I'd done with the duct tape.

Again, the Bowlers began to applaud, except for a trio who moved to the side, conferred among themselves for a few moments, then held up more placards: 9.5, 10, 9.7.

Magritte-Man gestured toward the judges' scores and applauded soundlessly.

I didn't know whether to laugh, scream, or just sit down on my ass and cry, so I did the next best thing: I stepped forward and shoved the barrel of the Mossberg under Magritte-Man's chin.

"Speak to me, right now."

He shrugged and stepped back down onto the walk, lifting his hands into the air. He bent his fingers down against his palms and began to strike at nothing—no, not strike; paw. He was imitating an animal *pawing* at something.

At the same time, two Bowlers took up places on either side of him and held up a small barred door taken from a cage. Magritte-Man pushed his arms through the bars and continued pawing while a third Pedestrian—the one who'd worn the wig before—held another placard over his head: SANCTIONED PER-SONNEL ONLY. All of them began opening and closing their mouths as if trying to form words—

—lips squirming in a mockery of communication, sounds that were a burlesque of language—

—I shook the image of the old man on the highway out of my head and moved back into the front doorway, the Mossberg still at the ready.

They were crowding around the bottom step, their hands pawing, their mouths working soundlessly, the thin bright red beams of their goggles creating laser-show patterns before my eyes. The mist became thicker, the faces of the countless animals within pressing outward like bas-relief masks. I couldn't lift my left hand to shield my eyes because that would mean letting go of the shotgun and I wasn't about to give them an opening to rush me—and *what* the fuck had I been thinking, coming out here like this?

In perfect synchronization, all of them—Magritte-Man included—reached up to loosen their ties and unbutton the tops of their collars.

Every last on of them had a curved scar that ran from one side of their neck to the other. They turned their "paws" toward themselves and began to claw at the scars, all the while still moving their mouths and—

—when there's this many, they cut out their vocal cords—

—Magritte-Man flexed his fingers, and with an overly theatrical flourish reached up to remove the bowler from his head.

Another placard: YOU GET USED TO THE SMELL.

He was bald. Not a stunning revelation, I know, but for a moment that was the only thing I would allow to register. He was bald. He wore the bowler because he was bald underneath. I suspected that all of them were bald underneath. But the old man on the highway, he hadn't been bald—hair extremely thin and sparse, sure, but not bald. I remembered that. I remembered that clearly. I remembered the way he'd grabbed my shirt pulled me toward him; I remembered his blood seeping into the cotton of my shirt as I lifted the bowler and showed him that it was undamaged; I remembered the way he looked into my eyes, lips squirming in a mockery of communication because his vocal cords had been cut out long ago—

—no, no, that didn't belong there, that wasn't right, it couldn't be, there hadn't been any scar running across his neck and throat, right? Right—I was getting confused, the Bowlers' little vaudeville had thrown me a curve, that was all. The old man on the highway *did* have some hair—not much, not shining, gleaming, glowing, flowing, waxen, flaxen, wear it down to *there* hair—but he'd had some. Magritte-Man was *bald*; shiny, shiny skin covered his head, except for the spots where matchbox-sized rectangles with electrical wires were implanted in his skull. The shiny, shiny skin of his bare scalp was crusty and red where it joined the metal.

Another Bowler began flipping through another series of placards:

CARE ENOUGH ABOUT
SOMEONE AND YOU'LL
FIND A WAY TO
HELP THEM
NO
MATTER
WHAT.

He waited a moment, then flipped through three more.

NO
MATTER
WHAT!

He wasn't repeating anything with this—he was issuing a threat.

He tossed away the third placard to reveal one more:

THERE OUGHT TO BE A PLACE

I felt my stomach tighten.

Magritte-Man turned his head to offer his profile, then used his index finger to bend forward his ear and give me a good look at the blue plastic tag attached to it. I didn't have to be close enough to read what was printed on it to know what it said because at that moment all the tumblers fell into place and the door of the safe swung open and out came everything from all those years ago I'd been forcing myself to forget every second of every day of every week, month, and year of my stale existence . . . until now.

Until this

(You're getting awfully close to leaving me with no choice, pal . . .)

moment.

Until this moment

(You did the wrong routine . . .)

of this day.

Until this moment of

(Dammit, I've helped people, you know? I've cared for them when no one else wanted to . . .)

this day where I'd watched an old man die on the highway for want of hat and crawled in blood-soaked clothes under the porch to comfort a dying dog as my nephew who wasn't really my nephew but an angel of Long-Lost because I had no sister Jesus God I had no sister, she was just a trick of Long-Lost's, something to ensure that I would be the guardian of his little special agent, his angel of the pencil and paper, but that hadn't stopped Carson from changing into what he should have been all along while Magritte-Man and his troop of players surrounded me and a mist crowded with bas-relief ghost-animals formed an impenetrable dome over my house and shrunk the boundaries of what I laughingly thought of as my world until I

(. . . might say they're not from around here . . .)

had to come out and watch my own private production of *Godspell On Crack* just so these bastards could rattle my cage and jar everything loose and I didn't *want* to remember these things about Beth and her aunt Mabel and their Its and what happened to all of them and to me during that terrible sick-making three-hour period the year I turned twenty-one and I only had a few moments to try and shove it all back inside and slam the door before it took over and swallowed me whole but I wasn't sure what I was going to do because I was hurt and frightened and my house was under siege and so much of it was *already out* and right there in my face and suddenly I thought

(There ought to be a place)

of something I'd read about Nietzsche who'd said there are times when things get so horrible that you have only two choices laugh or go crazy so I opted for the former and barked out a single laugh that sounded berserk even to me and then I did the only other thing I could think of to keep the memories from engulfing me again, like the jaws of some mythic beast—

—I opened fire.

FIVE

The first shot hit one of the Bowlers right in the center of his chest, opening a fist-sized hole that blew him back into the mist and almost knocked me on my ass, but I managed to stay upright, plowing off another shot into the next Bowler, and it was with this second shot I realized that I couldn't hear anything. It wasn't that the first shot had deafened me or that the makeshift earplugs were working wonders, it was that all sound had been sucked from the world; all I could hear was my own breathing echoing from within, and everything without was a silent movie.

The first Bowler stumbled out of the mist, frantically patting at the smoking hole made by the shell as it tore through his clothing and into his flesh. He wasn't bleeding at all. Neither was the second one. Oh, they were moving kind of slow like Uncle Joe at the Junction, were obviously dazed and in pain, but they weren't even close to dead. It was absurd that they should still be alive and moving, and to emphasize this point I shot each of them a second time. It slowed them down even more, but that was about it.

I backed into the house and kicked the door closed, locking it. The loud echo of the deadbolt slamming into place was reassuring. In here, there was still sound, I could hear them coming. It was only outside that they could steal the noise. So I'd take them on in here.

I looked out the window. They were scattering around the house, readying to come at me from all sides simultaneously. I might not be able to kill them, but I could hurt them, of that much at least I was certain. They weren't going to get her, absolutely not.

I ran into the kitchen and grabbed a large saucepan that I threw onto the stove and filled with a quart of cooking oil before igniting the burner and turning the flame up to high. Then it was back into the junk portion of the bathroom cabinet for a screwdriver and the large can of lighter fluid and a second lighter. In the linen closet I yanked down one of the wooden shelves and began scattering the towels and dish rags and other shelves all over the floor, dousing each of them in lighter fluid as I made a trail through the downstairs.

Some of the Bowlers were scrabbling up the trellis on the side of the house, heading for the roof, while another threw his weight against the back door over and over again. I grabbed the antique oil lamp from the end table and ran to the top of the stairs, emptying the oil on the carpeting all the way, then throwing the whole thing against the far wall where it exploded against my bedroom door with a loud, satisfying crash of glass and tin. One match, that's all it would take. One match and the whole house would be swallowed by fire within a few minutes.

"Go away!" I screamed. "Leave us alone, god-dammit!"

Back down the stairs and into the kitchen where the oil was bubbling up over the side of the pan and the Bowler on the back porch was about to break the door off its hinges. I grabbed the handle of the pan in the same instant that the back door splintered inward with the crack of wood and the shattering of glass. The Bowler was halfway through when I threw the scalding contents of the pan at his head. It sizzled as it splattered over his exposed skin, creating dozens of bubbles of boiling flesh. He grabbed at his face and body with wild hands, opening his mouth to scream but of course he didn't scream because he *couldn't* scream—when there are that many of them they cut out their vocal cords—and as he thrashed and flailed about I leveled the shotgun and emptied a round into his chest but still he didn't go down and I thought that was a bit rude, so I reached into my pocket for a lighter, realized I'd soon need it elsewhere, so instead pulled a kitchen match from the shelf over the stove, lit it, and tossed it at him.

He burst into flames, his arms pinwheeling as he stumbled back and fell down the stairs into the yard. As soon as he hit the ground he began to roll but the fire was out of control now, snapping and spitting and sizzling (though you couldn't hear it out there, out there the mist swallowed the sound, but I'd heard the deep hungry belch of the flames when he'd gone up inside and it made me smile), then he was on his feet once more, spinning around, arms raised, scattering smoky bits of charred material and meat in all directions as others gathered around him, pointing, nodding but not helping, and it was only then I realized that the burning figure was swaying side to side in perfect rhythm along with the other Bowlers, doing the Wave, mocking me—

—distracting me.

An upstairs window shattered. Then another. A pair of feet ran heavily across the roof. Something came through a window in the living room. The dog howled under the porch.

I fired another shot directly into the dancing flame, then turned just as another one of them leapt at me from behind, slamming us against the stove where the ignited burner still roared. I smashed against the side of his head with the barrel of the shotgun but I might as well have been bitch-slapping a medicine ball for all the effect it had. He grabbed hold of my head and began twisting my face toward the open flame. The dog's howl rose in pitch and volume, becoming a shriek of fury; I knew it wouldn't be long before they figured out she was in the crawl-space and went after her and I was not was not, repeat, was not going to let that happen, I'd known all my life that this day would arrive, that someday they'd come for me, I'd planned out my actions long ago, so if she and I were going down I was going to make damn sure I took as many of them with us as possible, but now the flames licked at my nose, I breathed them, felt the hairs inside my nostrils curl and singe and fill me with smoke and the smell of my own burned flesh, so I pushed up against his body with all I had and brought my knee up into his crotch and that seemed to surprise him because for just a second his grip on me loosened, but just a second was all I needed to snake my free hand down to my side, yank the screwdriver from my belt, and bury it all the way to the handle through one of his goggle lenses. He snapped up, his back bowing, hands grabbing at the thing jammed where his eye used to be as I lifted the shotgun and shoved the barrel right against his face and fired. Bone and tissue blossomed outward, hitting the walls, sliding moistly toward the floor, making wet trails on the way down.

His body crumpled onto the table, shuddered, kicked, then lay still.

So they *could* be killed.

Good to know.

I heard footsteps upstairs pounding toward the landing. I jumped over the Bowler's body and ran through the house, lighter at the ready. I looked up the stairway and saw the first shadow bleed across the wall as they neared the top. I struck up the flame and tossed the lighter upward. As soon as it hit the carpet a bright blue-orange line of flame vomited out in both directions; it fizzled out before getting down to the living room—I hadn't spread the fluid out as well as I'd thought—but it chewed its way up the stairs and around the corner so fast I knew they didn't stand a chance. I rammed the door closed, locked it, and spun around just in time to see a smoking, charred tower of meat come at me with outstretched arms. I lifted the shotgun but he was on top of me before I could get off a shot. He weighed as much an elephant, and when we hit the floor every breath I'd ever taken since I'd been born blew out of my lungs and I went numb. He grabbed at my throat with deep-fried hands and began to squeeze, pushing up and down to increase the pressure. I felt the world slipping away from me, felt my body handing in its formal resignation, my legs kicking out in uncontrollable spasms as I wet myself, but then he pulled up again and one of my legs jerked back, its knee bending, and I saw the handle of the dagger jutting out from the sheath strapped to the ankle. Take me, it cried out. I'm right here, so take me, fer chrissakes. I knew that I should but my arm wasn't cooperating—at least, that's what I thought, but then I heard the echo of Whitey's voice in my head saying *keepers gotta keep the kept kept, know what I'm saying* and I remembered the way he'd looked the last time I saw him and some beast composed of equal parts anger and sadness snarled to life in my chest; the next thing I knew there was my arm shooting out and my hand grabbing the handle and then the dagger was free; I looked up into the scorched ruins of the Bowler's still-smoking face and I did what I was taught to do with a roast when you had a knife—I began to carve. First a cheek, then the lump that had once been his nose, the charred meat searing my own skin as it fell off in blackened, dripping chunks, but I kept at it, burying the dagger to its hilt and then swiping sideways before pulling it out and hacking away until his grip loosened and he fell to the side, shuddering. I shoved the gristle-covered dagger into my belt, staggered to my feet, and disintegrated the rest of his head with a single shot.

Across the room, another window exploded in a shower of glass and wood. One of them was throwing rocks through all the downstairs windows in order to let in the mist. The mist swallowed sound. The mist obscured perspective. The mist had terrible faces in it, both animal and human, and they wanted to talk to me, make me listen, make me understand that it had to be this way and I really had no choice in the matter, it was an ancient thing when you got right down to it, a way for nature to make perpetual use of its organic systems, hadn't I figured that out yet?

I stepped over the broiled mass on the floor and made my way into the kitchen, grabbing the step stool and putting it to good use. Then I started back toward the guest bedroom. Underneath the house, the dog's shrieks of fury had become something so loud and primal and frenzied they sounded like the screams of a waking dragon. I knew there was a chance she might come after me once I was down there but I had to risk it. She'd come here for a reason; even if she wasn't completely aware of it, I was.

A flash of movement as one of the Bowlers darted across the hall. I lifted the shotgun and pulled the trigger; there was only an impotent *click!*

So be it.

I used the dagger to cut away the duct tape and let the shotgun drop to the floor, then removed the pistol from the back of my pants and clicked off the safety before transferring it to my ruined hand and using the remaining duct tape to hold it in place.

Then I just stood there.

I could hear them coming in through the back

door, through the shattered windows, pounding their way through weak spots in the roof. Two loud thumps from behind the door to the upstairs let me know that at least one of them had made it through the flames and was heading down.

Still, I just stood there.

I wanted them to see that I was still on my feet, that I was still fighting, that I was not going to go gently into that empty lonely, miserable, and not-so-good fucking night. They weren't going to win, and before I died I wanted to make sure they knew it.

Beneath the porch, the dog's cry became a high, clear song of triumph.

I smiled. I had long ago learned the words with which to name my own secret losses and shames, and the old man on the highway had whispered some of them to me as he turned his head so I could see the small plastic blue tag attached to the back of his ear.

I thought he was dead. No one could have survived being hit and dragged like that, but as I knelt down beside him his eyes opened.

"This is the way it's supposed to be," he'd said to me as his bloodied hand grabbed my shirt. "We can only wait for so long after . . . after, you know. I'm . . . I'm sorry. Will you forgive me? I just couldn't finish it. It doesn't seem right to do it like this. Can you . . . you . . . forgive me?' "

"Of course," I'd whispered, brushing his blue tag with the back of my thumb. "Of course I forgive you."

"I just wanted to look like a human being when this time came."

I offered him the derby. "I understand."

"They know," he said. "They've always known. Be careful." Then he whispered my name. And died.

I knew then he'd been following me—had probably been watching me for a long while (isn't that what they did with a candidate?)—but in the end found some reserve of compassion that stopped him from going through with what he'd been sent to do. Knowing what they'd do to him because of his failure, he'd chosen to die, dressed in his snappy suit with a dapper bowler hat upon his head.

I'd pulled the tag from his ear before the police arrived, then tossed it out the window as I drove home. By the time I pulled into my driveway his words were white noise in my memory. Then I found a dog on my lawn. A package arrived. Visitors came.

In the living room I opened the bottle of Johnny Walker I'd taken from its hiding place, lifted it in the air, and toasted the old man on the highway before drinking deeply. The liquor sliding so smoothly down, my throat felt like a dead limb suddenly tingling back to life. I made it a long, slow, deep drink, the only one I would take: I pulled the bottle away, wiped the back of my arm across my mouth, and shouted, "Come join the party. It's gonna be a real barn-burner, motherfuckers!" I threw the bottle across the room and pulled out the second lighter. End of tough-guy action-film moment.

A few seconds later Magritte-Man stepped into the hallway, dashing and stylish as ever. The mist was rolling in, covering the floor, creeping up the walls. In a few moments it would engulf the room and he wouldn't be able to hear me.

"I appreciate this chance alone with you," I said.

He reached up and gave me a respectful tip of his hat; as he did this, the mist began to twist and spread farther across the floor, swirling to our ankles. It felt like lead shackles, weighing down my feet. It was cold, so very cold, yet I could feel something like a damp pulse in its tendrils, one that was firm and strong.

"You put on a good show."

He spread his arms before him and gave a very theatrical bow. At my feet I could hear the reverberating echoes of the screams and gunfire the mist had swallowed, but more than that, I could hear voices, dozens of them, maybe even hundreds, whispering in rapid, anxious tones *of course I understand dear I don't want to be a burden I'll be fine here Jesus Christ who's idea was it to have your mother move in my God will you look at that child I wonder what happened to make it look like that did the mother do drugs you suppose Daddy will you play with me I don't have anyone to play with why does that kid cry all the time don't you know I need my sleep it's not our fault he was born looking like that who didn't feed the fucking dog the litter box hasn't been changed can't walk can't go to the bathroom by himself can't understand what he says half the time if we had money for the surgery don't you think we'd I wish I'd miscarried anything's better than this so why don't you call me anymore you put me here and say you'll visit but now the goddamn thing's barking all night and I'm gonna shoot it I swear to God* as the churning carpet of silver rose higher—almost to my knees now—and once again unveiled the bas-relief Magic Zoo: birds, cats, tigers, horses, dogs, sea creatures whose tentacles blossomed from the tendrils, bears, deer, elk, snakes, all of their faces and forms pressing outward, then came the faces of the chimera, the manticora, the gryphon and Minotaur and harpy and other creatures of myth.

Long-Lost's children.

From a world that was supposed to be but got fucked up.

When God blinked.

The creatures looked unafraid.

They seemed to recognize me.

I stared for a moment at the Minotaur, his hooves and horns—I knew something like this from somewhere—then was snapped back as the coldness of the rising mist touched my elbows; the room was nearly full. "I need to ask you a question."

Magritte-Man gestured for me to continue as other forms took shape, hybrids and monstrosities and faces of the malformed whispering *I want to, I want to, I want to, please. . . .*

"We really weren't supposed to be the dominant species on this planet, were we? That's why there were more animals than humans on the Ark, right?"

He pointed toward my feet to where a section of mist was pulling back to reveal something. I didn't want to look away from him, didn't want to chance being taken by surprise, but there was a stillness between us that seemed far removed from everything that had happened or was about to happen, as if, just for this moment, I was protected, safe from harm. I stared at him for a second longer, then looked down.

There at my feet lay a small gray cat, eyes opened wide in anguish and fear, its neck broken, legs kicking out and back as its body twitched and spasmed. It was just as horrible to watch now as it had been that day nearly three decades ago behind Beckman's Market. The silver tag on its collar was still covered in blood. It jerked to the side, looking at me, accusing me. I felt my legs begin to give out, and knelt down to touch it, whispering now, as I did then, "I'm sorry, kitty, I'm sorry . . ."

As soon as my hand touched its side, the cat became still; its body relaxed, the choking stopped, and it rolled its head toward me in that same lazy, easy, sleepy-eyed way that any cat looks at you when your touch wakens it from a nap. We looked into each other's eyes for a moment, and then it leaned its head down against the back of my hand and rubbed its face against my thumb.

At least you cried, said a voice, but who, where, or what it came from I couldn't tell.

The mist crept back in, blanketed the cat, and a moment later my hand touched only cold air.

At least you cried.

I rose to my feet and looked at Magritte-Man once more, my unanswered question still hanging between us.

He shook his head. He seemed genuinely sad about it.

Looking into the eyes of the creatures surrounding me, I sighed. It sounded like a petulant child's noise. "That's what I thought."

At least the cat had forgiven me. At least I had that.

I struck flame to the lighter's wick as the rest of the Bowlers came at me.

I shot at anything that moved as I backed into the guest bedroom. I couldn't tell if I'd hit Magritte-Man or any of the remaining Bowlers because I couldn't see a damned thing, couldn't hear a sound because the mist devoured everything, but I kept shooting until I was in the room, then slammed closed and locked the door. Everything stank of charred wood and melting plastic and burned flesh. I could barely breathe.

Above me, the ceiling was beginning to sizzle and smoke from the blames burning through from upstairs. I tore the tape away from my hand and shoved the gun into the back of my pants, then pushed the bed up against the door, nearly passing out from the effort.

Dropping to the floor, coughing and wheezing and choking, I fumbled my hands around until I gripped the handle of the trapdoor; I threw it open and dove down head-first, scrabbled around in the dirt, reached up, and pulled it closed. I looked over to where she lay under the porch, then began crawling toward her.

Her eyes were open and watching me. She did not bare her teeth or snarl.

We had maybe a minute, a minute and a half before they came through the trapdoor or found the entrance to the crawlspace.

I slid down next to her and pulled out the gun. Her gold-flecked eyes looked at me with something like gratitude as she moved closer and nuzzled against my chest. I reached into my pocket and pulled out the small blue tag that had fallen from the envelope.

"Still Mr. Slow-on-the-Uptake, I'm afraid."

She made a soft, pained noise in the back of her

throat and I heard the echo of her voice from the phone call that night: *If I put out, they didn't treat me like I was some kind of dog—and I'd spent so long being treated that way I started to believe that's what I was—I still do, sometimes.*

I tossed away the tag and embraced her. "You shouldn't have left the house that night," I choked into her fur. "I would've made it all right."

She rolled her head to the side, licked her lips, then pressed her head against my shoulder: *I know.*

I looked at the silver tag hanging from her collar. I wondered if anyone was watching us at this moment. I made a small wave and mouthed the words "Hi, Mom."

A loud crack from above shook the floor as they broke through the bedroom door and began shoving the bed out of the way. At the other end of the crawl space, one of them knocked aside the trash cans and knelt down, his goggles casting their eerie light on our faces.

I looked at the gun. How many shots had I fired? God, please let there be two bullets left.

I ejected the clip.

It was empty.

But one bullet remained in the chamber.

I looked into her eyes. She shook her head, raised a paw, and batted the gun from my grip.

I held her close as the trapdoor was wrenched open and the Bowler at the other end began crawling toward us.

Then I remembered Carson's question about swans, did I like them and did I know what made them different from other animals?

"Swans," I muttered to her. "They mate for life, don't they?"

Yes. Pressing closer against me. I would never let her go. Never.

"Then it'll be swans."

I closed my eyes.

Her breath against my neck was like summer sunlight. I could smell the cooking from inside. Mom and Mabel were preparing dinner. Dad was busy collecting eggs from the henhouse while Whitey butchered a too-loud rendition of "Hello, I Must Be Going" on the out-of-tune piano in the parlor. My sister and Carson were on the front porch. Carson was attempting to draw her picture. One of these days he'd get it right.

An old man is chasing his hat across the highway in a comic dance. Thank God there's no traffic at this hour. This will make a great story at dinner. I will tell it with perfect timing and make Whitey proud.

Beth is there, smiling, holding out her hands. I will take them, and we will dance in the autumn twilight, turning, turning, until we turn round right. I will say something funny, and her laugh will ring like crystal. We will look into one another's eyes. And her smile will linger; oh, how it will linger.

I touch her face, revel in the perfect texture of her skin. She moves closer. A moment, a breath, a sigh. *Now.*

The world is returned to the way it should have been.

Her smile and touch tell me all I need to know.

I kiss her gently in the lilac shadows. . . .